SAFE

ALSO BY RYAN GATTIS

All Involved

The Big Drop: Impermanence

The Big Drop: Homecoming

Kung Fu

Roo Kickkick & the Big Bad Blimp

RYAN GATTIS

PICADOR

First published 2017 by Farrar Straus & Giroux
18 West 18th Street
New York, NY 10011

First published in the UK 2017 by Picador
an imprint of Pan Macmillan
20 New Wharf Road, London N1 9RR
Associated companies throughout the world
www.panmacmillan.com

ISBN 978-1-5098-4375-6

Pan Macmillan does not have any control over, or any responsibility for,
any author or third-party websites referred to in or on this book.

9 8 7 6 5 4 3 2 1

A CIP catalogue record for this book is available from the British Library.

Printed by CPI Group (UK) Ltd, Croydon, CR0 4YY

Visit **www.picador.com** to read more about all our books
and to buy them. You will also find features, author interviews and
news of any author events, and you can sign up for e-newsletters
so that you're always first to hear about our new releases.

For my family

I went into one room and then I went into another.
I was in a room inside a room.
There I felt safe.

—Emily Berry

In this life, the only way to be safe is to be dead.

—Big Fate

Do not go gentle into that good night.

—Dylan Thomas

Fuck Dying

A Mix by Rose G. Stenberg

Side 1: You
1. "I'm Not a Loser" / Descendents (1:29)
2. "Rise Above" / Black Flag (2:27)
3. "I Can See Clearly Now" / Screeching Weasel (2:18)
4. "I Want Something More" / Bad Religion (0:48)
5. "Living for Today" / Pennywise (3:08)
6. "Instant Hit" / The Slits (2:45)
7. "Day to Daze" / NOFX (1:58)
8. "Hey Holmes!" / The Vandals (2:45)
9. "Just to Get Away" / Poison Idea (2:30)
10. "Big City" / Operation Ivy (2:17)

Side 2: Me
1. "Los Angeles" / X (2:25)
2. "L.A. Girl" / Adolescents (1:49)
3. "She" / The Misfits (1:24)
4. "Demolition Girl" / The Saints (1:41)
5. "Quality or Quantity" / Bad Religion (1:35)
6. "Please Don't Be Gentle with Me" / The Minutemen (0:48)
7. "I Love Playing with Fire" / The Runaways (3:21)
8. "What Do I Get?" / The Buzzcocks (2:53)
9. "I'm Not Down" / The Clash (3:08)
10. "In Love" / The Raincoats (3:05)

1

THERE'S ONLY THIS

Ricky Mendoza, Junior, a.k.a. Ghost

Sunday, September 14, 2008
Morning

1

I'm on First Street, eyes up but slouching down, parked across from the Rancho San Pedro Projects at the absolute end of Los Angeles. Not for the first time today, I'm thinking that if I get into this safe and they leave me alone while I'm doing it, I'm taking the money.

Not all of it. I'm not stupid. Just some.

They said 0900 hours. It's ten past. I've been here since 0850, but they're not here yet. This happens with DEA sometimes. They come when they're good and ready. No point complaining.

The idea here is that it's a Sunday so they come at church time. That's how I know we're hitting Spanish speakers. It cuts down on the numbers if some are up at church with girlfriends or mothers, and around here that's probably Mary Star of the Sea on Seventh. I've been there once. For a girl too.

DEA love them some Sundays. I'm a private contractor, so it doesn't matter to me. A locksmith job is a locksmith job. When they got intel that they have a safe on the premises and need it open, they line me up and I open it. I got my laminate across my chest, hidden under my shirt. OFFICER OF THE COURT, it says. I got black license plates on my Jeep. Can't ever have someone knowing I worked for DEA or FBI or the Sheriffs. Can't have them knowing I busted their shit all up, see me driving away and figure out who I am and where I live from some numbers on a plate. That keeps me safe.

As far as anyone's concerned, I'm a ghost when I do this job.

I said that once to Frank when he was first teaching me the trade. He laughed and liked it, so he made it stick. Called me Ghost after that. When he introduced me to anyone, I'd be Ghost Mendoza. Not Ricky. And it worked good because I got pale enough skin that maybe people don't expect me to speak Spanish but I do. That's just part of my street toolset now, another way to be under-estimated. But that nickname was cool anyways, since Ricky Mendoza, Junior, wasn't my real name, just one I took as my legal back when it seemed smart to. Like, the real me died back when I changed it and what's left of me just floats.

I'm a block and a half up from where we're hitting. I'll roll up close when they're done breaking the door in. The nose of my Jeep points down the hill towards the cruise ship terminal and a big white ship there. Behind it, and above it, are big cranes that might've been painted turquoise once if the sun didn't beat the hell out of them every day. Behind those, it's one of those gray mornings that'll get hot and burn off eventually but now is just shoulder-to-shoulder clouds.

There better be money in that safe, I think. Not drugs. I can't do shit with drugs. Back in the day, sure, I knew too good what to do with drugs, but not now.

If you wanna know where gangs hang out in Los Angeles, look for old white signs on stucco apartment buildings that say NO TRESPASSING, L.A.M.C. SEC. 41.23. That's the posted municipal code. Or there's newer signs, ones that say the area is closed to the public and violators will be prosecuted. That's how you fight gangs if you're a city with not a lot of options. You make it illegal to hang out outside.

There's one of those signs on every side of these buildings. It's all L.A. Housing Authority property, stuccoed from bottom to top and barred up on all its windows and doors. Security doors don't matter. If you don't open when they knock, that's when I come in.

If it's a Medeco or a Schlage Primus lock sitting there, you probably got an extra minute or two to jump your ass out a back window and run straight into an officer with his weapon drawn, just waiting on you to do something stupid. Or maybe you have a slider on the other side of the door. But DEA brings rams. Sliders don't last long.

The LAHA is cheap as hell and gangs won't put their own security doors up because that's like a neon sign saying WE SELL DRUGS HERE! So for normal doors, I got bump keys in my pocket and all it takes is two. One for the security-door lock. One for the front-door lock. They're my little sharks. I cut their teeth a certain way on the grinder so that they'll break down normal mechanisms when I wedge it in and give it a few hard taps with a screwdriver handle. Easy.

I can tell by looking at these doors they don't have anything that can keep me out.

A woman comes out of her place across the way. She's dragging a baby carriage out behind her before shutting the door in some grand sweeping motion. There's no kid in the stroller, though. Looks like pots and pans, maybe stuff to sell. I don't know. Don't wanna know.

Just being in these sorts of neighborhoods, my stomach gets that old familiar jump. Like the down-drop on a trampoline. The kind where you wonder if you'll ever go up again. For me, that bounce back up was never taken for granted. Never. In this life, nothing is rock solid. No guarantee you ever get back up after you're down.

I got this saying, yesterday's gone and tomorrow never comes. This right here is all there is. This moment.

I know the insides of every single one of these sad-ass little apartments without ever needing to be inside. With their broken-door closets that never slide right no matter how much you try to line them up. With their rusty sink taps that maybe got plumbed wrong so if you turn the cold one, it gets warm but never hot, and if you turn the hot one, you get cold, and you can forget about stopping that drip. There's rats or roaches or bedbugs or termites too, but hopefully only one of those. One you can live around. You can get used to avoiding traps in the dark, but please, God, not *chinches de la chingada cama*. Not having to buy an expensive-ass sleeve to stuff your mattress in for a year, or putting your bed's legs inside little plastic bowls you dust with powder you're not supposed to breathe or it'll fuck up your lungs. One you can live with, but not two.

Two makes you crazy. So crazy you never wanna go back.

A tall box of a Mercedes SUV that's got no business being in this neighborhood turns in off Harbor Boulevard and comes toward me on the opposite side of the street. It slows down like it shouldn't and I'm shaking my head like, *Don't do it, dummy.* I see the tanned-up, white face of the driver from here. He's scanning the other side, looking for his hookup, but I guess he didn't call ahead because there's no one coming out to meet him. So he keeps going. Because even this rich motherfucker from off the hill has the sense to go get coffee and sit around and wait to buy before getting high.

Him, I don't care about. But it means there's no one around doing business. And less people around to do business means maybe there won't be a shoot-out. Maybe DEA's right about hitting on Sundays after all. At least here, anyways.

Down the street, I watch the cruise ship go out. A floating skyscraper on its side is what it is. The gray of the sky hasn't moved any.

All of L.A. is bad right now with people losing jobs, but this place is bad without telling anybody. Pedro looks fine on the outside, but if you keep your ear out, you hear. How there's no casual longshore work. It's been months. Unions are hurting because trade is down and the port's not moving like it used to. And you can't do that shit to Croatians and Mexicans, dude. Can't have them sitting on cards with nothing to do. If those folks aren't working, if food's not on the table, trucks go missing. Shipments go out light or come in the same way. Corners get cut. That's the shadow you never see because you need light to see it, and this is shit that always gets done in the dark.

I read the papers because Frank reads the papers. I shouldn't because it makes me sick to my stomach, but I do. Some Lehman brothers are about to be in the toilet. Good, I say. Serves them right for fucking with the mortgage shit. Packaging and repackaging so much that they can't even tell what's in those things anymore. Fucking preying on people. Chewing them up. Taking houses away from families that do nothing but try to pay anything they can and calling it business. Nothing worse than that to me. Nothing. Not even murder. Murder is one person. Maybe two.

This'll be *millions* if it gets much worse. Families. Little kids. People getting tossed in the street. Bellies going empty. Here's what you don't read but most people should just know: when the economy goes down, crime goes up. Average people do what they can and maybe they don't drown, but people on the bottom got to make ends meet somehow. Mouths don't feed themselves.

Last month this dude in group hung himself when his bank started foreclosure proceedings. We heard his twelve-year-old daughter and her friend found him when they came home from school. They're adults now, basically. One moment is all it took to grow them up.

Stories like that stick to me. I can't shake them off.

Just as I'm thinking that, I see the caravan rolling in coordinated, in my rearview and in front of me. Two trucks coming hot. No lights, just speed. They don't say DEA, but they're DEA. I sit up. There's probably another one around back on Santa Cruz that I can't see, cutting off chase routes. This is them, the boot that kicks you when you're doing bad.

They don't care if you got no choices. Shit, they don't even know what having no choices is like. On their off-hours they live in Pasadena. Seal Beach. Irvine. They come from that bright world where everybody has them. Where options grow on trees and you can grab them down like oranges.

All's I'm thinking as I watch *la DEA* pile out of their trucks in their marked vests to bust in this poor fucker's door is *I'm taking this money.*

I put my Jeep in gear and coast down the hill.

How much money, I don't know. Much as I can get away with. Much as I can line the inside of my toolbox with. Much as I can stuff under the foam holder in my drill case. Much as I can put in my socks.

It probably won't be $284,353, but it'll be something.

It will be a start.

2

The money's not for me, if you're thinking it. I don't need $284,353 for a gambling debt or anything like that. I'll be sober sixteen years in November. I'm in the black and I got a job. A good job. I got a place to live. Rent's real low. There's no rats or roaches or bedbugs or termites. There's mosquitoes sometimes, but I can handle them. The money's for somebody else. Somebody who needs it.

I step into the spot, and I swear, it took me less than five minutes to roll down the hill, park, bump the shitty door locks, go back to my Jeep and grab my heavy tools (two drills, drill-bit bag, toolbox), lock up, and head back inside, but by the time I'm walking through the doorway, the place is already a screaming mess because DEA doesn't play.

All the vents are off the walls and there's a pile in the middle of the room of supermarket baggies that came out with them. Inside those are foil-wrapped logs looking like tiny burritos. The dog is in and already barking at a wall with a *Scarface* poster on it, and a wall he must've already barked at is getting chewed up. There's a guy with a stud finder and a guy with a circular saw working it. They cut huge chunks of drywall and then lift them out. Behind those is a whole lot of nothing, but they rip it up anyways.

The inside of this place is how I thought it'd be. The living room mashes itself into a kitchen counter. There's a ripped-up couch that has already been tossed. Behind that, in the kitchen, is a fridge older than black-and-white TV and next to that is a rusted-out range. No oven. It's camping, basically. The drywall and ceiling just hide that this is a tent for running what they run till they need a new one. I know it's true as soon as I see the only bedroom has two mattresses on the floor and two sleeping bags. Which is when I start thinking maybe they got a tip.

In the bathroom, the rippers find loose tile. Underneath that is a main stash so big they take the dog out and give him treats for being a good boy because if he stayed in when they pulled it, he'd lose his shit.

Even halfway full, the hole is a crazy sight. And I'm thinking that maybe it was all the way full before the homies had to split, and they just took what they could as fast as they could. Maybe.

If that's the case, it might not be good news for that safe. It might be emptier than a bad nut. My face burns just thinking about it.

"Is this," somebody says before they even finish hauling all the little foil-wrapped goodies out, "all black tar?"

Black tar heroin. If it is, it's guaranteed from Mexico. And if it's from Mexico, it's from Nayarit. I thought all that shit was running through Norwalk or Santa Fe Springs or Panorama City straight to Downtown these days. *And pounds don't really make sense in that context, since they don't deal in large quantities, but, okay,* I think. I don't need to know everything about everything.

But then that makes me think about the white boy driving by, and how that doesn't fit the profile of Mexicans from Mexico, because they *deliver* their shit like pizza, and my stomach doesn't like that.

I'm still thinking about that when Collins comes up behind me.

"Ghost," he says, talking over the drywall saw that never stops going. "Hey, Ghost, did you see that Diaz-Katsawhatsit fight last weekend?"

Collins is in charge. He's a cool fucker. Fiftysomething, give or take. Six feet tall with a crew cut that makes him six feet one. Ex-military, but what branch I don't know. We always talk boxing, me and him, and the name of this boxer he can't remember is Michael Katsidis, the Australian with a shitty sun tattooed on his back. You'd think TV boxers could get better ink for all the money they're making, but that's never how it is. You come up rough, your body always shows it.

Collins should know who Katsidis is, we've talked about him before, so I give the big man shit about it. "You know I catch all them Katsawhatsit fights. That dude is can't-miss television."

Collins gives a sour little laugh before saying, "All right, what's his name?"

"Michael Katsidis. Former lightweight champ." I get to say former because Diaz just took his belt the Saturday before last.

"That's it." Collins nods. "That's him."

"Oh, I know it's him, and you know what? The twentieth century's long gone and Jack Dempsey doesn't fight anymore. You don't always have to go in for the white fighter, you damn racist."

It's a good little verbal jab, and it rocks Collins back on his heels before he shoots forward at me.

"What? Fuck off with that!" He punches me pretty good on my shoulder, but he doesn't know I let him.

Turning and slipping it would've made him look bad in front of his guys. And I can't be having that. Not if I want them to keep calling me.

I get down on the living room floor next to the kitchen counter where some guy marked the safe for me with a chalk-dust circle. I can't see much, so I start yanking up the carpet.

"You telling me Diaz won? I thought Katsidis threw harder punches," Collins says, "and he bossed the late rounds. The split decision was harsh."

That's who Collins is. He says shit like *bossed*. He loves punchers, this guy. He loves guys without any subtlety at all. This, he thinks, is more honest fighting somehow. No guard. Just go. He doesn't know life's not like that for most people, especially if you're not a white dude with a degree and a regional DEA command. The rest of us are too used to getting matched up with bigger, stronger, faster opponents. And those advantages have got to be balanced out. You have to beat them with your mind and skill and will. Nothing else.

Me? I think going in with your hands down so you can trade power punches is the way to fight stupid and die young. That's why I like boxers more than punchers. They're in and out. It's about technique. Feinting. Footwork. Hit and don't get hit. That's the art of it. The only art.

"You're crazy," I say to Collins as I tear back the carpet to the point that I can see how these gangsters chiseled into the foundation to make room for the safe. Looks like someone trying to tunnel out of prison. "Katsidis never throws a jab. Can't win like that."

"He doesn't need to. Doesn't matter when you hit that hard."

I try not to make a face like that's the dumbest shit I ever heard, and I think I do okay by turning to look at the carpet again. Still, I can't resist saying, "If you can't judge a fight the right way with punch stats, multiple angles, and slow-motion replay, I worry about you."

He laughs at that. I do too.

He thinks I'm kidding him. I'm not.

I get back to yanking at the carpet, but in my head I'm thinking, *It matters*. It always matters. One day you run into someone who hits just as hard or harder than you and right then is when you'll need to work a jab to keep him off you so you can figure out what to do next. See, jabs are offense that is actually defense. They're multipurpose. They set up combinations. The jab is the least fancy, least understood, most important punch on earth.

I've got the carpet all the way back now. Me and Collins take a look. First thing I notice, it's big. Real big. Like a refrigerator that got shrunk in the wash. It's a key-lock safe with a twist handle. Old, too. Maybe an antique, but I won't be able to tell unless it's out of that hole.

I say, "I need this hoisted up and flat on this floor before I can see what I'm dealing with."

Collins nods, turns, and gives the order.

Rudolfo "Rudy" Reyes, a.k.a. Glasses

Friday, September 12, 2008
Morning

3

Getting everybody in the car first thing before the bank opens is this huge production, man. I'm outside putting my one-year-old in his car seat, but my boy don't want to be in it. Felix is squirming, bouncing off the side walls of it.

Right now, he's not about being good. And I feel that. I'm angry about having to go too. We're two peas, me and him.

He's my first kid. My little me. A soft little knucklehead always trying to stir himself into some business.

Right then, Felix proves it too. He does this duck-and-dive thing before I can get him buckled between his legs. He flops himself face-first onto my shoulder and giggles. I freeze for a second.

I wonder how this would've gone if I wasn't there to catch him. I don't even want to think about that. I get my breathing back and lock him in. I test the latching twice. He's still fighting the belt, but he's not gonna go anywhere.

This'd be funny if it didn't suck so much.

It'd be better if we had a garage so no neighbors could see. If we had a legit house, and not some rented back house on some-body else's lot. If we could show even a little money instead of staying on the same block, six streets over from where I grew up, sticking with the appearance of no money and never gonna have it.

That's how Rooster does things. When you work for him, you got to be invisible. One ant in a colony. One tiny speck among a million other ones.

I can't give anyone a reason to look at me. For anything. Which is why this whole bank thing's throwing me off. My father-in-law, he has a mortgage I cosigned on. And that means nothing can go wrong on it. Ever.

So getting that phone call about a missed payment and a col-lections service made me lose it. Made me figure we're not calling them back. We aren't calling the credit union where the payment should've come from in the first place. We're not dealing with no middleman. We go to the source, the bank. Straighten it out person to person.

My wife's out the door behind me, weighed down with a bag for Felix. It's got extra diapers. A picture book that don't even make sense, about a dinosaur egg getting hatched in the future. His stuffed yellow duck. There's a bottle too. And some guava juice he didn't drink from earlier. And a little green hat with a brim and two frog eyes on it.

And sunscreen. Which only makes sense to her. We're going inside a lobby with no sun and she needs sunscreen for his face.

I swear, Leya gets like a white lady with him. All overpro-tective. Sometimes, Felix has coughs and wakes himself up. He had them all last night. Leya stayed awake with him. Allergies, the doctor said. Pollen. Mold. What he's allergic to is everything you can't see.

Leya always stays up when he gets like that, since he almost died inside her. One of those twisted-cord things. But he's fine now and his brain is fine. We're super lucky.

When everybody's in the car, I go three blocks to Leya's dad's house, pick him up, and hit Atlantic Boulevard, then Martin Luther King.

I got the radio going. Nobody says nothing the whole way to the bank. Not even little Felix. We're all some combination of nervous, anxious, and unhappy, hoping it can get worked out today and just be done.

What this bank is, is two big redbrick squares and gray horizontal lines of concrete. Inside, it smells like newspaper and old cigarette smoke, like people used to be able to smoke in this building and then they couldn't, but it never stopped smelling.

I sign the signing-in form and we wait to get called. Leya has Felix in his little hat already. She's worried about him getting cold from air-conditioning. We sit for twenty minutes.

Felix won't take his sippy cup of juice from me even though I'm trying, and my father-in-law's just staring into the parking lot like he wants to be back out there and done with this.

That's when I'm done with waiting. I go up to this guy's desk that's nearby and not doing a thing but being on his computer.

"I need to see your loans manager, please," I say in my super polite voice.

He don't even look at me. No respect. He says, "Did you sign in?"

In the world sitting outside these doors, a guy like this should be scared of talking like this. There's consequences around here for trying to act above it, the type of things that come up behind you in the dark when you're walking to your car after work and staring at your phone. It happens so quick you don't even know what hit you, or from where.

I feel myself getting heated but I smile since I don't teach those types of lessons to random fools anymore. Not even when I want to.

"Yes," I say, trying to keep it all polite still, "but there's nobody else here. I'd appreciate if—"

"Excuse me," a voice comes from behind me, "perhaps I can be of assistance?"

I turn and see a light-skinned black girl in a real tight blazer. Skirt to the tops of her knees. Red heels.

She puts an arm out beside her to show me her open office door. On the glass beside her, it says MIRA WATKINS, BANK MANAGER.

I'm looking at her, but subtle, trying to drink her in. Almost looking at her without looking at her since I can't have my wife seeing me see her like that.

This Mira Watkins isn't what I expected a bank person to look like. She's built like maybe she hustled a bit. Like maybe this wasn't always her career. There's something I can't put my finger on about her, so I don't trip, I get everybody into the office and shut the door.

She's sitting behind her desk, behind her gold MIRA WATKINS nameplate, in a tall black leather chair like some type of queen.

She's staring at me, looking me right in the middle of my forehead and not in my bad eye. It's cool. I can tell she's just assessing. Seeing what I'm about. I'm wondering then if she can tell how real I am. If she has any clue.

Prolly not, I'm thinking. I'm just one more *raza* dragging my family in, needing help. Nothing more. There'll be twenty more of me through that front door today.

Mira Watkins kicks it off by saying, "What can I do for you all?"

What I do when I tell her the story is, I start with my father-in-law's name and account number so she can get to tapping on her computer before I explain the situation and how we got here. I say about the mortgage payment that got missed, the one we didn't know about. We got a call yesterday from the bank, a person with collections, saying my father-in-law's behind in his mortgage payments and had been for a couple months.

That tripped him out. Me too. We've never been late.

So I tried to check the payments with his credit union by phone, but they'd closed by the time I got off work. What I did then was try to figure it out myself by looking online. And I wondered what was going on since he'd just made a payment.

I mean, *I'd* just made a payment, but she don't need to know that.

And I was confused to see that I had a record of the payment this month and last month, but not the one two months before. That's where the missing payment was. I'd pushed SEND on the online credit-union form just like every month, but that one had never gotten there. I tell my father-in-law in Spanish to take the check out and hand it to her.

"It's for the missing mortgage payment," I say, "and we can pay any late fees too, right now."

She takes the check. Of course she takes the check. But then she gets up and says she has to go check on some things. "There's only so much I can see on my computer."

What this prolly is, is BS, but I'm trying to think of what she wants to check and where. I watch her go. Her ass in that tight skirt. Her shoulders back. Looking like she means to handle something.

Felix has his hat off and he's swinging it around in his hand like he's gonna shake the eyes off it. Leya lets him.

Hey, she begged me to cosign on this loan. It gets paid on time, all the time. I can't have nobody in my business. It's not safe that way.

Mira Watkins, you better not be messing with me. You better be fixing this. If you don't, things can happen. People I know can show up late at night where you live. They don't ask you to fix stuff then. They tell.

When she comes back, it's like she's a different person. Less businessy. Friendlier. On our side. Prolly she wants me to think that anyway.

She has a folder in her hand, a bunch of papers she's flipping through. She's frowning doing it too, but a good frown. "Six years and no late payments. Very impressive. We can take care of this for you, Mister Reynoso."

That's my father-in-law's name. What Leya's last name used to be.

Mira Watkins hands me a late-fee form I have to sign. I make my father-in-law write another check for the $95 fee. It sucks, but it's not like it's his money. It's mine.

"Things are a little crazy right now," Mira Watkins says. "I do apologize. I hope you understand how we need to be vigilant."

Vigilant? She sees me hate her last word the second it comes out of her mouth and she softens. She lets her shoulders go, leans forward.

"I'm so sorry this happened." She says it to me, with feeling, and then she says it down the line, to Leya, and Leya's dad too, topping it off with a half-decent accent on her *"Lo siento."*

Then she says, "Too many bad things are happening to good people right now. Clerical craziness, that's what I call it. You get a computer involved and anything can happen. You've never missed a payment before, and yet we jump all over it and send it to collections. I'll look into how that happened, and I'll make a note in your file that it was taken care of promptly, and maybe we should just give you a phone call next time instead of escalating it right away."

There's a tiredness to how she's saying it. Like this has happened a lot before, and she's had to give this speech before, but she seems real with it. There's shame in her cheeks. A double wrinkle in her brow too, like a bent metal hanger you used to be able to pop car-door locks with.

She means it, I think. I look at Leya and Leya looks at me. We agree with a look. We believe her.

I turn back and say, "Can I get something in writing today that says it's paid and you're calling off your collection services?"

She claws long fingernails at me in the air, like she's catching my words, right before she moves her hands back to the keyboard to start typing. "I'm all over it."

And she is. And that's good. For us. But for her too.

Ghost

Sunday, September 14, 2008
Morning

By the time the safe is out and up where I can get at it, the dope is already bagged, sealed up, and on its way to evidence somewhere. Flat on its back, the thing is sitting in the middle of the living room. It's got a layer of concrete dust all over it from where it got pulled out of the floor.

DEA's clearing out. They're giving me a wide berth. They left an outlet up for me, though, which is always good. I plug in and drill a few holes in the safe's door with a diamond tip that goes ·dull while I'm doing it, so I grab another one and plow through so I can see the mechanism I'm dealing with. Two tumblers, it looks like. I'm scoping it. Yeah. Two tumblers. Maybe.

I unscrew the anchor for the handle and take it off, thinking for just a second about all the hands that must've turned it through the years. I clamp my vise grips to the stump that's left over and give it a jar just to see if it'll hold. It does.

Collins hovers nearby. He wants a status update so he can make a decision about what happens next. He sees it's keyed but he's seen enough of this now not to ask if a bump will work. Because it fucking won't.

"Antique and weird," I say, pressing my eye closer to the scope and adjusting the light. "Foreign. Got to be."

The safe is beat to shit. No markings on it. It's a straight-up contraband safe. The kind that gets passed around from gang to gang when deals go down. That happens sometimes. Don't ask me why. I've opened a safe before and there was no use taking it in for evidence so we left it. A couple years later I found it again, in a different part of town, all patched up, so I cracked it again.

When Collins takes a step towards me, a little chunk of concrete shoots from under his foot like a pebble and goes skidding over the carpet. "Where do you think this came from?"

"Could be anywhere." I take my eye off the scope and look up at him. "Probably off a boat from just over there." I nod towards the port.

He huffs. "ETO?"

That's *estimated time to opening.* Pretty sure that's not official. It's just something I've always heard him say.

"Depends what it's lined with. If it's a fire safe, it could be a lot of things."

"Just a number, Ghost."

I shrug, but my heart's beating fast. This is where I have to sell it. Where he has to believe me. So I don't look at him. I stare at the safe instead.

"Forty minutes? I see two tumblers, but there might be three."

Collins waves the information away. He doesn't need to know it. But it's me covering my ass. He looks at me for a solid few seconds and then gives the order to round up the troops, grab up their gear, and ride.

"Call when it pops."

"Yes, sir. Always do." I don't have to, but Collins likes it when I call him sir.

So that's how it works. They leave me alone, and when I bust it, I call. I stay till somebody comes so as to preserve chain of custody, then I'm gone. It's not always like this, but this is how it goes down more often than you'd think.

Nobody that works outside the profession ever believes it. They think it's like TV where everybody gets watched like a hawk at all times. It's not.

I've been working scenes for eleven years on my own, and four before that with Frank. Eleven years means I'm long since trustworthy. I'm solid. And the fact is, DEA doesn't need to be wasting man-hours babysitting me while I crack. They got paperwork just like everybody else. Evidence to inventory. Maybe even pursuing more warrants. They might even be hitting another spot while they got their crew together. I don't know. It's possible.

After the security door bangs shut and I hear the trucks going out, I hear people talking in the street. I can't hear words. Just voices. I don't do anything different than I'd normally do. I get set to drill through the bottom and into the door. I line it up, brace myself, and put my full weight into it.

I've had guns pulled on me plenty when I'm alone like this. People that scattered when the badges arrive usually come right back after they go. It's why Frank never went alone. Always had me along to call or at least watch the door. But I don't got an apprentice and I won't be taking one.

Tell you what, though, takes work to talk someone out of trying to shoot you. Believe that. Funny thing is, I never tell anybody that they shoot me and get the death penalty, because that threat never kept anybody from doing a crime.

I get raw. I tell them I'm an officer of the court, motherfucker. I tell them the government takes this shit personal if one of us ever goes down. I tell them the address I'm at is known, it's in official court documents already, and that whoever's hitting it *will* be back, and that means the fool standing in front of me and aiming is known too. And if I get shot, it's not like some kid getting shot in the hood. You *will* get caught. Not in days, in hours. Guaranteed.

You'll bring so much heat on your *clica* that they'll fucking turn you in because you're bad for business, it's happened before, and then next thing you know, you're getting booked up, charged, held without bail, and chain-walked the fuck into court for pretrial so fast you'll wonder why all of a sudden the system is actually *working*. I usually pause there. I let it sink in before saying, because I am the system. That's why. You take a swipe at the machine, you get chewed up. And that's all there is to that.

It works too. I mean, I'm still standing here. There's no trick to it. It's simple. I tell a story and wait for it to hit.

See, people will kill if they feel like they can get away with it. That's why it goes down. Conviction rates in the heavy gang areas are the worst. Detectives don't got resources to clear cases there. Poor communities don't help the cops because they're more afraid of gangs coming back on them. Everybody knows which motherfucker killed somebody on the block. That info goes around.

But when you tell somebody that he's going into handcuffs quick and forever if he pulls that trigger, then that's worth thinking on. It's a stone-cold motherfucker that still pulls it after that. I've met a few of those in my life, and I guess I'm just damn lucky it's always been a low-totem homie that walks in on me trying to crack.

I feel the drill punch through the bottom of the safe and go into the door with a lurch. I look at my watch. Not even ten minutes. *Good*, I think. *Real good.*

I grab one of my rounded-off drill bits and push it up through the hole I made. Too many people think cracking is like how they see it in movies. People standing around with a stethoscope in their ears. That's *picking*. And there's no point to it if you ask me. It's not time efficient. What I do is boxing. There's art to this too.

Safecracking is with your eyes and your hands. Not with your fucking ears. But people don't always see it. In the ring, they only see a dude getting knocked flat. Like, how you might see me open a safe and think it's all about the last punch and not everything that came before it.

Like how I had to make the opening and now I go through it. Not with a hook or an uppercut. Nothing with an angle. I jab away at it till I get that mechanism off its angle, then I give it a straight shot to jolt it. If you were in the room, you wouldn't even hear it pop. But me, I feel it give under my fist and go through. Like, I had an opponent in front of me and I lined up a combination but he went down with one shot so after that I'm just swinging at air.

That's it. I'm in. Just like that.

I check my watch. Almost sixteen minutes and tomorrow never comes.

This moment, that's all there is.

I breathe like I haven't been breathing all morning, take my vise grips, turn them like they're the handle, and there's no clank sound because there's no mechanism connected to it anymore. There's just me opening the heavy metal door straight up to the ceiling and letting in the air.

I don't even look at first. I can't.

I'm putting gloves on. Little blue plastic specials.

The kind you can get at any drugstore.

5

With the safe's mouth busted and just hanging open in the middle of the carpet, I reach in, hit paper, and pull my hand right out like it's hot. That's when I look in and see every shelf full. Six of them, deep like a library bookcase. I even pull both little drawers at the bottom up and out. One is empty. The other has coins in it. Coins, I can do nothing with, so I drop that back down into its slot, but then I stand up because I got to stand up or I'm going to go all light-headed, and I walk over to the front door and look out the peephole. Outside, neighbor voices are going, but nobody's standing in front of the apartment, or near my Jeep. The coast's clear enough.

I'm feeling it. Adrenaline burning in me like getting tattooed on the inside. That's how I know I'm still taking the money. As much as I can get away with.

I kneel back down at the safe and pull cash out by the fistful. There's a problem, though, as I'm laying it out, and I feel a knot getting tight inside me. This isn't small bills from street slinging. It's not a mess of tens and twenties or wadded-up fives pressed flat from junkies. It's all fucking *hundreds*. Too neat.

Safe guts never look like this, all clean.

This is good news, but also it's very bad news.

All this cash might mean a delivery was coming. Cash on hand to get sent back to Mexico. That's the likeliest. I'm still wondering why the runners didn't take what was in here when they bounced, but then I get to thinking that maybe they didn't have the key. Maybe only their boss had the key and he wasn't here or couldn't get here quick enough before *la DEA* came knocking or—

I tell my brain to shut up.

I even say it out loud to calm me down, "Shut up. Shut up. Shut up."

That tattoo machine's still going inside me, ripping my lungs up. Making it hard to breathe.

Thinking won't do anybody good now. Only taking will.

I check my watch. I'm at twenty-five minutes.

Shit.

Fast and messy, I unload my drills and pull their foam linings. Last week, I cut some deeper compartments into the plastic underneath, enough to stick about eight stacks in each, so I do. Thick as eight books. I overfill it, though, because when I put the foam and the drill back in, it won't close, so I have to take some out.

Half a stack comes back on the floor, and then I fill the other drill case and get both closed up. The loose stuff goes into my toolbox, in its false bottom that I added.

My brain's back on again. All this cash, it's trying to tell me, there's no way I get away with it. There's too much here.

The owners of this cash will come looking. They'll come looking *hard.*

"Shut up," I say to my brain. "I don't need to get far with it. I just need to drive."

Getting caught, that's happening. As sure as breathing, that's happening.

You can't take from these people without consequences. They'll catch me. The only problem is, I definitely have less time now. If it was just a little money here or there, I might be able to go on for a while. That was always the plan. Like that Johnny Cash song Frank's always humming, "One Piece at a Time."

But not this.

This is the kind of thing that makes me glad I took some precautions, so I can stay moving. When I take this money, there's no going back.

I know that as I wrap my ankles with rolls and then pull my socks way up like I used to, back in the day.

Me, I'm not worried about. I know I'm going out the bad way now, but there's power in that guarantee. I've been doing bad almost my whole life. Hurting people. Innocent people. People that never did deserve it. Like how I said at group once, when I was on drugs, I was a Tasmanian devil of pain and bullshit. All through my growing up. A whole mess of people got caught up in my tornado.

So now, knowing this is it for me, it's a gift. It's a chance to go out clean. And that's all I need. A chance. Like a tablecloth getting pulled off a table without disturbing the plates or forks on it. That's the best case. Because I lived messy too long. And I done so much shit I should've been dead for, twenty times over. How I even made it to wearing this laminate on my chest without a criminal record is a goddamn miracle. Because I've been up in some shit. And I got so dirty living stories where I'm the villain that they're all sunk into my bones now, and never letting me go.

"So fuck it," I say.

If this's the end, it might as well be a good one.

I get up, go to the sink, and I'm surprised to find there's more of them decent-sized plastic shopping bags in there. I take the biggest one, from a cowboy-boot store, and stack almost three whole shelfs inside. I eyeball it, smoosh it down flat, tie the top, and test it to make sure it'll fit under my passenger seat. And then I walk outside. I carry it to my Jeep and get it situated before locking up and taking my phone out as I walk back in.

I call Collins at thirty-two minutes. "It's open."

"Sending someone now," he says before hanging up.

I mess up the rest of the safe. I make it look like any other we bust. Not neat. Not stacked. Crumpled up. Thrown in. I even pull the coins from the drawer and toss a few around inside to hear them ping.

I pull my gloves off and stuff them in my back pocket.

And then I wait.

Sure, there were eyes on me when I walked that bag to the car.

Doesn't matter if the block was looking. The people that put that money in the safe in the first place will know I took it anyway. Soon or late, they'll find out. They got people to hand over police or Fed reports. That's a given.

They'll know I walked a bag out. And then they'll read those reports and know the numbers that went confiscated by the government don't match up the numbers they know for sure were in the safe. They'll suspect me first but will be real thorough. They'll check to see if somebody on DEA is dirty and they'll run with that till they're sure. And maybe they even *got* somebody dirty on the inside already. Somebody that can help them get to the bottom of it even quicker. They'll check with the house runners too. Just to make sure nobody is taking off the top from inside the house. When they're done with their inventory, after all that, they'll know for sure there's only me. They'll know I'm the only one that makes sense.

And then, they'll figure out what to do about me. A problem like Ghost.

Maybe then they'll rat me out to DEA or Sheriffs or anyone else I work for so they can get me thrown into prison so I can get dealt with while I'm in there. But most likely, they'll just find me, scoop me up, walk me out somewhere quiet, and after I tell them where the money is hid at, they'll shoot me low caliber under the chin so it doesn't make a mess before pushing me in a hole that maybe they don't feel like filling up. It's not rocket sciences. It'll happen. There's too many of them and only one of me. That's just how it will go down.

And I'm okay with that.

Fast is how this needs to go so they don't focus on someone else. Not Frank. Not Laura. Definitely not Mira. Just me. They got to catch my ass first, though, and I intend to jab and move, and jab and move, and do a whole lot of damage before they corner me. More damage than they ever thought one dude could.

Glasses

Saturday, September 13, 2008
Evening

6

Three hours into my niece's *quinceañera* party, things are popping off pretty good. Most everybody's eaten, and the XV girl's done her choreographed dances with her little court of *chambelanes*. The theme color is pink times a million.

People of all ages have been through the Caballo Dorado line dancing, going faster and faster to "No Rompas Más Mi Pobre Corazón." Leya went out there with her sister and got through three plays of it, but I don't go in for that type of stuff.

Bateman Hall is across from the Senior Center on Ernestine in Lynwood. What I like about the front of it is, they have a whole row of fountains on either side of the entrance.

For most events, they're all bubbling up like little geysers. But they don't have them on tonight for some reason. Just lights and still water.

Walking in, I remembered Hosler Junior High close by, how fools used to jump the fence to ditch out of there, how security would chase us and we'd run across the street and through Bateman since it was open during the day. We'd run in and out of the big room, bigger than a basketball court. White ceiling, white tile floor, brick walls painted white with tall brown wooden slats breaking it up every few feet.

Stage up front, where the DJ is right now. He's got all his lights up and running, shooting pink snowflake patterns over the Lynwood banners hanging in the middle of the room, and onto the big wooden clock in the back that tells me I got maybe ten minutes left to be here.

We're sitting on the right below one of them banners, closest to the back wall so I can see the whole room and every person in it. My sister-in-law got mad about it and said I needed to be in the middle, but that's not a good idea. Too exposed.

So I'm with Leya and Felix in some little headphones like guys at the airport wear when they're waving planes around. That's not something I fought Leya on. I was all for it. The older I get, the more I hate this type of party. The music is always too loud at these things.

"*Disculpe.*" This guy off to my left almost shouts it.

I turn at him and he's got a long-sleeve, button-up pink shirt, open three buttons too many. His face's a little red from dancing but he's still paper-bag brown underneath. His hands are shaking from being nervous to meet me. I don't know the guy.

He introduces himself in Spanish and says hello. Turns out I know his brother. He smiles at that and asks how I'm doing. Always the answer is good. Am I enjoying? Yes. *Por supuesto.* Do I need a beer, or anything? No, but thank you. He leaves backing up, with a smile and too many nods.

Hey, I know this is just paying respects, more to Rooster than to me, and I'm just the way it gets to him. I'll be asked about it later too. I'll have to remember which of them said what, and which didn't. I always do.

But this is the fourth guy tonight to come up acting too nice like that. I don't like people seeing it in public. Leya always notices. Her family does too. It's this thing they don't like putting up with but have to. The worst part is tonight it's taking attention from the XV girl, and that's just about unforgivable.

The only thing saving me right now is that the food is good.

Big tin trays of tangy beef *birria* in a red sauce, *pollo al pastor* with half cuts of pineapple in it, *carnitas*, rice, beans, salad, and marinated vegetables that Leya picks the cauliflower out of.

This type of *birria* reminded me of corned beef a little. When I said that to Leya, she gave me a look. What it said was *Birria es birria*. Also there was the decision in there that I been spending too much time with Rooster. Prolly she's right about that.

But it's not like I can do anything about it. I'm just happy the food's good since I was *padrino* of it. I didn't pick it but I paid for it. Can't be working for Rooster and having anybody upset where food's concerned. That's just not happening.

I wanted to be cake *padrino* since it would've been cheaper, but Leya's sister wasn't having that. There was no *recuerdos padrino*. I asked about that too.

But the Reynoso ladies made those sitting up in their living rooms for three weeks, doing beads and drinking too much coffee. It's like a rosary bracelet strung together around a cross with wings on it, for your wrist. The beads are pink too.

The good ticky-tack sound of *cumbia* comes on the speakers then, "El Viejo del Sombrerón" by Sonora Dinamita. Since that's one me and Leya danced to at the restaurant after our wedding, she's grabbing my hand and telling her mom to watch Felix as we pass the main table.

The clock says I got four minutes as we take the back right corner of the dance floor, and it fills up with older couples but there's some kids too. The *chambelan de honor* is right next to us, dancing with my niece. I look at him there, so serious as he's doing some steps, thinking about getting them right, not yet feeling the music.

I tell him to make more room between them. Don't dance too close. Leya digs a finger into my ribs since she wants me to shut up, and my niece looks like she's never been so embarrassed in her whole entire life, but he does it, he backs up.

What I think by looking at him, I can't help seeing Felix being that age someday, being some girl's special little *chambelan*, wearing the hat and the suspenders and the bow tie. Memorizing dances. Doing it for a woman.

It makes me happy and scared at the same time, like maybe I'll never get to see it, him being that old. And I must wobble a little or something since Leya can tell I'm thinking sad things again, so she turns me and I spin her.

I pull her close then. She knows I'm not that guy that gets out there and does the twirls and the two-steps and junk like that. I hold her. I focus in on her eyes so she knows I see her.

Even with all the lights around, the three shades of pink, light, regular, and dark. Even with all the other women around, I'm only looking at her for the good seconds I got left.

After, I'm looking to the clock and seeing it's time, and then to the back doors, where Big Danny is already standing, blocking the view of the courtyard. I know he's got the stuff in the car. I know it's time to do something I don't want to do but got to.

Big Danny might not always have been big, but I only known him since he was. He's almost six foot, up over two hundred pounds, all in the neck and shoulders, since he lifts. He's got a gut to him too.

He eats for real. I seen him eat half a pig once. Two feet. Legs. Most of the side of it. It was a small pig, but still. Backyard roast, homemade barbecue sauce. He couldn't help himself.

But he's not interested in anything other than leaving now, the way he's standing by the door, in front of the dimpled yellow glass, looking at me but not looking at me. Rooster sent him. It's definitely time.

The song's winding down with some horns, and then REO Speedwagon's on just after. The dance floor empties. What it is, is "Take It on the Run" as a break. After this song, they'll play the stuff the kids want. Rap. Club music. It's a good time to leave.

Leya knows I'm about to go too, the way her hands drop off me when she sees Big Danny hanging out. She gets how that was our last dance.

I kiss her, good but quick, and drop her off at the middle table with her parents and sister. I push Felix's headphones back a little to kiss his head and then slide them back forward. I say my goodbyes while everybody's trying to throw guilt my way, take one last picture with my niece in her wide pink dress, and then I'm gone.

The 710's good at night going south. Fast. It feels like in no time we're on the 47 and those harbor lights and cranes are throwing themselves at us, in reds and blues and yellows. I prefer them to the flashing ones inside Bateman Hall. I like them better when they're still, not moving, not trying to get crazy.

Me and Big Danny, we don't talk on the ride. Neither of us is the type. He chews gum. I look out windows. It's what we do all the way there.

Big Danny pulls up on First Street in San Pedro into one of the resident spots that got cleared out for us. He gets the bag with Rooster's 10 percent, the ninety-two gees, out of the trunk, and we go to the door of the apartment building that's about to be given up.

Next to that door is a guy smoking. A guy I recognize.

"Gafas," he says to me. Sometimes people call me that.

"Hector," I say back.

He puts his hand out, not to shake. To hand me a key. I take it. It's wet from his sweating palm, warm too.

Late twenties and already he's got a belly on him like he's eight months pregnant. The rest of him's skinny. Almost twelve years I've known of him and he's never looked this sick, just bloated out. Bags under his eyes from not sleeping. Skin looking a dirty-milk pale from never going outside during the day.

He's never been the same since he got back from Mexico. I get why too. The work he was doing down there would turn anybody into a zombie.

I mean, even looking at him right now makes me almost chuck my *birria* up, and all he ever did was tell me a story about barrels when he got back. Barrels, and what gets put into them.

I tripped out on it. And what's worse is how it's stuck to me. I get nightmares about it. Leya says I scream sometimes in my sleep.

I take some antacids out of my pocket and chew on them. My stomach's been messing with me lately. Some type of flu prolly.

Me and Hector don't have time to talk and that's good with me. The door opens without Big Danny needing to knock.

They're waiting for us. Four of them. Long Beach is there. Watts is there. Wilmington. And one I don't recognize too. Santa Fe Springs, prolly. I make a note in my head to check. The others have already been and gone.

We go in and say our hellos the same to all of them, real respectful. The safe's open, almost full. Seems like it's three quarters of a refrigerator down there, all big in its spot that's chiseled into the concrete foundation like a little grave.

I sit at the foot of it, on my knees. I don't like doing it like this. I never like it, but I do it. I put the money in, one stack after the other until it'll be almost all flat to the door.

Big Danny's got my back. In this life, you trust people, but you don't trust people. Sometimes, you can't help it. You have to.

And then, it's about doing it as fast as you can and getting up out of it. My stomach still don't feel good. It won't until we leave.

I mean, there's a lot of juice outside this room making sure this goes right. A lot.

What this is, is the sixth safe I've done like this. We do about one a year, sometimes two. It depends. But the looks on faces are always the same when it goes down. It's a weird feeling being in a room where almost every fool is being professional but still is daydreaming at the same time.

Thinking about that money, what they'd do with it if they had it all, how good it'd be. It's like they're here and not here at the same time.

When I'm done, I test the door to make sure it'll close. It does, so I lock it. I snap them out of it with that. I put the key in my pocket, for later, to give to Rooster. That's when everybody starts breathing normal again.

Big Danny wipes for prints and we say our goodbyes one by one and then we go. As we're walking out, a vacuum goes on. I say bye to Hector on the way to the car and tell him to keep looking after his mother. He just nods.

There's always that one story. The warning story that happened to somebody that everybody knows, and it keeps other fools from getting the smart idea of stealing.

For stuff like this, it all comes down to this fool named Cuco.

Everybody knows Cuco now. He's cautionary, a super special example.

What happened was, he used to work for a South Gate crew. Back in the day, he ran a house for them. First it was for pimping girls, but then he moved up to a little spot on the edge of Cudahy and it was mostly drugs, but some guns too.

So this fool Cuco, he gets it in his head one day to rob the safe after everybody's put their money in the pot. He thinks he'll do it when everybody's gone.

This is how Cuco got to be the reason we have to sit people on families and girlfriends now. You know, as insurance until everything's settled.

So it gets late and Cuco's only there with one other lil fool that he sends out for food, which is never how it should go down, but the little one don't know any better, so he goes.

After that it's just Cuco and no combination for the safe, since you can't be leaving people around it that know how to open it. So this dumbass, he drives a forklift that he'd been hiding down the block into the garage, and he picks the safe up and puts it in a truck he had stashed from before.

I don't even remember how much was in that safe. Maybe a hundred gees. Not more than one twenty. Low numbers. Nowhere near what we put in now.

But anyway, this fool gets in his truck and drives it over to his girlfriend's spot and they decide to celebrate there.

Just real quick, you know? Little bit of *perico* for heisting it right. Never mind that he hasn't opened anything, hasn't even got anything real in his hands yet. Or that he didn't even tie his loose strings up.

Back at the spot, the lil homie walks into an empty house holding a bag of food. Nobody's there. Not in the kitchen. Not in the back room. And definitely not in the garage.

He saw all the money go into the safe, so he knows something bad happened, but he don't know it's Cuco that did it. For all he can tell, somebody rolled in, kidnapped Cuco, and took the safe, so he makes a call.

That lil homie was Hector, the smoker outside, the one with the gut. Being quick for calling got him a good promotion for a while too. Before he got deported back to Mexico anyway.

Like lightning, some hood detectives from various clicks swoop down to see what's up. Any gang that put money in that safe sent somebody.

They start looking around too. A guy from Bellflower notices how there must've been a big truck parked out back in the alley, from the tire tracks in some dust.

What was supposed to be tactical, the garage facing the alley and making it easy to roll up and load or empty the safe and go quick, got shown as a big weakness right then. Especially when there's a abandoned forklift sitting right there too.

Neighbors get asked about a truck after that, and somebody's seen one, a moving truck. Word goes out. Everybody tells everybody to be on the lookout.

What the first stop is after that, is Cuco's girl's house she shares with her cousin. There's a truck there fitting the description. And it's locked too.

So some homies show up with snippers and get that lock off and the truck gets opened. There's a safe in it. Our safe. With our money.

So those same homies go in the house by the back door then. It's locked but that's nothing to people that want in.

And they come through too. Four of them. And they find Cuco in his girl's bed since everything ended up getting bigger than one little celebration.

But he's sorry. He's crazy sorry. He was just, like, messing with us. Exposing a security problem, yeah. And it's not like he opened it. Not like he ever could have. So it's all good, right?

He got told to shut up. The girl got told if she wanted to live, if she wanted her cousin to live, she had to go into that gross-ass kitchen nobody ever cleaned and get the biggest knife she had in there to cut his throat up.

Cuco's face right then, people say it was like he died a death right there just looking in her eyes, knowing she'd do it to him.

Prolly this's why it's not a good idea to be with a girl that hustles. A girl that knows odds. A girl that survives by nature. She'll do you. If she has to.

And she did too. Of course she did. She got up, went to the kitchen, came back with a knife. When you hear this story get retold, it's a butcher knife, some six-inch, super sharp thing you can buy from TV.

Man, it wasn't. It was a small little steak knife. Four inches, if that. One of those thin ones with a black handle was all she had in the spot. Serrated edge with the tip broken off. Wasn't even clean.

I mean, Cuco tried to run first. But, see, he got pinned down. A knee on the back of the skull will do that to you. And she went into him.

She didn't look, but she sure stabbed him up. Did it until it bent and broke, that little blade. Right there on the floor. On the raggedy brown carpet with cigarette burns in it, and a patch that turned yellow from bleach put on it years ago.

She got beat after that. Choked. Not just to do it, but to give her a story. For the Sheriffs.

She did time for sorting out Cuco. Voluntary manslaughter. No contest. Mitigating circumstances being that she was a domestic abuse victim and all.

She got time served, plus her sentence reduced to one year at Sybil Brand. Got out in eight months, right before they closed it down due to earthquake damage.

She did that time right too. Kept her mouth shut. Never said nothing to nobody.

Now she's back in Lynwood, working four days a week at El Paisas on Long Beach. She has a kid. They both get taken care of. She's doing real good. Staying clean.

I should know too. I still roll through. I still say what's up to her.

Neither one of us ever mentions that I was in the room, that I had to watch all of it, or that I was the one that told her she had to do it. We'll both be taking that weight to our graves.

Ghost

Sunday, September 14, 2008
Late Morning

8

I'm on the road and I'm settling. Like, I was a Jarrito, all shook up and fizzy while two DEA jackets came back and logged the safe's contents and bagged it without saying shit about any of it, because of course they wouldn't. I'm trusted. Now I'm out and I'm driving, and I'm letting the bubbles I had trapped inside me out in a big-ass yell as I take my foot off the gas and cruise down the far side of the Vincent Thomas Bridge with my windows open. One of the best rides in all Los Angeles.

The port's on both sides of me with cranes like long-legged dragons all lined up in rows above oil tankers and container boats from China. Up this high, I can see where most of America first gets its everything. Where the big metal boxes land and sit before getting driven off to Iowa or Washington or Fresno.

Driving's a *gift*, man. Freedom is what it is. I get to go where I want, when I want, and I love that because the times when I never had nothing still stick to me. Like concrete between my ribs. Because those heavy spaces never forget being hungry. Never forget L.A. potholes on a bouncing bus. Shit, the bus is like being in a room with a bunch of people you'd never wanna hang out with but you have to, and the driver's driving at his pace, on his schedule, and the route is the route. It doesn't change. Not even if he wants it to.

Up ahead, the stoplight pops red on Terminal Island and I push the brake in real easy as I roll up my windows and get the air going. It doesn't help, though.

I'm smelling smells again.

I try to ignore it. I swipe at my nose hard like that's going to do anything, and I end up just looking like a coke head to the lady in the car next to me. I laugh when I catch her glance at me real quick out of the side of her bug-eye-looking sunglasses, because it's not like that's untrue. Long as I got this body, I'm an addict. That's how I'm programmed. That doesn't change.

The light goes green and I let her beat me off the line. Speeding happens all the time on this stretch. I don't do it because it's a hassle. CHP know better than to stop me, but Port Police don't. They don't see blank black plates much, I guess. I never get ticketed after the lights go spinning behind me. I just got to pull over and jaw. That's a Frank word. He jaws with people, and now I do too.

Because if you get pulled over with nothing plates that need explaining, you got to jaw and show ID and then trade a story about the time we opened a safe in Compton and besides drugs and cash, it had a bunch of unexpected old *Playboys* in it because some young gangster was a serious collector. They were all from the seventies, all pristine and in little plastic bags. Sheriffs didn't feel bad opening the bags because they said there might be evidence in there, but all there was were little bookmarking receipts from where they got bought. Maybe you leave out the bit about how you heard later that the kid that owned them was second-generation gangster and his dad had died in the cracked-out eighties, and the only thing left of the old man was this collection. The kid kept it perfect, like his dad might be back home any minute. It's the family stories that always kill me.

Nearly all the stuff coming out of safes I bust for law enforcement is MDMS: money, drugs, metals, and stones. The first two and the last one speak for themselves. It's the metals that are interesting, usually. You got your golds, your silvers. I've never seen platinum on its own in a bar, but I've seen platinum-plated handguns, platinum teeth grills and jewelry and watches, even a platinum-and-gold abacus out in Monterey Park. No shit. Been seeing more metals lately. Maybe because people think the economy is going to go full meltdown and it's better to have the real stuff to back it up.

Weirdest thing I ever found: some dildo made of horn. Like, animal horn. Rhinoceros or antelope or something. I was glad I had my gloves on for *that*. The agents in the room that day still tell that story. If you can't see it coming, nearly all of them end with some joke about being too horny or how the only antidote to being horny is horn, and then everybody listening laughs louder than they're supposed to. That's kind of how it is in this life. On both sides, you take funny where you can get it, and you don't question it.

I put the accelerator in and leave T.I. behind, climbing up the Desmond Bridge toward Long Beach. This side's not as pretty as the Pedro side. More gas stuff. More buildings. Fewer dragon cranes. The engine of the loaded-down semi in the lane next to me is grinding pretty hard as he downshifts, and I push past him, get in the middle lane.

Saddest thing I ever found, and this was back when I was still apprenticing for Frank, was a pair of baby booties knitted with alternating blue and white thread, straight Dodger colors, all looking like somebody's *abuela* put serious love into making them. Each one like a little reminder that gangsters got kids too. That even if you're on the hustle, you don't stop fucking or making more humans. Just maybe you do it faster than folks with plans ever do, because in that life, there's only go, go, go.

Anyways, these booties weren't bigger than my palms when I picked them up. But that's when I saw that there were these spots on them. Little brown-red dots on the white, and little brown-purple dots on the blue. It could only have been blood.

I remember I said, "Oh, fuck," when I saw that, and then, "Excuse my language please, Frank."

Frank didn't say anything.

Out of anybody, he knows what having a dead kid is about. And you don't push a man when you can see he's thinking about things he's been through.

Of course, those dots don't mean the baby is dead or anything, but that's sure the feeling I got holding them. They were heavy in my hands, heavy like rocks, so I put them back all gentle, and I tried not to think about them being in an evidence lockup somewhere.

It took a while, but me and Frank talked a lot about those booties afterwards. Maybe that's why we asked around about them to anybody we did freelance for. Tried to match up any crimes or deaths of minors to that address. Never came up with anything. It ended up being a mystery we had to get comfortable with. Because that's life. You can't know everything. Only some of it. Only the parts that ever find you.

So we speculated how it might've went down, how they ended up in a safe. The short answer is because they're precious, and whoever put those there wanted that tiny little piece of that baby's life to stay safe forever, sealed up, nearby. And that always made me think of Rose. How her one regret was never being able to have kids. That was my regret too, not for me, for her. Because goddamn, the world is going to be better off without any more of me in it, but it sure could have used a lot more of her.

I'm smelling sunscreen again. Coconut and leaves and glue. Hawaiian Tropic. The oddness of it is, I never wore that sunscreen. Never wore any kind. Show me a junkie that ever did and he wasn't any kind of junkie. I still don't carry any in my Jeep, but that's besides the point. The point is, now I'm smelling it. So strong it's like someone's holding it under my nose. And I'm smelling the sea with it too. Like, salt air. And they're mixing together inside me while I stare at this goddamn scented cutout of a tree on my rearview that I just put on this morning, and it promises me it's Pine Fresh, but all I smell is Rose wearing her sunscreen and I'm thinking about us at the beach for the first time, and I'm speeding up on the 710 North, passing the hauling semis, going fast, but that's just stupid. I know I can't outrun the smell. I know it's inside me. I know *she's* still inside me, and it's shit like this that makes me feel like she's still here, even a little.

Like, maybe she's a ghost too.

Like she'll never let me go.

9

Back in the summer of '92, I was seventeen, with shiny new scars on me, still sick to my stomach a week after what the doc called just-to-be-safe chemo, when I first saw the Pacific Ocean. I knew she existed. I knew she was close by. I mean, I saw seagulls all growing up, but never been to where they came from.

I didn't even really know what the word *beach* meant till I was standing on sand, just staring out at the moving blue and watching waves. Like, I'd seen maps, I *got* how the world was mostly water, but there's a difference between thinking something and seeing it. *Feeling* it, really. Being caught up in it because everything you thought you knew is actually growing bigger by the second, and you're not saying anything, or even breathing, really, till you get reminded to take your shoes off and your socks too.

And so I did. That sand was hot. Gritty. Sneaking between my toes. It was too much, standing there like that. Sun on me. Feeling like I was seeing California for the first time even though I'd seen nothing else my whole life.

Rose held my hand, I remember. She kicked my heels till my feet were in the water before handing me that sunscreen, telling me to rub it on the bald parts of her head, the ones that weren't Mohawked. She didn't really have one. Just tufts down the middle, so blond they were almost white. Like the thin feathers of baby pigeons.

"We've come a long way, Saint Francis."

The hospital, she meant. Sometimes she just called me that after the place we met.

We couldn't have been more different from each other, but everybody else was older than us or so young it made you sad, and after kind of circling each other, we talked because there was nothing else to do when Uncle Scam paid to pump me full of anti-infective, antitumor chemicals. And she was there. Half-broken with a smile on her face. Gray-blue eyes. Her left lid a little lower than the other. She fell asleep sometimes when we were talking. Said she felt safe with me. And no one had ever said that about me ever. It still kind of fucks me up to think about it.

"Far as we can get," I said with my feet in the ocean. "We ran out of land."

She didn't say anything, but her eyes told me, *Good*.

It was easy to see she was sick. She had Hodgkin's. "I got Hodgkinned," she used to say. She was terminal. This was why she brought me to Cabrillo Beach. Said she wanted to look past Angels Gate lighthouse to Terminal Island and see if it called out to her to swim to it and never come back.

It was the kind of thing I never knew if I should laugh about.

I wish I had. Because seeing the gleam in her eyes when she knew she'd made me laugh was, like, everything. Yeah. *Everything.*

Rose hated her name. Hated being named after a flower. The way she saw it, that wasn't who she was or what she'd become. She liked me calling her Rosita. Liked the half roll on the *R*. She said it made her giddy, made her forget where she came from. Made her feel more like who she really was.

She was canvas Converse, and ripped T-shirts she sewed back together by hand. She was caramel corn, sweet and salty and hard to chew sometimes if you got down to the kernels. She was box matches. She was men's hats. She used to say she was just crumpled-up tinfoil. Some glittery trash, and pretty soon God was going to throw her away in a garbage can. It hurt hearing that.

Her name wasn't the only thing Rose hated. She hated her nose. Too flat. Her arms. Too skinny, too freckled. Her rogue eyelid. She wanted to cut it. She thought she was the furthest thing from beautiful. Nothing I said ever made any difference. Took me years after to figure out that trying to convince a woman that doesn't think she's pretty that she actually is, is like throwing coins in a well with no bottom. You wait for it to hit and pile up just so she can see it over time and start believing it because you believe it, but nothing ever lands. Nothing ever adds up.

Rose didn't have time for anything to add up. She only had that present. Her yesterday was gone, her tomorrow would never come, and she lived like it. She was like this exploding sun all the time, the closest thing a bone-skinny girl got to being a thumping bass line walking and talking. No surprise, she got me into punk rock. Bad Religion mostly. Through them, she made me see how punk spoke my language without me even knowing it. Punk didn't come from where I came from, but it knew how mad I was before I even did. It just reached in, hit all my fuel I'd been building up, and lit it on fire. Bad Religion were a whole different L.A. One I'd never known before, and for two months that summer we drove everywhere we could in her beat-up Wrangler with the tape of *Against the Grain* smashing our eardrums.

That song off that, "Turn On the Light," that was her. Still is.

When we went out together, she just wanted to take and then give when people weren't expecting it. And me, I just wanted to be with her and I didn't care what we did or who we did it to.

We'd go to Santa Monica Pier and cut people's fishing lines when they weren't looking. If you could do it and not get caught, the other person had to put a five-dollar bill in the fisherman's fish bucket. If we ever did get caught, Rose just pulled her hat off her head and people saw she was the sick kind of bald and she said she was real sorry, just playing a prank, trying to feel alive for a few more days and then she forced them to take one of the fives. Wow, did people ever crumble.

Because what was it really? A lost bit of plastic? A hook? What was that compared to a cancer girl about to cry because you're yelling at her. Nothing, that's what. It was silence and embarrassment and turned backs, no one wanting to take the cash. I knew before, but I knew it for real then. People don't like being confronted.

And I learned something else too: death has a power. Death-coming-soon has even more. It changes up the rules of things. It creates breaks and slides where there might not otherwise be any. It's a knife for this world. Opening things up. Letting things slide through. Giving you shortcuts when you don't have time to go the long way. Especially when everybody can see on you that it's true.

10

I texted Frank about tamale breakfast and he wrote back *yes*, so I told him Tamaleria La Doña in Compton. When he didn't reply, I knew it was because he was already on his way so I needed to be there first.

I'm pulling off the 710, getting down onto Alondra, waiting to turn left. I've been pushing it away, but it's been piling up inside me, how the first time I was ever in San Pedro, it was with Rose. How the first time I ever really went anywhere but Lynwood, it was with Rose in her Jeep and it was to Pedro.

Already I'm thinking about how every moment I ever spent with her got stuck inside me and changed how I saw things. The city. Even me. She did that. Just by being her, she came in with this invisible crowbar and broke me out of this jail I had inside myself, one I didn't even know about. Rose took me to my first NA meeting. Sat next to me. Held my hand the whole time when I wanted to run. My world was like eighteen blocks wide when she met me.

I bust a right on Atlantic while I'm staring at Dale's giant bumpy donut he's got on top of his shop. I go past a muffler place and a pet shop and a whole mess of tire shops clustered together. Ralda's. Atlantic Tire. Vargas. Rios. It's like the buildings are sitting still and staring at each other all day.

My heart's kind of hurting, more than usual. There's a badass rose I got on my chest because her name never felt like enough. Tattoo is like thread under skin. It makes invisible stuff real. It catches up dreams and wishes and memories and ties them to you with ink so you can carry them and show people, but only if you want to.

Going east on East Compton, I pass the spot when there's no street spaces, hit a right on Gibson, and park just down from the do-it-yourself car wash. The cart pushers are out already, pushing rigs they stole from North Side Market, going through the car wash Dumpster, trying to fill up on the leanest day of the week. Tomorrow will be better. Mondays are trash days. There will be bottles and cans for the digging, and maybe food too. It'll be good again.

If you're worried about it, don't be worried about it. It's not a great neighborhood, but it's not the worst. My Jeep's fine. It's only got a tape player in it. I eject Rose's tape out of that, put it in its case, put the case in my jacket pocket, button it closed. When I get out, I grab the heavy grocery moneybag from under my seat, move around to the back gate, and open it up. I combo out the big lockbox bolted to the floor back there and push the moneybag down next to my tools before locking it back up. Couldn't have done that in Pedro with DEA watching me leave.

The outside of my Jeep is clean, the paint's good enough on it, but it's definitely no kind of target. It's an '87 Wrangler, same as the one Rose used to have. First big thing I ever bought. Took me forever to find one. You'd think you could find any car on earth in Los Angeles, especially with the Internet, but I had to do a deal with a guy in San Diego and take the train down to pick it up. Coming back was one of the best and worst drives of my life. I could feel her so near me and so gone at the same time.

If you're thinking it, yes, I know I'm living in a time capsule. Shit, I'm driving it. But I want to. At least I know I want to. I think some people aren't much different from me. They like how things used to be more than they are now. But that's gone. I know it's gone. I just try to keep what I can.

You wouldn't know it by looking at the Jeep now, but I've had the entire guts taken out. New engine. New tranny. New everything. It's also LoJacked. Only sticker on the back of it is a little one with that logo, and the VEHICLE RECOVERY SYSTEM typed underneath. Smart gangsters know better about that. It never stopped the baddest ones, but that level knows enough not to touch anything with black plates.

When I walk past the car wash vacuums, I look to the lanes on my left and see some dude sitting in the cab of his truck and messing with his phone while his girl is out blasting over the hood with water from the long metal wand. She's short. Like, five foot. And she's arching the spray to reach the roof and a little unexpected rainbow's popping out of it. I watch it for a second, water and air and colors, till I notice him looking at me like maybe I'm looking at his girl, so I nod my head up at him, turn, and go.

Fresh corn. The smell hits you first, then gets inside you, tells you life is going to be okay today. And I'm so damn thankful I can smell it right now. Being inside La Doña is like being inside the littlest food factory on earth. Every inch of the room is full up. In front, it's a standing and waiting area with a few scattered tables in front of a counter with a register. Behind that is a shucking station where at least three men are always pulling the husks off corn in rhythm. Sometimes there's more. Next to them are boxes for unshucked and shucked, naked corn still on cobs, where another man picks these up and whisks all the kernels off them with a long-ass knife: quick, quick, like he's playing a guiro or something.

Behind him, ladies shape each tamale on big metal tables that have some kind of wax paper spread over them so the tamales don't stick or get dry. To their right is a giant mixing thing to shred the corn up. It's taller than the lady putting stuff into and taking it out. On the back wall a whole army of steaming pots is cooking up masa, and other ones steam up tamales.

Men shuck. Women shape. That's just how it is. Together, they make thousands in a day. No lie.

Most people don't eat here. They just pick up. I go grab a table on the far wall, so my back is covered and I can see the door. Above me, there's a map of Mexico and black-and-white pictures of Zapata and Villa. It's that in-your-face kind of *raza* place I can't get enough of. No AC. *Champurrado* on the whiteboard menu. Wrinkly *tios* waiting in line, holding their cowboy hats in their hands.

I got corn for me and a cheese. For Frank, two *carne de res*. He shouldn't eat beef anymore because his doctor said so, but he won't eat anything else, and Frank is Frank. He'll keep being who he is till they put him in the ground.

I kind of get lost watching the men shucking. Hands flash and green gives way to whitish yellow, again and again. It's hypnotic. They're all masters. No wasted movement. After the corn threads are thrown into a trash bag just for them, each husk leaf gets set down gently in a curved stack to be used for later, because that's what the tamales get wrapped and cooked in.

This place has a hum to it. I mean, there's the drinks case with Mexican Cokes buzzing its buzz next to the front door, and fluorescent lights too, but neither of those is it. It's just a feeling that people are doing what they do in here because they want to, and maybe some of them even love it. People are smiling at each other behind the counter while they're doing what they're doing, and that's good, I think. That good feeling goes right into the food, which is fine by—

"Earth to Mendoza." Frank must've come in without me noticing, which is rare and he knows it. "Sometimes you're just out there orbiting, you know that?"

I definitely know that. And me looking down and smiling about it tells him so.

He doesn't smile back. Just shakes his head when I push his paper plate and wrapped tamales in front of him. Half his hair's the color of steel and he still lifts weights three times a week. Pretty good for an old guy with a sandpaper face. He could shave at five in the morning and have stubble after breakfast. He's got kind eyes, though, if he likes you. And if you know where to look.

11

Frank's never been to La Doña before, and that can be a problem because he doesn't always like going to places he's never been. He's mostly a La Fiesta Carniceria guy, this spot on Marine by Frank's shop that does some killer carne asada tacos. He must not hate this place too much, though, because he almost smiles when he sits.

"Jesus," he says, "why make me drive over here? We got tamalies in Hawthorne."

Tamales are *tamalies* when Frank's saying it. And why here, because I'm not as known here, but Frank doesn't need to know that.

"You got Mexicans all around you right now, Frank. You can't be taking the holy son's name like that." I move my plastic knife up from doing surgery on my *elote* to wave in his face a little. "You're liable to get cut. And I might even *let* them."

Frank laughs at that. It's a good laugh. Strong. Like he has to go somewhere deep down to bring it up.

He's laughing because he knows if somebody ever for real tried to hurt him, I'd lose all sense of right and wrong. A light would go off inside me and I'd be that whirling devil again. Not like he'd need me to, though. He's an ex-army engineer from the Vietnam days. He did some stuff back then. Stuff he'll never tell me about, but I know it's bad. Bad under orders is still bad. He's killed, I'm pretty sure. It takes one to know one and I see it in his eyes sometimes. The weight of it. How he'd never want to do it again but would if he had to. Keeping that look on your face is just part of this job. Keeps people from messing with you. But if someone did, he's got a gun on him right now in his ankle holster. CCW. Legal concealed carry.

I kick his holster with the toe of my boot under the table just to show him I know where it is, and when I do, the rolled money wriggles around my ankle and I set my foot back down, quick and flat, so nothing falls out.

I say, "You'd probably just take care of that yourself, though, huh?"

He scoots back fast in his chair and shoots me a warning look, a you-fucking-know-better kind that I feel in the bumps behind my ears, and I know I shouldn't have gone so far. Frank's the kind of guy that when he looks at you wrong, you never want him to look at you that way again.

I look at my tamale. I stab a little corn kernel. "Sorry, Frank."

I feel stupid. Like a kid saying sorry to his dad. I'm not looking up, but I know he's still giving me the look to nail it in. I can feel it. We go a bit not saying anything. We just chew.

He finally says, "You're acting squirrelly."

That's Frank's way of asking me if I'm all right. He asks questions with statements because he can see inside me too good. He mostly always has. He knows about my tumors on account of my visible scars and me not lying when he asked about them. I'm not about to tell him I'm smelling phantom smells again, for the first time since before. He can't know that.

And I'm sure not about to tell him I just betrayed all the trust he ever put in me since he's had me running his shop, and that the evidence of that is locked up in my truck. And I'm not about to tell him that I don't even know how much money it is. Almost don't want to know till me and Mira can count it.

"I guess I just been thinking about some stuff," I say.

He stops midbite and puts an eyebrow up at me. Like, *Stuff?*

Frank's face asks you questions too. He keeps chewing when I don't say anything, swallows, and says, "Spit it out."

When I was young, being cool was about being wild, not giving a fuck. Basically, it was taking shit way past the point it needed to be at. When I was using, that's just how it was. Drugs *ran* me. I didn't even know half the stuff I was doing when I was doing it, and I remembered even less if I was lucky. All of it was shameful. All of it coming out of pain. I didn't know that then.

I know it now, though. And one of the things I've realized about getting older is shit like that was never cool to begin with. Growing up, *real* growing up, regardless of how old you are when you do it, is about discipline. Trying to be deliberate, I guess.

"I don't think I can run the shop much longer, Frank." My ears start ringing before it's even all the way out of my mouth. He can see my face get red.

He'll never say it, but I swear the first thought that flashes in his eyes is I got cancer again. That it came back.

"When you say *much longer*"—his words come out slow, like he's working cherries around in his mouth and only spitting the pits when he wants to—"what are we talking?"

I don't know, I'm thinking. *Depends on how long it takes them to catch me.* "Two weeks?"

Frank's brows go down and don't come back up.

Frank's sixty-three. He's only ever had two apprentices, and Glenn fucking Rios moved to San Bernardino to open his own shop forever ago. There's just been me and Frank these last eleven years, but it's really been us together for fifteen total. So, this is basically me stabbing the man with words. Doing everything I never wanted to do but was always afraid I would, eventually. This man right here did everything there ever was to do to give a fucked-up kid some purpose, a new life if I worked for it, and here I am throwing it in his face like I don't care and never did. Worst part is, he thinks I'm pulling a Rios too.

He'll take this personal. He'll take it to his grave.

Betraying this man, I've never hated myself so much in my life as now. I feel shame bursting up inside me, telling me, once a junkie, always a junkie. Telling me, I can't ever be loved, or trusted. Telling me, I'll break his world and everything in it if I haven't already stolen it first.

It's what I am.

Stupid.

Selfish.

Worthless.

I grab a big breath and use it to try to kill this negativity inside me. Or at least get it quieter. Because if I don't, I'll spiral. And I can't do that. Not now.

"So this is you telling me you don't even know." Frank pushes his plate away from him. "*Soon*, you're saying."

"Yeah." I want more words. Better words. Strong words.

Words that can say how fucked-up and sorry I am, and that it has to be like this if I'm going to protect him at all, and that I can't tell him why because I can't have him knowing what I did and I can't have anything ever coming back on him. No matter what, he'll be disappointed in me, but at least it's for thinking I'm an ungrateful piece of shit instead.

He's waiting for me to say something, but I'm just blank-facing it because I'm exhausted and I got nothing left to hide behind.

"Jesus, *Ricky*." How he says that name hurts more than him punching me in the kidneys. "You could've at least had the class to get me drunk first. Bought me a fucking steak. Tamalies are no kind of goodbye."

' He's absolutely right, but I don't say that.

I can't.

When he gets up and walks out without even looking back, I can't breathe.

And I never want to again either.

12

That feeling lasts all the way to the Jeep. And when I get in, I just have to turn the engine over and blast the AC, because I'm feeling like I'll fucking throw up if I don't. So I just got to sit here, and breathe with my mouth wide open, but it's still coming at me, so I throw it into drive and shoot down Gibson.

Sometimes driving is the only antidote for anything. When I feel stuck, when it feels like I can't breathe or move, I get in and go. When I hit the 710 South, I'm good for a minute in the fast lane so I blast it, and when I put my foot down, I'm trying to put my anger there like I'm stomping out a bug, and the engine's roaring, and for a good few seconds, I'm free.

That doesn't last, though.

Late lunch traffic of people sneaking back to work creeps in around me, and my eighty-five drops to seventy-five, seventy. Nobody wants to go this slow in L.A. Never. You see an open lane, you take it. Because if you don't, somebody else will. They'll fucking pass you on the right to take it too.

By sixty-five, I'm not outrunning anything anymore. My stomach knows it. It's acting like I've only ever fed it hot sauce, this burning thing inside me. And I can't stop thinking about Frank's face when he told me I should've bought him a steak if that's what I was going to tell him. Fuck.

I want to scream, but I don't.

At sixty, I start looking for concrete dividers to plow into. But I don't see any big enough to wreck this thing and kill me, and the feeling passes. I'm telling myself, *There's also the money and how it's for somebody that needs it, but maybe there's so much now that it's for a lot of somebodies*, so I just drift over to the 91 West ramp, which is all jammed up. Cars left. Cars right. A bunch stuck in the middle.

In L.A., people know their exits, but never which direction. They never plan ahead. It's epidemical. So they're cutting each other off, which knocks on to everybody else. Like, right now. I have to stop on an on-ramp because some old lady in a 1970s Celica with a THE WORLD NEEDS MORE RAINBOWS sticker on it needs to get all the way west for no understandable reason.

Sometimes, you just gotta know your lane and stick to it. I'm in mine and I'm stuck, staring at the sign for the West.

My face is sweating. The AC is to max, and I'm *still* sweating.

I need Rose with me so I go in my pocket and pull out her tape, the one she said I had to take because she made it for me, and if I didn't take it and listen to it and memorize it and let it get down into my soul, it'd be the rudest thing ever and she'd never talk to me again, especially after she was dead. She even made me promise to keep listening to it when she was gone. I put it in the deck and hit a full rewind.

When it stops and rolls forward, I imagine Rose pushing the PLAY and RECORD buttons at the same time on her stereo. I can almost hear her silently counting the five seconds before the guitars and spit of "I'm Not a Loser" start. I smile and ride it for a couple miles. It fades out, ending in a small tap. That's her hitting PAUSE, and compressed down into that tiny sound is the knowledge I got of her changing to the new song, and then the pause comes off and I count the five seconds with Rose again, and then "Rise Above" puts me on its shoulders and picks me up.

Took me too long to figure out that she was trying to tell me something with the songs she picked. Trying to say I was worth something and I could do better than I was doing. I could *be* better. I was her project. Her good thing to leave behind in the world. I couldn't let her down. All she left me with was this mix tape and some stories to tell.

It's Rose's fault that I think stories are one of the most powerful things in the world. More powerful than knives and surgeries. More powerful than bullets. Because stories live past you. Stories can get into other people and live there too. Stories are like glasses, kind of. They change how you see the world. Rose's stories made me want to find her dad.

I never told Frank I looked him up the first time because I'd been reading the obituaries every day since Rose stopped calling me at the Piñedas' place down the block and telling me where to meet her.

"If I stop calling"—she used to smile as she'd say this to me— "I'm dead or in the hospital."

I saw his name in the *Times* in Rose's obituary. "Survived by her father, Franklin Stenberg." Donations were received for her funeral and I ripped off a dealer I knew but didn't like called Harlem Harold for almost four hundred bucks, put it in an envelope wrapped up in tinfoil, and sent it to the house in Hawthorne. I knew the address from the clipping. I still got it in my wallet. It got pretty ratty before I laminated it. But her face is still there in black-and-white, shining underneath blond-white hair that went down to her shoulders. I never knew her like that. Unsick.

Months later was the first time I took three buses to Prairie Avenue in Hawthorne, across from Jim Thorpe Park. I didn't even know what I was doing. I would've gone sooner, but I was high all the time. I stole. I fought. I got sent to Youth Authority. Burned almost a year in there before I came out and wanted to see Frank's face just so I could see Rose's in it. You know, see where she came from. I was crazy. Really fucked-up. I missed her so much I wanted to die.

Going up to Hawthorne was the only thing that got me out of the neighborhood. I hung around that block enough that Frank noticed me scoping *tortas* at the Mexican Mini-Market there. Noticed me reading newspapers out in front of it on this little metal bench. Noticed me looking in his shop window once or twice. All that before he ever called me out on it and wanted to know how long I was planning on casing his shop before I tried to run up in it with a gun and rob him. I don't blame him for that. I would've thought the same thing.

This was before Glenn fucking Rios, but it was after this dude named Jeremy. His mom got sick and he had to move back East, so Frank needed somebody to carry his tools and that was it. The first few months were unpaid, but he'd buy me food when I was on the clock. And I never told him. I never even hinted at what made me find him.

He'll never know his little girl stopped me saying *cuz* and gave me *becauses*, stopped me saying *don't* for everything and gave me *doesn't*s too, or how his little girl gave me a better life when she led me to him. That's how I see it. It was her ghost guiding me. Never letting go. And she's still not. Her brain is still here in this mix. Every track she picked. The ordering of them. I can see it. Feel it. And I count the five seconds again, and Screeching Weasel comes on, a cover of "I Can See Clearly Now."

Frank knows I got a rose tattoo on my chest. He never asked why. Lots of Mexicans love their roses. If I was him, I never would've thought twice about it. I'll never tell him it's for his daughter, though. Not ever.

It's the only thing that would kill him dead on the spot. Anything to do with Rose. Anything to do with how I met her. Especially me never telling him all these years. And that's the one thing I can always spare him, so I always will.

I'm almost to Crystal Casino when my phone rings.

I got to bite my lip when I see it's Collins. Well, a blocked call means DEA or FBI, anyways. And I just know it's Collins.

When I click to pick it up, and he comes on the line, he says, "You notice anything weird about this safe?"

Panic snaps onto the bottom of my stomach like a bracket and tries to pull me down into my seat, but I know I got to answer quick, so I just act like I need clarification. "What kind of weird?"

"*Weird.*" Collins says it like his emphasis is actually helpful. "Bad weird."

"I don't know what that means," I say, and it's the truth. "I just open them."

"Okay," Collins says, but he's not convinced. I can hear it.

I don't know how he knows I took anything, but he knows.

I say, "You see something I missed?"

Something's going on in the background. Voices. Maybe somebody talking to him. He gets distracted for a second and then stays distracted. He signs off with "I need you to come in. You've just got to see this."

It's not a request.

And I know it, but I'm distracted too. I'm smelling smells again, grilled cheese this time. Haven't had one in a week. I miss my exit on purpose and keep going. As I pass Crystal Casino, I watch it go by like a cruise boat I won't be getting on. It's so close. But it's too damn far.

I pick up my prepaid phone and call Mira's prepaid.

"Going to be late," I say.

She sighs on the other end. "Just don't make me waste a baby-sitter day for nothing."

Glasses

Sunday, September 14, 2008
Early Afternoon

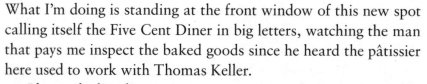

What I'm doing is standing at the front window of this new spot calling itself the Five Cent Diner in big letters, watching the man that pays me inspect the baked goods since he heard the pâtissier here used to work with Thomas Keller.

I learned what that was ten minutes ago in the back of a Chrysler 300 with bulletproof windows and a reinforced body since Rooster cares about stuff like chefs and pedigrees.

So we're here, watching the man stare at some type of cut cakes in trays and Danishes under a glass lid while I ignore the severed mannequin heads with frosting hairdos set out around the food like a art project.

I look up Main Street to Fifth, where two raggedy people are yelling at each other near the bus stop. A man and a woman. He's wearing two jackets. She's got on something looking like it used to be a long dress, with one of its straps tied in a big knot on her shoulder to keep it up.

Both of them are so dirty I can't really tell what race they are from here. She's super in his face too. Her chin's up so high that she's shouting at the sky above his head. "Plastic, you dumb bucket of crap! Plas-*tic*."

He's shaking his head at her, saying, "No!"

Downtown Los Angeles has a special type of crazy to it. It's got so many people with problems, drugs or liquor, or even medical. Street theater, that's what Rooster calls things popping off like this.

Sometimes it's sad. Sometimes it's funny, but it's never boring. A big red bus pulls up at the stop and blocks my view of the couple, so I turn to check on the car.

It's parked at the curb next to a meter that isn't working. Lonely's inside it, still cramped behind the steering wheel, just watching the street be the street.

I've told Rooster he needs something bigger so Lonely isn't so smashed in the seat when he's driving, prolly an Escalade, but Rooster likes this 300. It's in his ex's name. It's his lucky car.

Besides, Lonely never complains. He's a no-maintenance type of soldier. I don't think I've ever even heard him excuse himself to go and use the bathroom. He never has questions, always does what he's told.

But the guy sitting next to him in the shotgun seat? He's the opposite. Terco's one of those controller types. Every hair on his head slicked back with a little wave to it. He carries a comb on him too big for his back pocket.

He has opinions for everything, the type to ask you stuff not so much to get answers, but just to see your face and if he's pushing your buttons or not. That type of behavior might be funny if he wasn't hungry to be bigger than he is.

Hey, he's smart, I'll give him that, but the kid's early twenties, too young to remember how bad the drive-by days were, how safe everything is now in comparison. That's what bothers me about him. He's got no gratefulness to him.

Me and Terco, we're oil and water and he knows it. That's why whenever we're together on account of Rooster, we don't talk. Not like how me and Big Danny don't talk. That's comfortable. This is the opposite of that. I mean, we don't even look at each other. It's better for everybody that way. Less stress.

I take my prescription sunglasses off to clean with the cloth I always bring in my little jeans pocket. Twenty times a day I'm doing this. The reason is, I got long eyelashes. I'm forever getting stuff on the lenses. I get them swiped off and put them back on and look to Rooster, but he's lost in thought on some type of donut. When he does this, we wait it out.

I'm good for that normally, but I'm hungry now. My mind's on sandwiches. I could do a French dip, but Cole's isn't reopened yet from getting restored. They promised it'd be ready for January's hundredth anniversary. Nine months later, still nothing.

If I got a vote for today, I'd have said Langer's for pastrami or Eastside Deli for meatball subs, but when you ride with Rooster, you're on his schedule and you only eat where he wants to eat.

"What's up with the name of this place?" Terco points at the sign on the window with his comb. "Does that mean, like, everything in there is five cents, or what?"

Obviously the answer's no, and Terco knows that, but he's asking just to ask. That's who he is.

"Fifth Street gets called the Nickel." Lonely always talks when you don't expect him to and I like that about him. "So this place is called Nickel Diner."

I sniff. Of course he'd know what it's called. He drove us here.

Terco's looking around still. He says, "But aren't we on Main Street?"

We are.

When this don't get a reaction, Terco sort of scoffs before saying, "That's dumb then."

What Fifth Street is, is a artery for Skid Row, where a good amount of the homeless and junkies hang. Next to the diner is the Community Action Network, so it's a spot homeless go to, and standing where we're standing? It's like we're on an invisible trail for street people.

Junkies, I can do without. But I'm not mad at homeless. Hey, my dad was one when he first came here. He crossed the river over in Texas, near El Paso. What my mom says is, she came the same way a couple months later with her brother. Took us years to move all the way west.

There was Socorro in Texas, where I was born in a filled-up bathtub. There was Las Cruces and a different Socorro in New Mexico before Albuquerque. We hit those before Pueblo in Colorado, where we stayed for only one snowy winter in 1979 and we all hated that.

After, it was Flagstaff, where the gardening and odd jobs was finally good for my dad and uncle and that got us saved up enough to make Ontario, or *Onterio* as I always heard it, in California.

After that, it was like getting thrown up into the air and bouncing again and again, never landing for long in one place. Chino, then Watts, Cerritos, back to Chino. That was the time we went back to our old landlord since my uncle got snapped up in a raid outside Walmart and sent back, then it was Downey and then Lynwood to stay. Lynwood wasn't so much where we stopped as where we landed and stuck.

Most people passing on the sidewalk avoid us here. They either got tunnel vision for wherever they're going, or they're junkies that can smell scary a mile away.

Either way, nobody's going near Rooster. Nobody except the guy from the bus stop, the one wearing two types of coats.

I'm watching him walk his way toward us, trying a story about his car running out of gas on an office lady with her hair up, and then on a girl with arm tattoos that came out of the diner and went his way.

Both don't say nothing. They just keep walking.

What I do when he gets closer is, I put myself between him and Rooster. He sees me do that and changes direction. He goes straight for the car instead, straight for Terco, his arm hanging out the window.

Up closer, I see this guy is missing the top of his right ear. It's squared off on a angle, clean, like prolly a good knife did it. He's short like me, couldn't be more than a hundred pounds. And he's light-skinned black like that manager lady at the bank. Mira something.

"Good-looking gentleman like you," the guy says to Terco, "I know you got change."

Lonely looks to the man before looking to me to see if I want him hurt. I shake my head. Lonely sees this and sits still where he is.

Terco brings his arm back into the car and puts on his best tough-guy face. "Get the fuck out of here, *mayate*."

The guy ignores the slur, or don't even know it is a slur, and keeps pushing. "C'mon, I know you got money for hair cream, so you got some for me."

I want to smile but I don't. Even if he's ripping Terco, I can't be having that out on the street, so I step up behind him all obvious. I want him to know I'm there. When he feels me get close, he turns quick.

I say to him, "Hey, I need you to keep walking."

He hears in my voice how there's command, like military or cops, except he's smart enough to know we don't have to wear uniforms or worry about holding up any laws. I see this guy look at himself in my sunglasses before he turns and goes, past the CAN. Towards Sixth.

When he's gone a few steps but not so far away he can't hear, Terco laughs after him and says, "See ya! You have a delicious day."

I guess Terco didn't realize how Rooster's beside me now too, not looking in the window no more, and he says to Terco, "Get out."

Meaning, get out of the car. Terco does it, but his look shows anybody looking how much he don't like doing it.

Rooster lets him stand there and wait for what's coming before he says, "I know you got more class in you than saying 'delicious' to somebody that probably doesn't get enough to eat. What's your problem?"

"Nothing's my problem," Terco says, sounding like everything is.

It don't help that he tries putting his comb away in his back pocket before deciding to stick it in his front instead.

"Apologize to him." Rooster holds out a twenty-dollar bill to Terco and makes him take it.

What the best part is, is that Terco actually tries to argue. He says, "But that hype'll just put it in his arm!"

At that, Rooster just leans in close to Terco. "Then we get it right back."

Rooster leaves it there. He's not the type to ever tell somebody to do something twice. Terco knows this. He's just trying to swallow his pride. I can see it stinging in there behind his eyes.

What I'm hoping is, this'll teach him something, but I know it won't. He's not the learning type. Still, I'm about to enjoy the sight of Terco apologizing. Already he's walking stiff and fast, going after the guy, trying to catch up before the crosswalk goes for Sixth Street.

But what happens then is the phone I'm carrying rings when it's not supposed to. Rooster hears it and shoots me a sharp type of look, the type I feel in my chest, the type that reminds me how real he is.

Me and him, we both know this call's bad news. So I cross the sidewalk to the car, open the door to the backseat, and get in before I answer.

14

What I'm thinking first when that phone rings is *Prolly something's off with the money I set up.* My guts know it.

I let it keep ringing. That it's going now means a problem is finding us, one that's about to be Rooster's to fix. They don't call unless they messed up or need something big. Or both.

Hey, I don't have to tell Lonely nothing. He's already getting out the front and taking a short walk to the curb by the time I pick up the line. I don't say hello.

I say, *"Bueno."*

That's it. Nobody says names. If you know the number, you know who it is you're calling. On the other side, it's just a guy like me in another crew confirming the connection.

"Yeah," he says, and that just means we're here. We're ready.

I move over, making room for Rooster to get in on the near

side and sit beside me in the backseat. When he's settled, I put it on speaker.

He don't carry a phone, so I carry it for him. I run all the phones. This one is in Leya's cousin's friend's name, and I give her cash flat, plus a little extra, to pay the bill each month when I take it.

I say phones since I rotate them. Single women are best. They use their phones a lot. The world is a scary place. It makes more sense for them to request blocked numbers and use them.

I run about thirty lines at once, borrowing them a week here or a few days there, picking them up, taping camera lenses over, until I drop them back off with people that use them like everyday phones.

When there's no dedicated line for business, not even a pre-paid, it's like putting a bunch of little toys outside in a snowstorm. They get buried. What I like to call it is random layering, since I'm hiding a few short calls from blocked sources in plain sight every second month or so on a law-abiding citizen's bill.

Rooster don't know I copy down the call log dates and times before I hand the phones back so I know exactly what call came or went when, and then I make notes on who got called and for what. If I know where it happened, I write that down too. He wouldn't like that if he knew. He'd hate it.

Rooster never talks on any phone about business, on the chance it's recorded. He listens. He uses American Sign Language to tell me what to ask back. This is so he'll never be on paper.

It's the same on the other end, but I don't think they use sign. More than likely, they're writing stuff down for the speaker to say. This way, if someone DEA like Collins was overhearing this call right now, he might think it was two people having a conversation, me and the other guy, not four.

Even if he thinks it's more than two, it don't matter. He can't prove it. There's no words on tape to use as evidence.

This call kicks off with us getting told what we already knew was coming. DEA came, busted everything up. They got in the safe, but, and here's where everything got messed up, they didn't confiscate all of the 920 gees that was in it.

Rooster's calm but inside he's tripping out. I can see it in his eyes. He signs, *Why not?* So I say it.

There's not much of a pause before the answer comes in, so I'm thinking they'd worked out a few things to say before they called.

"Because the money was gone. We saw paperwork. Thirty-three thousand, it said. We know the safecracker took it. We got somebody saying she saw him walk out and put some bags in his Jeep before the dog came back."

Dog's DEA. What my first thought is, I can't put down without cursing. That's all Leya's fault, getting me to tone it down for the kid. My second thought is what type of idiot gets seen like that?

Rooster's already thinking what I'm thinking. He signs, *No*.

It's shorthand. What this means is, don't repeat on the phone what I'm about to sign to you. Then he signs, *Nothing organized. This clown not planning to steal.*

There's not really a sign for *clown*. It's *peabrain*, like *stupid*. But if we were talking, he'd say clown. So that's what I hear in my head.

There's so much tone you can put on sign, so much body language and flavor if you want to. It can be the most emotional language on earth if you let it be. Rooster's super calm, super reserved when he says it. Precise, I'd say. Monotone hands, if that makes sense.

I agree with him, but I'm more agitated. I sign back, *He sees money, he takes.* The way I sign this says I think this thief's greedy and stupid.

Rooster raises his eyebrows, but don't disagree, so I speak up and ask for everything they know about the safecracker. I need a description. As soon as they say it, I memorize it.

Rooster signs, *What else?* So I ask it. What comes next is a bad surprise.

We get told about two holes and dynamite dust that got poured down inside the door of the safe. Even I'm not cool enough to keep my scoff from coming out when I hear that news.

That was definitely not something I seen when I was there.

Rooster looks at me and I look at him at the same time, both of us super pissed off. That wasn't the deal.

Rooster signs, *Who did it?* I say it.

"I just found out," the guy on the other end says.

There's no way this's true, but we have to act like we believe him.

Again, Rooster signs. *No.* Then he signs, *Safe. Later tell me how we got it.*

This time, anger jumps in his fingers, like he's knifing words into the air. As he's doing that, I'm thinking how I definitely don't want to be the guy that got this safe for us. We knew his cousin got shot through the spine and paralyzed by some sheriffs on a wild bust in Hawaiian Gardens last year.

If anybody put the powder in there, it was him trying to do some type of random payback on anybody with a uniform, is my guess. That's gonna haunt him and the dumbass deserves it too.

Rooster's signing again. *Anything else?* Basically, he's wondering if there's any more we need to know before we handle this.

When I ask it, they say, "No." I say, "Okay." And that's the end of that. No goodbyes, just a click.

Rooster needs thinking time, so I step out of the car onto the sidewalk. Terco's back and looking like a wet cat, so I send him into the diner to get one of every pastry type so Rooster can do his tasting later in private.

Terco likes taking orders from me about as much as he likes getting told to apologize, but he does it without acting like a little kid so I'm good.

Outside's hotter than I remember it being, and my stomach don't like that. It don't like that Rooster's not happy with what he heard either, but even when things go good, he's not happy. You don't get to be Rooster being happy.

You get to be him by being unhappy, by whatever he has never being enough. He's always after ways for things to go smoother. He's always after ways to get more.

But I'm angry. I put Rooster's ninety-two gees in the safe with my own hands. If I'd known there was something stupid going on, I never would've done it. How this whole thing happened was

Rooster sent me down to negotiate. We knew DEA was coming since I told them to come.

When I stacked that money in the safe, I knew it was never coming back. That was the plan. It was meant to get taken, to buy us time. DEA could take what they wanted. It was for them.

How much, we couldn't say. It was an offering, almost *cariño*. They could skim however much they wanted to at the scene or Collins could find some paper way to add it to his budget down the road, however they do that.

Rooster has always known I kick Collins scraps. He put me up to it. A lot of times, I give Collins wrong information before something goes down for us, or I give him right information but too late. I tip him to Rooster's enemies too.

Sometimes, we even have to set up a bust, like this time. It was supposed to be a big one and now it's not. That's a problem.

Rooster organized it so nine of the other crews would put in 10 percent each. The idea in pooling is to keep losses down by going in together to make something big enough to satisfy the DEA since they need their dope and cash on the table from time to time.

What Rooster calls that is feeding the dog, and this safe was supposed to be a little feast. It's the type of thing that makes them proud and sluggish.

The safest and best time to move something is after DEA has a big bust and they're all congratulating themselves on TV about keeping streets safe for kids. That's when you run it hard and quiet, when they're full and slow.

You feed them an offering to move much bigger shipments somewhere else. This type of thinking is why people talk criminal business like it's chess. But it's so much bigger than that. Not even watching a grand master playing eight games at once against eight opponents comes close. It's bigger than that too.

Hey, in our world, every small game is linked together into a larger one. Except with this, there's no such thing as boards with squares. There's only a map of the land and a mess of pieces.

For Rooster, his whole crew is split up into different parts, all going at once. Lynwood, Cudahy, South Gate now, and a chunk of

Long Beach too. In all of those places, there's pieces moving all the time, doing work, and there's no maximum to how many he can have.

What I mean is, there might be forty pieces in one city and thirty-two in another, all linked up by orders they might never understand all the way, but they do work anyway. Where it gets crazy is, you have to bring in the idea that there are other people with the same rank as Rooster all over the city, like in Rancho San Pedro for example. And when you add more people, you add more places, and all of these things impact on each other. It's not anywhere close to chess then.

What it is, is territories and war zones. It's strategy. Troop movements. It's straight-up Risk, but with chess pieces. It's giving up lil homie pawns in one neighborhood to move three bishop lieutenants anywhere you want. It's picking up a *caballo* from one zip code and putting him on another by sending him on an errand, like when me and Big Danny get sent out to put ninety-two gees in a safe.

That's the only way it's explainable, and now one greedy little weasel just stirred himself into the middle of this business like he matters.

He don't.

I get a couple tabs of orange chewable antacid going and hope they can get this stomach thing settled. The holes in the safe door, that's information we can use. I just don't know how yet. What's messing with me now is, did the safecracker know about the money? Did he just open it, see it, and decide it was his day to break on it? Did somebody tell him about it or was it just dumb luck?

I don't believe the dumb-luck thing, but right now there's no telling how he knew, and the only thing that matters is finding him. The key to that is not caring what happens to him.

Hey, the easiest way to survive in the drug game is never catch a conscience. I think there's some real truth in how that's said. It makes it sound like your conscience is something outside of you, not part of you. It's basically like a cold, something that can make you sick. Something that can even kill you.

It's not like it isn't true. When I was young, it didn't matter. Drugs were something that always happened to someone else, somebody far away. Once it was out of my hand, what somebody did with it was on them.

What my problem with growing older is, is that you realize you're tied into something bigger than yourself. Your actions have consequences, and even sometimes nonactions have consequences.

It's possible to hurt somebody you never even met that way, hurt them pretty bad. The biggest problem with putting off a conscience for years is when you finally do catch it, it comes back in the door with interest. Bad interest.

It gives you a rash of sores on your chest that a doctor says isn't psoriasis but presents "psoriasis-like symptoms." I didn't realize until then that I'd actually have something real to get off my chest.

Nobody but Leya knows that whenever I put money in safes like that, I get wild thoughts. She calls them "get-out thoughts" since they're about me getting off this track I've been on almost my whole life and running free, not being tied to nobody but her and our little man.

If you want the truth, I'm more jealous of the safecracker than I'll ever say. I mean, if he's smart, he's gone. I hope so too. Man, I don't want to have to see his face. I don't want to have to handle things if he gets caught when I'm still around. That business of sorting him out will fall on me, and I don't know if my body can even take it anymore.

I didn't always run numbers for Rooster. I did other things too. There was the Cuco thing, but there were others. I pointed a gun and I used it when I got told to.

Those things, they add up in you. They do. They got a weight you can't move. If it's not some sores over my heart, it's my stomach.

Before Leya, it was about me being ready to do whatever at

any minute, but being with her and having Felix, seeing my face in his little face, that makes me want to get old. It makes me want to get out.

I turn back to the car and show Rooster with my hand that I'm gonna call Collins. For Collins, the sign we use is *dog* too.

Normally, I'd make a *d* with my index up and my middle finger on my thumb, then I snap those before I make a *g*, but we're in public so I pat my leg twice and act like I'm just looking for my keys. That means *dog* too.

Rooster's only rule with sign is never show it in public in case you're being watched and taped. Never let anyone know you even know it. Only do it if you play it off like it's something other than sign.

Rooster nods up at me when he sees this. He knows it needs to happen, but that means do it and be quick.

The sign language thing was Rooster's idea from years ago. We use ASL but he's thinking of changing it up to the *español* LSE. His daughter's deaf, so he had to pick it up, and once he did, he knew it could change the game by taking him off the map completely.

She's thirteen now, sharp in science and funny as hell. And no one even knows her dad exists, so I'd say it's working. He turned what so much of the hearing world calls a disability into a serious criminal ability. I respect the hell out of that. I always will.

I switch phones to call Collins on the special number, but I don't dial yet. What's difficult here is, Collins didn't know how much money was in the safe before his guy ripped it, so prolly with all the heroin involved, he was thinking it was a decent bust and it didn't raise any red flags for him at all.

I dodge a couple people going the other way before I know what to say about the holes. I think it'll play, so I call in.

Some secretary guy answers. I've never heard his voice before, so I just ask for Collins. When I get transferred to the man and he picks up, I tell him there's something he should know about the safe if he don't already know it. But first, I ask him what he knows.

"A safe's a safe," he says. "You fill them, and we confiscate them."

That's ignorance and arrogance is what that is, just a quick way to be wrong 100 percent of the time.

I say, "This one had powder in the door of it. I don't know how old it was but I'm told it can still blow. You're super lucky it didn't."

I turn the corner on Sixth and walk down it as I hear him put me on hold. He's checking. This means he's not sure if he believes me, or if he does believe me, he don't know how he feels about learning it now and not before.

If I'm telling the truth, he might jump to some type of conclusions about why it was there in the first place. He might wonder if we're trying to kill him. This is a stupid thing to wonder.

Rooster would never go that route, but if he did, it would look like a car accident, or something messed up and personal, like that sex self-choking thing, and if Collins is breathing right now it's because we want him to. I think he gets that, since he comes back on the phone and confirms what I said.

After, he says, "What's the best way to deal with this?"

Me and him, we have some separate business together. He's asking since he thinks this might put other things at risk.

"Call him in," I say. "Put it in his face. See what he tells you about it. I'm sure he'll be slick. If that don't give you enough reason to take him off what he's doing, then find one. Is he DEA?"

"I can't disclose that," Collins says, but he says it in a way, like, *Keep digging.*

I don't need to dig. There's only one other option.

"So freelance then," I say. "How about you call his boss and rat him out about messing up. Act concerned. Fish for a reason why he missed it. I bet they give you one. After that, cut him loose, but do it like it's protocol."

"Does this endanger the wedding party?"

That's what Collins calls this thing I'm helping him out with. I don't know why he picked something so stupid. I never bothered asking.

"It could," I say. "It could mess it up bad, but it won't if you get him out of circulation."

That's the end of the conversation. We don't say goodbye. I'm right out in front of Mr. Cartoon's tattoo shop when I hang up.

I look in and there's a guy reading at the front desk. Behind him is a big white poster of a smiling clown looking dangerous. Seeing it reminds me of peabrains and Rooster signing that at me, about this safecracker being one.

But seeing this, this just reminds me that there's different types of clowns, with different types of faces. Smart clowns put on masks for all sorts of reasons and prolly this safecracker is smarter than we think.

Collins could make this whole thing easy. He could give us a name and a address. He won't. That's not how it works and that's okay. I'm not even tripping. I'm turning and walking back to the car already dialing another number.

This is me spreading the word. We know city and county workers up and down the ladder. We know dirty cops with databases.

We know delivery drivers, postal workers, garbagemen. You know, people with daily routes all over the city. People that know addresses.

We don't know everyone but we know a few. If all it takes is six degrees of separation, Rooster likes saying we know four of them and can break into the houses of the other two.

Hey, people aren't needles in haystacks. They have phone numbers, a house or a apartment. They have connections. They live in neighborhoods and walk around.

They buy groceries. They drink at bars that have bartenders, security, regulars. They get found since somebody will know somebody that knows them. This is why we will find out who he is and where he stays.

We've got a description too. He's five-seven or five-eight. He's some type of brown, likely *raza*. He has no visible tattoos. His nose is a little bent.

We would have more but he's smart. He wore a hat and sunglasses. What we do have, is he drives a white Jeep with blacked-out plates. As big as this city is, there can only be one of those in it, two at most, and when we find it, we find him.

This safecracker, he broke the rules. There's no doubt to that.

He's guilty. How this is playing out makes me think of that movie *Dead Man Walking*, since that's what he is now. It's only a matter of when and how.

That's not on me either. That's on him. He knew what he was doing. Putting that money in a bag and walking out like it was his? That was him putting a gun to his own head and pulling the trigger. It's just suicide with a slow-motion bullet.

Ghost

16

I'm on my way to an ulcer when I do my check-in, sign for my visitor pass, and get escorted down to meet Collins in the basement of the federal evidence lockup. It used to be all theirs alone, but because of budget cuts and a government building across town getting condemned for being the opposite of earthquake-proof, they share with another agency now.

I get buzzed through a door and Collins is there on the other side of it, surrounded by metal shelfs full of all kinds of shit. I follow him down a row toward the back wall. It smells like mold and plastic baggies down here and not like grilled cheese, which I'm glad of. The mortar of the back cinder-block wall is going dark gray in places. Water always wants to get in. Always does get in, somehow. It's why so few places got basements in Los Angeles. Too close to the water table or something.

When we're almost to the end of the row, we go by a stuffed big cat on the bottom of the shelf. It's big and awkward and barely fits. You can tell whoever put it there had to take the shelf above off its pegs and remove it to make room. It's, like, a cougar or something, and it's creepy as hell seeing a frozen growly face and big-ass bared fangs bagged up in a clear sheet. Almost like it suffocated to death.

Collins hears me slow down. "That's crazy, right?"

Careful to hide the bulges on my ankles, I kneel down slow and press the bottom of its nearest cougar tooth with a thumb tip and have to pull my hand away because it's still sharp.

When I'm down there, I scratch my ankle like it's itching, but I'm checking the tape on my socks. It'll hold. The money's getting wet from me sweating, but this way was the *only* way. Couldn't transfer it to the lockbox on the street or in the parking lot of a government building. That'd be stupid. Couldn't pull over and do it earlier or I'd be late and I wasn't about to give Collins anything to wonder about. So this was it. Me, walking through a federal facility with wads of cash taped around my ankles. Going in confident. Like it's just another day, and I didn't do *shit*.

I give the cougar one last look, stand up, and say, "So, taxidermy's illegal now?"

"It probably fucking should be," Collins says, "but no. There's a crew running drugs in dead animals like this because the formaldehyde smell throws off the dogs. But if it's freshly done and one of the baggies inside pops and soaks some up, it's nothing but bad news for whoever ends up sniffing it. Sometimes those junkies just get sick. Catastrophe sick. Corrodes the upper gastrointestinal tract, apparently. Other times, they just die. This fucker's got trafficking *and* murder charges on him now. No points for guessing which one the U.S. Attorney's licking her chops over."

This is the irony of doing what I do. I've been clean so long, nobody knows I'm an addict. Nobody knows I got empathy. That junkies aren't *them* or *they* to me. They *are* me. And dead is what I could've been many times over. I could've sniffed the wrong shit very easily. Or cooked bad stuff. I wasn't what you'd call discriminating early on. I'd do anything. I've dosed out three times in my life that I know of. I've blacked out twice that. Maybe more. That's not the kind of thing you can know exact numbers of.

We hit the end of the row and follow the back wall to a series of small rooms no bigger than closets. I've been here before, but only once. In the second small room, on the floor, is the safe, sitting on its ass with the door open toward us. As soon as we walk in, my relief almost knocks me over.

Collins doesn't know I took anything. He's trying to *show* me something.

And it's the safe I cracked a couple of hours ago, the one I stole from. Two holes have been drilled into the top of its door, like a giant Dracula sunk his teeth into it. It's not terrible for me, but it's definitely not good.

It means I fucked up.

"On-site dusting didn't come up with any explosives residue, as you know, or we'd never have you popping it otherwise. But it did come up positive here. And we noticed these."

He nods at the holes. "We're guessing they've been in there a damn long time. That it's been moved a lot and maybe whatever residue was on the outside got swiped off. Who knows?"

He's waiting to see if I'll say something, but there's no point now.

I missed it. At the very least, I should've seen and reported it when I cracked it, but I didn't. I was a little busy.

"They put dynamite powder in there. Just like it was god-damn Looney Tunes." He points to the spot where they drilled and packed it in, but he don't need to. It's obvious.

I don't know shit about explosives. I know what I've seen in movies. Like, vibration and heat are bad for them. Only reason why I can think of, is that this was a precaution to explode anybody trying to blow the safe door. I don't do that stuff, I'm a drill-and-punch guy, but some other gang might not know any better and try to, if they knew where the safe was at.

"Good thing you came from the bottom," Collins is saying. "You know how lucky you are? Could have blown up that whole building."

He's smiling when he slaps me on the back. "The fuckers that did this are never getting out of prison. Possessing explosives after nine-eleven? Man, that's some special kind of stupid. We're going to hit them with some terrorism shit now. They are stone-cold fucked."

All I can think about is how there's nothing I can do about

that. Some dude wants to spend his time drilling into the top of the door without any sense of how it might affect the lock mechanism, gets blind lucky he doesn't hit anything and the door happens to be solid where he drilled and not pocketed, so he can dump some dynamite dust in there? I don't know the odds of that, but I'm guessing he was probably more likely to blow himself up than me.

Collins's faced up to me now, angling his chin at me. "How'd you miss that?"

I missed it because it was on the top of the door, and the door was sealed, concealing the holes. I missed it because I drilled up from the bottom. I missed it because I didn't do an inspection on the door moat because I was down to steal everything in it that I could carry, but even if I did eyeball the moat, there's no guarantee I'd have seen it, and even if I did, I might not have called in for backup or even thought to run tests, because who the fuck drills into their own safe door and dumps explosives into it? First I've ever seen or heard of it.

None of these things will make Collins happy, though, so I decide on some version of the truth.

"My girlfriend and I have been going through it," I say.

"I get it," he says, and he does. Far as I know, he's on wife number three. "But you got to be a pro. It's not just you out there."

Well, I'm thinking, *it* is *just me when you leave me on-site by myself.*

"You're absolutely right," I say. This sentence is one of the most useful sentences in the English language. It backs people off. It's a jab that doesn't seem like a jab. And I say it sincere too, so he thinks I mean it. And then, just to nail it in, I repeat it, "You're absolutely right."

That's a double jab.

Collins stares at me to gauge how sincere I am and smiles when he thinks I'm still trustworthy. I don't smile, though. I frown and look down at the floor to show him I'm still mad at myself for not catching this. It's exactly what he wants to see.

"Good," he says, "because we both know this can't happen again."

I tilt my head and nod. I don't ask him how many times he's seen it, because I've been doing this pretty solid for near eleven years and this is a goddamn first, but okay. I'll make sure it doesn't happen again.

Collins gestures toward the door and turns the light off behind us. "Sorry to hear about your girl, though. That's rough."

"I think we gotta break up soon. Actually, I know we do."

He nods at that, all solemn.

But then I say, "Her husband's coming back."

And Collins damn near cracks a rib laughing.

17

I've got no hands. They're full with the heavy gear I got from the Jeep. The only way to bring it up was in one go, not attracting attention—well, as little as I can, anyway. So I drag my kit boxes and a suitcase that's got wheels on all four corners of its bottom. I push 6 on the elevator push pad, doors close, and I go up.

What I said to Collins, it's no lie. Not something I said to deflect and get out of there. Not completely. When I key into the hotel room door of 626, twist the handle, and kick it open with my foot, Mira's there, red around her eyes and acting like she's not just been crying.

She gets like that after video chatting with her husband. He's in Afghanistan till next month. Seventeen months he's been there. She doesn't do it much because it's so hard to get the timing right. It's like a twelve-hour difference and that's if he's back and safe at the base and not out doing maneuvers or whatever American soldiers are doing over there. Shooting terrorists, you'd hope. But it's probably things like setting up offices and scheduling convoys and having dumb conversations with dangerous people that never go anywhere because they just want us the fuck out of their country.

I don't know what her husband does. Never even asked. That's not something I'm allowed to talk about. She's never said not to, but I feel it.

The door's on a spring and it's swinging back towards me so I reach my hand out and bang my drill case into it because that's all I can do to keep it open. Mira sees this and she's up off her spot on the king bed quick, through the little hall, and grabbing the door so it won't shut on me and pulling me in.

I must be smirking or something because she says, "What?"

"Nothing," I say, but it's something.

A whole lot of somethings. I kick this wheely suitcase she got for me as a kind of going-away present toward her and it stalls on the carpet and tips. She sticks a foot out before it falls flat and catches it.

I'm in then. I set my kits down on the bed and lock the door.

She's already got the luggage rack set up in the corner by the dresser, this thin-legged metal thing that looks like it's going to bust when she puts my suitcase on it. It's got everything I need inside. Socks. Shirts. Pants. A toothbrush. A comb. All the things I need to never go home again.

This was always our plan: the moment I took anything, I'd go to places where no one who ever knew me would guess I'd be. And nobody I ever knew would look for me at the Crystal Casino hotel in Compton. Not Frank. Not Collins. Not anybody. I hate gambling. I can't stand not being in control of the game.

Now, being mobile like this, it's even more important. Mira doesn't know entirely why just yet, but she's about to find out.

"So?" Mira's saying *so*, but she means, why are you late? How did it go? What happened? Why did you make me wait?

I just look at her. I smile. She loves this and hates it at the same time.

See, between Mira Watkins and me, it's like this animal thing. I always know where she's at in the room. Even if we are both looking at something else, it's like I can feel her movements, you know? I zoom in on her, even without looking, and I know how she's feeling about something.

It's not love. It never will be. It's *recognition*. We see each other. We know we're survivors. We know where the scars are. We get what made them.

She's in a T-shirt and jeans, and I know what's underneath. Out of heels, Mira's five-three. When she's not eating celery lunches, she's one-thirty with Cs, curvy like real women are, the best women. Soft in the right places, firm in the rest. Black hair hanging in a banker's power cut, she calls it. It sways a little as she shakes her head at me for wasting up all of her time. It's this short, sharp bob that frames her face and it's clippered on the base of her skull like her hair's afraid of her neck.

"You don't answer questions now?" She makes this squeaky *tsk* sound like she's kissing her teeth at me.

"*Paciencia.*" I open my tool kits on the bed. "It's good for you. Makes you a better person."

She scrunches her face up. "Don't be pulling that Spanish on me like it's gonna work. I'm mad at you."

Mira never lied a day in her life. She is mad. And that's okay. I like it. She can see I like it, though, so she crosses the room to me and stares me straight in the face.

18

Mira knows her name means *look* in Spanish. She abuses it. Growing up speaking Spanish and English, me meeting her was like meeting someone named Look. Of course I looked then. I paid attention like it was a command. And she's worth looking at. Some women just are, commanding your eyes, promising secrets.

Nobody would ever look at Rose twice, not when she was sick. I saw it firsthand. People would even try *not* to look at her even once. And I think somehow that that's why she acted out. To be seen. But that girl, she could rearrange your whole soul with a look. Mira's different. She's natural. Just seeing her reminds me I'm still here. That I'm human. That I got needs.

See, but Rose was a switchblade that could open you up to anything, anywhere. Mira is a billy club wrapped up in warm towels.

Rose was air. Mira is all earth.

Rose was punk. Mira is hip-hop.

Rose was white like Frank, white like new plates. Mira's cocoa—that's what she calls it, like it's her own race.

And maybe it is. She's black and something else, something lighter. Something she'll never know. Her mom got raped in the early eighties and had her anyway. But Mira's not sure how much of a decision that actually was. Her mom was a junkie, just like mine. And she and I both know too well that decisions don't get made when you're using, decisions make you.

"Just tell me you got it." Mira huffs as she puts her hands on her hips like this is my last chance. "Tell me it's good."

It's time to put up or shut up, but I still feel like I want to string her along a little more, make the surprise that much better at the end.

Rose's middle name was Grace. Mira's middle name is Rose. When I heard that, it was just over. Any walls I had to keep this from being a thing between us were just exploded into a million pieces. It was too weird. Too true and too sad, at the same time. Like, I knew that right away. Because I'll never stop looking for Rose in other people, least of all in Mira.

"When you say 'it,'" I say while pulling a face like I got no idea what she's getting at, "do you mean, like, milk shakes or what?"

Her response comes quick, but not quick enough.

I roll my right shoulder and lean back as the slap's coming in. I'm already smiling and she hates it, but she can't stop the swing. She's committed to the force. Already on her toes, already a little off-balance. Her hand ricochets off my shoulder bone and I catch her wrist in my left hand, not hard, but just to let her know I can. I squeeze before I let go, not in a gloating way, but more like *Cálmate*. Like, *Don't worry. I got this.*

It doesn't help anything. In fact, it does the opposite.

A complicated look swirls up in her eyes, a mix of surprise, anger, hurt, and being impressed at me. Even I know not to push it much further. You push that look too far and she's taking her earrings off and swinging. We've never done that, she and I. Come close a few times, but never fought for real. And I know that stuff is always hiding in the corners of her brain, ready to pop off if it goes there.

When I let her wrist go, I can see she's made up her mind that asking questions or even swinging at me isn't working and she needs to try something else if she wants to find out how it went. She gets close to me and does something I don't expect.

She hugs me. She says she's glad I made it, that I'm safe. That dazes me, and as I'm wondering if it's the only thing that could right now, I hug her back.

She's told me before that she's with me because she knew I'd never hurt her, not physically, but that if something happened to her like that, something real bad, I'd kill whoever did it. I know her husband's the same way. I know I'm just a type. A plug for a socket. And that's okay. I don't need to be more.

Some women need that kind of protection, need to feel safe to function. I'm talking about women that've been through it. I can't explain it to you if you don't know what it's like to get beat till you black out and wake up somewhere with a busted face so puffed up that you can't see out your eyelids. That's why I'm here. You can't leave a woman like that alone with a hole in her life.

Sooner or later, she fills it. She has to.

I pull her arms off me and reach down to my socks. I rip the tape off the tops of them and pull the rolls of wet money off my ankles and out into the air in front of her. Before she can grab them, I toss them on the bed. It's maybe forty grand. Her face tells me she's happy, but there's expectation in it. Like, *If that's in your socks, what else you got?*

When I pull the kit linings out and empty them, she has to cover her mouth. I pull the plastic bag full of cash out of the bottom of the suitcase, turn it over on the bed, and she grabs a pillow, covers her face, and screams with every bit of her lungs for seven seconds. I counted.

When she takes the pillow off her face, it's got a wobbly O of brown-red lipstick on it and she's throwing it to the floor so she can use both her hands to grab me and bring her mouth close to mine, because she's got a kiss coming up on her lips that she needs me to take.

19

Mira and me take almost three hours to count it twice, to pile it, and repile it on the bed to make sure we got the count right. We cover the king comforter with stacks ten grand high—a hundred hundred-dollar bills each.

When we're done counting, we're staring at each other and then staring at the stacks but still not saying anything. Like we're scared to speak because it might break a magical spell. Like any words will make it all go away.

For real, it feels like I'm hallucinating, like this couldn't possibly be sitting in front of me, because, shit, I've only ever seen this in movies. Ten thousand dollars in cash, though, even in twenties, wouldn't fill up a regular briefcase.

A hundred hundreds standing up tall looks like thin books sitting there. That's what ten grand looks like. And what's crazy is, there's eighty-eight of them. Eighty-nine with the one that isn't all the way full because I had to peel a few bills off it to crumple up and throw back in the safe. Still, that's eighty-nine stacks in rows of ten. Eight hundred eighty-seven thousand.

That's $887,000 point 00, like how Frank showed me to write it when I got all sheepish in front of him once because nobody ever taught me how to write a check.

All we needed was $284,353. That's $70,353 to John to finish his house payments that Mira wanted, and $214,000 for Frank's outstanding debt.

"Wow," Mira says.

"Yeah," I say, slinging her word back at her, but the Spanish version, "*guau*."

Because there aren't words for this. Not really.

All this money.

Shit.

All this *dirty* money.

That's what's making me nervous right now, so nervous that I know I can't ever tell Mira, because this kind of stash isn't how these Nayarit black tar dealers do business. Their whole model is to keep it small-time on purpose.

They deliver product only when it's needed and about to be distributed so that drivers driving around with heroin balloons in their mouths never carry enough to be seriously charged for drugs. It's genius. Because if these fools get caught, they just get deported back to Mexico and replaced in the next day or two because there's always an endless supply of rancho boys wanting to come up here and live the American dream, all quiet with their heads down, till that time when they can go back home and be big-time at the local *feria del elote*. Wearing 501s. Spending up big money on mariachis and enough smoky-tasting *mezcal* to drown anybody that ever doubted they could make it up north.

And these black tar runners never, and I mean *never*, have money like this lying around, dude. Not that I've ever heard of. They're straight flower to arm, always riding the edge of demand and nothing more.

And *that's* what makes me sick to my stomach. Like, I don't even know if this cash is real. *Could be counterfeit*, I'm thinking. But it looks real. It *feels* real. And it smells . . .

Well, I can't smell nothing but grilled cheese again. And rotting strawberries now too. Like bad cheesecake, kind of. An oily, cheddary, berry cheesecake stuck inside my nose.

Mira doesn't know what we walked into with this money, but I do.

I know I don't have weeks anymore. I got *days*.

Four, maybe three. At most.

I'm not worried about Collins finding out anymore. If he does, fine. I sit in a lockup and die in a prison hospital. What I'm worried about is the people whose money this really is. About how quick they'll be looking for the dude in the Jeep because you know they already talked to people in the neighborhood and they know I took a plastic bag out that I didn't take in.

Shit like that doesn't get missed.

The only good thing about all this is that I know my outbound ticket's already punched. Doesn't matter if it's a bullet or a knife when I can't smell and I know my cancer's back and making itself at home again. One or the other is the same to me. Either way, I'm going out on my back, but at least this way I'll have done something half-decent with my life. Something to make Rose proud. Something to save her dad from drowning.

20

See, Frank doesn't know I know he's been putting everything on credit cards lately because there's some wage garnishing going on. And he doesn't know I know about the adjustable-rate mortgage he took out five years ago. About how it went into foreclosure. How it's the bank's if they don't get about $150,000. Frank would kill me if he knew I read the mail he left in the upper left drawer of his desk.

That ARM's from 2003. He's never said, but I think his idea was to buy a building and get renters in and get out from under the loan by the time Laura, the only daughter he has left, was ready for college. That way, he'd never have her worrying about student loans. So Frank goes in for a twelve-unit apartment building near downtown Long Beach and waives inspections to get it from two other bidders. Usually, Frank's careful, but he got greedy there. He must've heard Laura drop Stanford into the conversation too many times and thought he had to grab it. So escrow comes and goes quick, and then it's in his hands when he's finally doing diligence. That's when he finds the underground plumbing's rusted out.

He's pissed, but it's his problem now, so he bites the bullet and refinances the other building he owns, the one I live in, to pay for the repairs. That's how he went from one loan to two. After that, it was downhill on a ride he'll never talk to me about. So that's what the $214,000 is for. To make Frank free and clear on two separate loans he's underwater on. To help him breathe. And I couldn't do that, at least do it and not get caught, without Mira.

We're both sitting on the floor and looking up at the bed with all the stacks on it, partners in some serious crime now. When I first asked if she wanted in, she laughed. She thought I was joking. When she figured out I wasn't, she made it real clear I couldn't get her involved without agreeing to something she wanted. She said anything beyond the number Frank needed had to go to people in danger of losing their houses. People she sees every day at her bank. People trying to do right. People that never broke laws. People that got jobs, maybe not good jobs, but jobs. That was the deal. The first name on her list was John. She knew that would get me. It did. The rest of the list had eight families: four we knew from NA, the others from her bank work.

I said I'd do it. But I told her I didn't know how long it'd take once we got going, I told her I wanted to do a trust too, and I sure as hell didn't think I'd pull that much money out on the first go. That was just luck. Or fate. Call it whatever.

Sure was a gift, though.

I swipe at my nose but the oily cheesecake smell is staying stuck there. It hits me how taking $887,000 is nothing compared to the crazy corporate shit going on every single day.

I try to pull one of those numbers up from memory, one I've heard Mira say from before, but it's not coming and I'm starting to wonder how much tumors can affect memory too and I get a little paranoid, so I keep my voice calm and say, "How much were you saying those Enron motherfuckers stole?"

"One point one billion." This shit fascinates Mira. Always has. "Killed twenty thousand jobs at the drop of a hat too. They basically dropped a bomb on Houston. Just, boom. Fallout for *years*."

Mira has always told me that's what's happening right now, more fallout, with all this shit on the news about how Lehman

Brothers is about to blow up like Bear Stearns did. That this whole thing is going to be worse than Enron even. It's not going to be one company going down. If they go, they'll drag down other shady companies. Ten. Maybe twenty.

Rose used to say that nobody's safe in this world. Not ever. And when you think you are, that's when you're not. One big truth of life is that all the money you ever get in it is a rental. Everything's risky.

For months Mira has been talking about how she's going to fix everything up for anybody we help. Apparently, there's a way to do anonymous checks that will apply directly to existing bad mortgages. The ones with interest rates that get higher and higher till there's no way you can pay it.

She's a bank manager now, but she used to be a teller and moved up to home loans. She'd compile notes on applicants and send them to superiors. Then she had to sit by when people got rates by skin color. Ghetto loans, they're called. Each one that went out peeled off a chunk of her soul, she said.

She saw it and kept her mouth shut, learned the system. When she got promoted again after finishing her nights' accounting course, she did some investigating work, basically learned how people used her bank to launder money. She met criminals. Even interviewed them sometimes about what went where and how so she could document it and pass it on to prosecutors.

So now, Mira's got this guy she knows who owns convenience stores all over the Southland. He'll kick down with money orders in any amounts she wants under $1,000 so long as she brings him the cash to back them. He'll even spread them out. Different dates. Different amounts. Issued from different locations. It's a ton of work, but it's enough to pay off houses without anyone knowing who's doing it.

Mira takes it from there, putting those checks in envelopes and having some trusted conspirators she grew up with put on hoods and sunglasses and drop the envelopes in the night-deposit boxes of her bank's various branches, some of which she'll see as a manager and report up the chain about their receipt. She already knows the policy, though.

There's nothing illegal about paying someone else's mortgage. The checks can get cashed and go straight against amounts outstanding. All the bank needs is names and addresses, not even account numbers, and a note of instruction about what the money is for. Turns out banks never say no to free money.

Benefactor notes, Mira calls them, Good Samaritanism in an envelope.

21

Mira learned about benefactor notes through a colleague who told a story about a rich old married dude paying off an apartment for this young piece he had on the side in Redondo. See, he didn't give the money directly *to* her. He gave it to a middleman who slid checks to a banking corporation instead and then she got to live free of the debt they were holding on her.

Because the maximum amounts for money orders are low enough, they don't trip tax triggers, and the U.S. government apparently doesn't have a problem with them. Or, it's not that they wouldn't have a problem, it's just that it's a low enough threshold that it's not worth their time to go after it. Kind of like how the Xalisco Boys figured out that less heroin on delivery drivers was better, I guess. Pretty much always they carried below the "intent to distribute" amount they could be prosecuted for, even though distributing is exactly what they're always doing.

I know my nose is clearing up when I can smell Mira's lemon body spray close. Faint at first, but growing.

I notice how she's not talking anymore. She's just staring at me, bringing her hand up to touch my face, but then saying "Shit!" when she looks at her watch and sees the time. "The damn babysitter leaves in a half hour!"

She moves to the other side of the room to put her face back on.

I don't move or go with her. I flip a few piles of money over. I hold them before I start saying bye to them and putting them in the gym bag Mira brought. Back when I was using, I had a million hustles. But I never had a hustle as smart as Mira's, as untraceable. I've ripped and run, stabbed and stolen, and burned people like you wouldn't believe. Me on drugs was nobody you'd ever want to meet.

And I know people who did way less than me sitting in San Quentin right now. I was the luckiest fool you've ever seen. Coming through my drugs years without one arrest is, like I said before, a miracle.

They wake me up at night still, the things I did. They get all mixed up in my dreams. Harlem Harold getting robbed of his stash. Me swinging a baseball bat at his head, making sure he never takes revenge for it. Me finding out what brain looked like when pieces leaked out. Liver meat without the color. A mash of skull bone looking like chunks of big eggshells in the one-bulb light of his garage. The blood sticks with me. I can sometimes still smell the wet metal of it.

See, you don't get forgiveness for the things I've done. I can't come back from them and be a normal member of the human race anymore. And all's I can do now is try. Try to help some people, but even more than that, try not to hurt even one more person for as long as I got left.

First, do no harm. Like John always says in group.

See, I always had it backwards. I did all the harm first, when I was young and stupid, and now I'm trying to make up for a slice of it. As much as I can. For Frank. For Rose. For anybody else too. I guess for me, it's like: Last, do no harm. And if I can do that on my way out of this life, then I really did something.

I used to tell Rose that in boxing you keep getting up till you can't anymore. That the only honor there is in punching people for a living is you just keep getting up till you can't. And that's it. It's a good run then, and when it's done, you hang your gloves up and hope it was all worth something to somebody other than you, that your sacrifices made people's lives better because it sure as hell shortened yours.

From the other side of the room, Mira says, "This is enough, right? More than enough money. For Frank. For John. For helping people."

I zip the gym bag up and walk it over to the door, where I drop it on the carpet. That's our goodbye, me and this money. It's going to a better place now. Better hands. And that makes it worth it. The risk. The running. The bad way it's all going to end.

"No." I turn to her and say, "We need more. For more people. More houses."

Her eyes get wide at that. Her nose crinkles up. She doesn't get it. I can see her thinking risk is one thing, but this is just crazy.

Before she can respond back with anything, I walk to one of the hotel chairs that faces the windows and sit in it. We've never talked about this before. Never needed to. But Mira's smart. She knows there's something I'm not telling her, and she knows the relationship part is over between us too.

From the other side of the room, Mira says to me, "So this is the last time? Or just the last time till the last time?"

That's how she calls me out. Tired, almost. Not quite sad but getting there. She might mean the money. She might mean us, together. Could be both. But she knows real good how all this money changes things. Makes everything more dangerous. Makes it real likely she'll never see me again. That's for sure.

I hear her digging in her makeup bag by where the bathroom mirror is. There's a half wall between us, but it feels like there's more. Distance. Barriers. Whatever. And it's not clean or perfect, but I'm happy with how I did it.

It was my call, not involving her in any kind of heist, being real firm with her about how she couldn't be there when I did it. That was me protecting her. And she knows I'd *always* been planning on seeing this out. I just never told her the whole why. Never told her about the memory smells, about the cancer. Never told her that doing this is for the time I got left. And I want to tell her. I owe her that. But I can't yet. Not here. Not in some fucking casino hotel with a busted window overlooking the 91 Freeway.

What I got to say is depressing enough as it is. It doesn't need any more help. And I've held it so long on my own because I'm not about to give Mira the chance to pity me or think about anything like having a future with me instead of her husband and her kid like she should. She needs to forget me.

"It's going to be whatever it's going to be" is all I can say. "Can't make promises."

That's true too. No guarantees I get any other safes. Even if I do, no guarantees I can get it to her to distribute. From here, it's all chance. And, really, it's the only one path worth taking.

See, I can't tell her I fought so hard to do something different with my life and this cancer coming back to take a bite out of me again means I don't get to have it anymore, because I can't look at her face when I say it. I can't say to her that I'm already out living on this bridge between this life and what comes after it, and I know, I've always known, that I have to go as fast as I can because there's no going back for me. Shit. Even if I wanted it, I got no-where to go back *to*. Everything behind me is already burnt. There's no Reverse now. Only Drive.

I hear her drop whatever she was working with back into her little makeup bag, where it clacks against some other thing, and she steps out from behind the wall, so I turn my chair back her way. She's looking at me, and nodding, but it's heavy. The good feeling of counting all that money is gone and it's not coming back.

This is probably good, though. It's how it has to go. The fantasy happy ending of us running off into some sunset with bags of money is dying on the carpet between us, in this quiet when she's stopped nodding but her eyes are looking like she's waiting for me to say something.

I don't, though.

She says, "You know, you're a hard man to know."

"I'd trust you to know that."

That gets me another of her real good *tsk*s and a look that can't make up its mind whether she wants to kiss me or punch me.

I don't even get up when she goes. I want to, but I know better. I watch her leave wheeling the empty bag she brought with her. The one that's full now. That was always the deal because I can't be having the money on me. The hurt sets in when the door shuts behind her. I'm smelling her body spray too much now, the kind she leaves in every room she ever walked in. Lemons, everywhere.

I turn my chair to the window, imagining how she'll be walking down the hall, how she'll be pushing the button for the elevator, and then in the elevator, how she'll wait, how she'll exit and cross through the lobby, and out the doors through to the parking lot, and to her car, locking the gym bag in the trunk, getting in the front seat and turning it on, and putting it in reverse, driving out, going back to her little boy, and that's exactly how it should be. From the window, I'm looking for her driving out, hoping I can catch a sight of her car, if not her driving it, but there's too many other vehicles down there going in every direction.

I'm still looking out that same window an hour later and seeing what there is to see of Compton putting on its dusk. Not that it's much. The dry bed of Compton Creek with a tree in the middle. Above that dark greenness, the backside of Gateway Towne Center has fresh paint and empty loading bays. I slide my eyes from that to the parallel asphalts of Artesia and the 91 Freeway cutting through the city like an open artery and an open vein that blood cells with headlights and brake lights roll through in different directions. Past them, in the far south distance is the port of Long Beach, where cranes have their necks up, looking blurred and purple and ready to do work.

I check my regular cell to make sure I still have no calls on it and then I use my prepaid to call the shop so Laura won't recognize the number.

She picks up on the third ring. "Stenberg Locksmithing."

I say, "What's got more legs than cents?"

She doesn't want to talk to me, though. I know from the huff of breath she hits the phone mic with, but also because she says, "I don't want to talk to you."

Some people say "wanna." Most do. But Laura? She enunciates. She grabs her words and says them the right way and puts them in the right order because she's proper.

Laura Stenberg runs phones and schedules jobs. Hell of a name for a little Asian girl. She's sixteen and been hearing that pretty much every year of her adopted life. Frank and Marcy adopted her from the Philippines after they lost Rose. Five years later, Marcy was gone. Not leukemia. Lung cancer. Also genetic. Same thing happened to her aunt. I'd been four years at the shop when it happened.

I'd never met Marcy myself. She'd been sick for so long and Frank kept to himself outside of work. But going to that funeral and seeing what Rose would've looked like as an adult in that casket was about the hardest thing I ever saw. I was in pieces. Just busted up. It gave me everything I never got when Rose passed. Gave me a chance to say goodbye. Not all the way. But a little.

I repeat myself so Laura knows I'm not doing anything till she guesses. "What has got more legs than cents?"

I know she's mishearing it *sense*, and I want her to. I also know she can't resist. We've done this since she was ten.

"Are you really attempting this right now?"

I am. "What has got—"

"Okay! Fine!" I feel her looking out the front window, scanning the lot and the street, maybe to see if I'm there, maybe to see if this is all some elaborate joke I'm pulling on Frank and that real soon I'll come clean and everything will be okay. "A spider that makes friends with a lizard?"

I give it a few seconds and then I say, "No," and I pause there to sharpen up my delivery. "A yak that forgot her change purse."

Silence is what she hits me with. Not a smirk or a snort. Nothing.

"*Stupid,*" she finally says.

"You're right, it was stupid of her to leave it on his dresser before she went to the savanna bar."

She doesn't appreciate how I twisted that. "That's not what I—"

You got to keep teenagers unbalanced. Can't let them think they're running things. "Anything come in for me? Any calls?"

"No." Her voice goes a little tight. "Not a thing."

"Liar. Frank's taking them, isn't he?"

"Why are we even talking? Didn't you quit?"

"I'll quit when I'm dead." It started as a joke in my mouth, but now it's out, I know it's true. And knowing it's true hollows me out a little.

"Real funny," she says back. "Dad said you were giving notice, or, he wasn't exactly sure what, but he said you were leaving."

"I am leaving."

"But you haven't left?"

"Right."

"So, when *are* you leaving?"

"I'm leaving when I leave. Till then, if a call comes in, put it my way."

"Dad's not going to like that."

"He'll love it. It'll mean he's not having to do it, but he's still getting forty percent of the billable."

"I think he just wants to know what your deal is. What I mean is . . ." She halts there, and Laura's not usually like that, a pauser. She's as straight-ahead as a person can get. "I want to know too."

"It's got nothing to do with you."

"Oh, I know that."

"Do you?"

Her silence tells me she doesn't. Not all the way.

"It's a thing I have to handle." I already hate myself for saying that much. "It's not about you, and it's not about Frank. I promise."

I'm thinking that's enough, that my tone was good and firm and she'll have to accept it, but she doesn't.

"Is it cancer again?"

I'm wincing where I'm sitting.

"If you don't answer, it just means yes."

I saw Frank thinking it before. Of course he told her it was maybe why I was doing what I was doing.

"It isn't," I say, and I know it's not convincing but I don't care. "Tell Frank I said hello, and that I owe him one, no, *two* steaks. Keep sending me calls, Laura. I'm not even playing about that."

And in my head right then, I'm thinking, *Nah, fuck two.* I'll get him a whole box of Omahas. I wait a second and she doesn't say anything. But then she exhales, and whatever reason Laura has for deciding not to fight me on this, I'm grateful for it, because all she says is "Okay. I'll run it by Dad, but you know I have to do what he says."

"Always. Adios, Spider."

Bringing the joke back is how our calls get ended. It's how we show each other we were listening. How we care.

Since she doesn't want to say bye, Laura says, "I hope I'll be seeing you, Yak."

I say, "I hope so too," before hanging up, and just because it's true doesn't mean it's going to happen.

It took Frank a month to ask me about how hard I was crying at his wife's funeral, and I was forced to give him some good bullshit about how my mom died when I was little, and that I was made to go to the funeral and seeing Mrs. Stenberg like that brought a bunch of memories back, which was just true enough to convince him. It did bring memories back. Of Rose and me. And my mom *is* dead, but I never went to her funeral. She didn't have one that I know of.

So, now Frank's just got me and Laura.

Well, not me.

In the beginning when we were planning, Mira and I fought hard about Laura. I wanted to give her money and Mira said I couldn't. I said yes or I wasn't doing it. Mira just sat there all calm and said no. No way. If I do that and get caught somehow, people come in and find the money I stole. Forensic accountants, they're called. And if any of it got connected to my former employer, well then, he'd be going to jail too. That, I finally understood.

So that's how the trust came to be. Mira will put in 10 percent of whatever I can get above that original amount we needed. As of today, that's about $60,000 to the Rose Grace Stenberg Memorial Trust for young women who got cancer but got better from it. It's not much, just whatever the interest is off the lump-sum investment that will be spitting out annually in 2018, but the awards will help them go to college, buy books or whatever. It's not too particular, but if the students want to study music or arts, they get special preference. It's what Rose always wanted to do, so I'm making good on that.

The executor on it is a lawyer named Henry Willis-Jackson that Mira knows. When I'm gone, he'll send a letter to Frank informing him that some long-lost Stenberg relative from Sweden or something set it up on his deathbed. It'll be the last good thing I can ever give him and he'll never even know it was me. I'm imagining Frank's face when that letter shows up. How he won't understand it at first and then maybe it'll creep up on him. Maybe.

And I already know yesterday's gone and tomorrow never comes.

There's only *this*.

11

¡SIN VERGÜENZA!

Ricky Mendoza, Junior, a.k.a. Ghost

Monday, September 15, 2008
Late Afternoon

23

All day till now felt like I was floating. No calls from Laura, from Frank, from anybody. No jobs. No text from Mira even. So I slept till I couldn't sleep anymore, checked out of the Crystal Casino, and then just rolled out. By the time I got to Wilshire, Bad Religion was screaming at me about wanting something more. Like, *mooooooore*.

I still had an hour before I could check into my next hotel, so I went by LACMA to *Los Angelenos*, this Chicano art exhibit my tattooer told me I had to go see. The Chaz pillars were cool in there, his Chinese dragon too. What really snuck up on me though was something in another show, *Phantom Sightings*. There were these two coffins, one white, one black, done up by these dudes Ochoa and Rios. They were all angular, like an adjustable bed stuck sitting up. Speaker-box fabric was used, the little plaque said. It was a nice way of maybe going out, I thought, sitting up, not lying down, Rose's mix around me forever.

I'm still thinking about those things as I'm finishing off my corned beef Reuben from Canter's in my room at the Ramada across from St. James Episcopal in Koreatown. That's where group's always held. This is the closest I've ever had to commute to be there. It doesn't even take me five minutes to cross the street and duck upstairs. I'm early.

But coming into the group room, I can already tell it's going to be packed. I just feel it. Bad days mean more people. That's how it is. Weekends can be rough and everybody comes in on Monday to put things back together. We don't get the main worship area like the alcoholics do, but we're heading that way, getting bigger every couple months. Even five years ago, there were maybe twelve or thirteen of us here, mostly old-schoolers from the seventies looking twenty years older than they are for real, or kids like me that got caught up with it in the late eighties/early nineties. There's too much new blood in here these days, though. Teens doing their court-ordered NA. Little fools in their twenties that got caught up in pills. Oxy, mostly. More of them are whiter than you'd think. All the way white, even.

We all come in through the parking lot off St. Andrews Place and go up the back stairs, turn right, and go down the hallway to this little room on the right that fits maybe forty or forty-five of us with a squeeze. We got to set out metal chairs with green cloth backs for everybody. I'm doing that, taking five at a time, setting them down on a spot and letting go of the bottom one and then moving to the next spot beside it, and then the next. I do six rows like that as people are filling in, talking about how the stock market pulled a samurai move and cut its own guts out today.

Over five hundred points.

Mira schooled me already on Lehman Brothers going under and Bank of America buying Merrill Lynch and AIG going in the toilet, but to me, it was just chickens coming home to roost for some greedy motherfuckers. Far as I'm concerned, they get what they deserve.

But with the people at group, I can hear fear riding on their words as they're getting coffee and sneaking cookies into napkins. The older ones, anyways. They don't care about stocks. There are probably eight people in this whole spot with 401(k)s. They care about what happens only because it means there's a tidal wave coming and what to do when it hits them. They care if they'll get washed away with it. If they'll even have houses when it's done. They care if they'll be on the street. If their kids will be okay.

And I feel *that* in my stomach. It's a hot coal cooking down there. And I'm thinking, *This is why I did what I did, and why I'm going to keep doing it.* More. For people like this. I got no shame ripping off drug dealers anyways.

Sin vergüenza, I'm thinking, and I haven't even thought about that in forever.

I remember being a dumbass little kid with no parents ever around in our tiny little apartment on the block and how the Piñeda family took care of me, lumping me in with the three brothers and feeding one more kid most nights. Mrs. Piñeda used to say, what was a little extra beans? They were good to me even though me and Beto and Javi and Squeaker were a bad little crew, always getting into mischief. Stealing shit. Scrapping with anybody that wanted some. I remember how their grandma with the glass eye always used to say how these Piñeda boys (and she meant me too) had no shame. Like it was a bad thing.

After a while, we just took her scolding words and said them when we did bad shit, but turned them around like it was a good thing. Like, ¡*Sin vergüenza!* It became a call, sort of. A rally cry. Like, *Yes, I am doing this and I don't care if you see me, because I got no shame doing it!*

That's how I feel right now. No shame for stealing. Never. Not if it helps people like John. He's already sitting two rows in front of me, slumped a little on the left because ever since his car accident in the eighties, his back's bad and his pelvis is so wrecked that he can't even sit flat. All of him is on a slant now.

It started with opiates for him. That's true of more and more people here. It started with bad pain, and then it's about trying to take that away so you can function, but then, as you're doing that, tolerance goes up. First it was the legal way, with pills, getting bumped from Vicodin to OxyContin, and then it was other stuff. You don't wake up one day and decide to do heroin. You fall down the ladder to it.

Sitting in rooms like this, man, you learn everything you ever needed to know about human weakness.

How we lose and how we try. How we get back up.

John's white. A Vietnam vet. He used to be a doctor but he got disbarred or whatever it is because he was an addict too, and his wife and three kids got caught up in it and now two of his kids are dead (one killed herself, the other dosed out in the backseat of her car up in Topanga), and his wife was back on her struggle again and that's why she wasn't here tonight, but he was still fighting to stay off. He's always fighting to stay off. Same as the rest of us.

I know his story backwards and forwards. I hear new bits and pieces every week. The kind of talking that goes on in rooms like these isn't conversation. It's confession. It's little axes of words getting sunk deep in your heart.

And you can look around while it's getting told and see those axes in everybody else's hearts too, and that's how you know this group works. Being able to be seen, to look in another person's eyes and not just hear them, but listen and feel it. You get to sit with their truth, to really feel their pain. And doing that takes my mind off mine. And I walk around with it afterwards too. Their truth and pain and mine too, all wrapped up. I carry all of it together.

Rooms like this is where I learned that stories are worse than bullets sometimes, because bullets can pass through you or be taken out but stories can't. Stories stick. Good stories don't just do that, though, they can rearrange you inside. There's no getting them out. And once they're in, they can roll around and grow while you think about them and they can get bigger. They can change your mind about things, your thinking, even your heart. Sometimes years after you heard it, a story can change *you*.

Hearing John's made me know some people got it worse than me. Sure, I'd never have Rose. Me and her would never get married or have a family. But I didn't have to watch her die either. We didn't have kids only to lose them. Knowing you don't have it the worst has been more help to me being sober than anything. I still got Rose with me. I got her spirit.

Out of the corners of my eyes, I see Mira come in late, grab that apple-cinnamon tea like she always does, and sit in the back. We never look at each other. Nobody even knows we met here, or that we see each other, or that we started this plan because of this room, because its stories stayed caught in us.

When this girl talking finishes up, I raise my hand and catch a nod from the leader and say what I always say, what I've been saying every week since I was eighteen, using a name I made up on the spot the first time and been stuck with ever since, "My name's Ricky, and I'm an addict."

24

Because I am Ricky, and I *am* an addict. Even if part of me died when I changed names, the sick part inside me lives on. It never goes away. It's always down for more. And it's being in rooms like this one at St. James after Rose died, letting myself be seen by people that know what it's like to go through this is pretty much the only thing that's been keeping me together for years.

It used to be if you had something, I'd put it in me. And once it was once, it was twice, and then it was ten. I'm like a busted blender that way. You put anything in me and flip the switch, I won't stop till I short out. That's just how I'm built. So I had to unplug. It's the only way.

I'm not a stupid teenager anymore. I knew I couldn't keep hurting myself and other people. That shit catches up to you. And when one day Saint Peter reads my ledger out to my face, I don't want him to be reading only bad. I'm not saying I can balance it. I'm just saying, I can't be all bad on my day of judgment. I refuse that shit. I got to find some good in me. Whatever good Rose put in, I've been building around it every day I'm sober. I've been doing it these years. Having a job. Paying taxes. Trying not to be a taker my whole life. Trying not to be someone that never cared about anybody.

And for me, these meetings are glue.

They patch me up. Keep me together. Only place on earth I can say I still get dreams that I used again. And when I wake up, I'm so ashamed my sobriety's gone that I want to kill myself, and afterward I get hugs on top of I know *s*, and *It's okay* s, and *We all go through that* s.

"Hi, Ricky," everybody says in unison. John too.

I nod at him and swing my eyes around the room so he doesn't think I'm only focusing on him. John doesn't know me and Mira paid off his mortgage today. That he's good on that forever. Sure, it doesn't solve any of his other problems, but he'll have a place to live no matter what, and hopefully, that's something.

"My struggle for these days is," I say, "I met a girl."

There's nods at that, like the group already knows where I might be going. There's a million things that can go wrong there when you're in permanent recovery. A *million*.

"I told her right away too, said I'm an addict, and she said, 'How long?' And I said, 'All my life,' and she said, 'No, how long you been sober?' I told her sixteen years last month. She said she'd take her chances. Didn't ask what I did. Didn't want to know where I'm from or what my growing up was like. Not right away, anyways."

People are listening hard now. Cheering for me, almost, but in a silent way. Everybody in here wants everybody to succeed. And if they do, it's almost like you can too.

"I mean, sitting with her, I just feel like there's no point in her talking to me. Like, I told her not to invest in me. To put her time and energy into something shiny and new. And you know what she said? 'I'm into fixer-uppers.' "

This gets a laugh. Even from Mira. She did say that to me the first time. I don't tell anybody the person I'm talking about is in the room, that we actually met two years ago, or that she's still married, but this is how I can talk to her in a safe space. Say the things I never can while we're together.

"Some of you remember Rose. How she first brought me here and sat with me and held my hand when I wanted to run. She was my second chance." I look at John and say, "John, you remember her." I look at our group leader. "Sandra, you met her too."

Their eyes get sad and they nod heavy nods back at me. I don't bring up Rose often, not in over a year, but I got to now.

"There's never any replacing Rose. She made me who I am. She's why I'm still here. And I've been thinking about her a lot lately. And sometimes with this other lady, I feel like I shouldn't be feeling what I'm feeling because of Rose."

Nobody interrupts you here. Nobody tells you to stop talking.

They let you have the time you need.

"I guess that's especially because, and this is the hardest thing, but my cancer's back. I don't need a doctor to tell me something's going wrong. I'm having problems like before. Smelling smells that aren't there again. I'm forgetting things. I know I don't got much time left and I don't know how to tell this girl any of this. I guess I just want to disappear and not deal with it."

But this is me telling Mira right now. Putting it into the air of this room so I don't have to do it somewhere else.

I can't look at her, so I don't.

"So, all's I'm saying is, if you don't see me next week, or the week after, just know this group means something real to me. That it kept me going even back when I had to take three buses and go almost two hours one way just to get here because Rose wouldn't have had it any other way. She wanted me out of the neighborhood, away from where I'd been using. She was always smart like that. And that trip helped give me a life. So. Just." I don't mean to stop there, but my words are clogging up inside me. I got to look up at the ceiling and hold some emotions in before I can finish with "Thanks."

It's rooms like this that taught me pain is what makes people act the way they do. We're afraid to get more than we already got. Or we're trying to forget it for a minute. But pain is the driver. And it doesn't have brakes. It only lets its foot off the gas once in a while.

25

After group I got twenty people wanting to talk to me on my way to the parking lot because they followed me out to tell me it's okay, to tell me to go to the doctor because, well, it could be anything, and I know enough not to self-diagnose. None of them is Mira, but we agreed on not ever being seen together in public, so I take all that and say thanks, and then I walk across the street to where I'm parked and I just get in and drive because that's all I can handle right now, Rose's music and Wilshire going east.

We never did it, me and Rose. We wanted to. We tried. But she got too sick. We were going to do it anyway, gently, even when it got real bad, but one night she went home and never called again. I knew why. I wasn't stupid. And after that I was so sad we'd never been together, but now I wonder if it's better we didn't, that maybe it would've fucked me up worse. But she was so beautiful, though, even skinny as she was. Under a hundred pounds near the end. Cheekbones poking out. A skeleton queen. A living *catrina* when she put on a ton of dark eye shadow—

My ringer goes and I look down. Collins's calling on my regular cell.

I pick it up, put it to my ear, and for a full second, I wonder if talking on a cell phone like this, pressing it to my head, brought my cancer back. Radiation, or whatever. Not that it matters now.

"Yes, sir," I say.

"I'll cut to the chase." Collins says things like this thinking it's cool, like he lives in a seventies cop show, but then he surprises me when his voice gets softer, like he's actually got some sympathy. "I'm real sorry to hear about your medical condition."

Soon as he says it—dude!—I feel anger light me up inside.

All's I can think is *Fucking Frank dropped a dime on me.* I could've heisted two, maybe three more spots with no interference. Nobody would've gotten hurt. Now, though? It's a whole new game.

"Frank told you." I don't make it a question.

"Hell, no! You think that old hoss would say shit to anybody about you?" Collins laughs down the phone at me. "It was Laura. She's worried about you."

"I'm sure she is." But I'm thinking, *Maybe she is.* I'm willing to give her that.

But see, Laura's smart too. I'm sure she heard about the safe from Collins, the one with the explosives in the door that I missed. And if she thought I was working myself too hard, and that was why I missed it, or if she had any feeling that I might've been pulling some shady maneuverings, she would've wanted the business kept out of it, and the best way to do that is cut me right out.

Intended or not, it's a slick move, but it's also the right move. And I admire that. For real. Because if I was in her shoes, I would've done the same thing to me.

I say, "So, she told you what exactly?"

"Just that you're not working for Frank anymore, and why."

There it is. She basically fired me from everything freelance with that phone call. I don't blame her. And I'm not mad at her.

Still, though, it's bad fucking timing. It changes everything. Makes the next step way more dangerous.

It doesn't take much to get Collins off the phone. He was uncomfortable anyways, but he was giving me the respect of at least calling me to let me know I wouldn't be on any more DEA stuff. This will go for every agency from here on out. The word has been spread. I won't be getting calls on anything anymore. I'm cut off. An island, floating on four wheels in the L.A. night.

My phone beeps when I set it in the shotgun seat. I pick it back up to see I have a missed call and a voice mail that came through before I was even in group, both from Stenberg Locksmithing. When I listen to it, Laura's in tears. She tells me how she had to do it, how she talked to Frank and they both felt like if they kept giving me jobs, that I'd just work my way right into the grave, and how they don't want that, how they hoped that by making this tough decision that I'd go get treatment. At the end of it, she said she loved me like a brother, and I should come back and see them right away.

It takes my wind out. I crack the windows on either side of me, and the night pours in, but it's not helping. Not enough. So I pull over.

I don't delete the message, but I put the phone down. I have to. I have to focus.

From my prepaid, I call Janine at home. I got the number by heart.

She has that caller ID, and she's seen this number once, so she knows that it's me. She picks up without saying hello, and I just ask if a woman named Francesca is there, which is code for me telling her she needs to meet me up and we've got to talk. She doesn't ask when or even where. She knows it's now, she knows where, and she knows I'm about to be headed there.

"Sorry," she says, "you've got the wrong number."

And then she hangs up.

There's no way her phone's tapped. Not even a remote possibility, but we don't take chances.

I could take the 10, but I'm almost to Vermont. I see the street sign for South Berendo flashing past and I think about that dude I read about in the papers, Walter Vega. I didn't know-him-know-him, but I've heard of him. He got killed down that street in November, last year. He was like eight days out of prison too.

Through Vermont and I can already see the old Bullocks Wilshire, standing up tall like an art deco temple—rectangular spines pushed out past the windows, guiding your eyes up to the top. With its gray stone and copper squares that rusted turquoise between banks of windows, that was Rose's favorite in all of L.A. Turquoise was her favorite color. The place is a law school now, but it used to be a fancy department store, the kind where ladies in old movies buy hats with feathers.

Wilshire's playing nice tonight, putting me on green after green, passing me—intersection by intersection—on a chain to Downtown.

I push PLAY. On comes the little whisper of tape reels turning and I'm feeling Rose counting in that space between. "Instant Hit" by the Slits plinks in, with its beat going over scratchy guitars. The girls start singing to me about how I'm going to self-destruct.

How they know it because it's how I'm built, how I've always been built. Rose put this song on there as a warning for me, just to say I got that in me, but there's also a line about how I'm "too good to be true" and that's pure Rose. From her to me forever.

I ride on that for a while before it ends abruptly and then me and Rose count the seconds. The time in between. Her in 1992. Me in 2008. Together.

NOFX butts in with their guitars and their beat. Putting out anger. Hitting me with a song that stings, "Day to Daze." It's another sad warning not to use again.

See, Rose knew me inside out.

She knew I needed to keep hearing this stuff every day of my life, every day I got left, so I'd know what I could become again if I ever started slipping.

Knowing I got darkness inside me no matter what. That it doesn't go away the older I get. That it's just sleeping. That it can wake up anytime.

Especially now.

And I've got to take it. Got to put a saddle on all the stuff that makes me be me and ride it. Strategy. Lying. Cleverness. All the gifts I ever had that made me a damn good junkie have got to be used for good now.

Even if I have to do some bad things first.

Rudolfo "Rudy" Reyes, a.k.a. Glasses

Monday, September 15, 2008
Morning

26

Collins didn't tell me I had to valet in order to go into the Beverly Hills Hotel. He just said meet him at the Fountain Coffee Room inside at 7:15 a.m., but he didn't say where it was or how to get there.

So I pull up at 6:55, anxious since this is nothing I'm used to. What happens is, I have to unlock my door so they can open it for me.

This kid does it. He's taller than me by shoulders and a head. He's dark haired, stretching his pink polo just by standing there, like it's a size too small.

He says, "Are you checking in with us today, sir?"

"No, getting coffee."

He tears some type of ticket and puts it under the near wiper before holding the stub out to me. He wants me to take it.

I seen this type of thing on TV and I seen Lonely do it, but I never had to do it by myself before. It's harder than I thought to trade the ticket for the truck and trust this guy to take care of it for me.

"You be good to it," I say as I take the ticket. "It was my

dad's." A 1975 Chevy Silverado. First truck my dad ever bought. I brought it back to being blue and white myself. Had to replace the steering too.

"Of course, sir. Absolutely."

I watch him drive it off and disappear on a left turn into a lot before I go in. In the lobby, I go left but figure out quick that's the wrong way.

At the front desk, I ask for the coffee room and they tell me to go to the right and take the staircase down on the left. When I get to the bottom of the stairs, it'll be on my right. I can't miss it. They tell me it opens at seven.

I go where they told me to go and find a chair by the top of the stairs. I take some time soaking up the carpets and the patterns on them, the light fixtures that must get dusted every day.

I even look at how the writing for the POLO LOUNGE curls above its closed doors. Everything looks expensive here, even the doorframes.

At seven, the doors to the Polo Lounge open but I go downstairs. When I walk into the Fountain, there's no other customers yet.

The waitress up front tells me to sit wherever I'd like, so I sit on the furthest end of the bar on the right, putting my back to the wall so I can see everybody walking by in the windows and they can't see me unless they turn and look back over their shoulders.

I put my arm on the seat next to me so people will know it's taken. I feel stupid I wore a nice guayabera, light blue, some khakis, and shined shoes, since everybody I seen go by so far is in T-shirts or hotel robes.

Maybe that's a reason Collins picked it. If I showed up wearing a T-shirt, staff would just think I was staying here.

What a government agent's doing picking a place like this, I'll never know, but it needed to be open early and it needed to be way away from Lynwood.

It's definitely that. Took me almost an hour on the 405. There was a big slowdown at La Tijera for no reason I seen.

Sitting here now, I get it. It feels like a different planet with its white walls, green fern paintings on them, and a man coming in and ordering cottage cheese and tomatoes for breakfast.

I think it's prolly the safest place I ever been in my life. I'd even bet nobody has been killed here before.

I check the stock price for BBY. It was $43.20 at the open but I don't get any service underground like this.

The waitress comes by. "You know what you want, sweetie?"

I don't even know what to say to that. An old white lady in a pink uniform with smile lines in her face looking at me and calling me "sweetie" is like being on some type of TV show. I look at the menu again but nothing jumps up at me.

"No," I say it more to the menu than her, "not yet."

"Well, you just let me know when you do." It sounds like she says it with a smile.

I look up and watch her go. She turns and slides behind the chef to go fill water glasses for two new people coming in. It's a small space they've got back there, just a little bar aisle, but they make it work.

The chef's got his little hat on and he's cooking right in front of me. I seen him whipping eggs and pouring them out onto the grill. The chef's *raza*, and when he sees me seeing what he's doing, he asks me in Spanish if it's my first time here.

I tell him yes and he laughs. He tells me not to worry, that he'll take care of me, and that I'm having the silver-dollar pancakes. I don't argue. I just say thanks.

He tells me it's nothing. To be polite, I ask where he's from. When he says Morelia, I can't help smiling. My parents are from there, I tell him.

He gets a look like he wants to talk more about that but it's best not to, since too much Spanish makes people nervous in a place like this. I understand that look, so I just nod. That's when I seen Collins walking past the windows and turning inside.

He's got a leather bomber jacket on over a blue collared shirt unbuttoned two buttons too many and no undershirt. He's in jeans and some gray-and-white running shoes with giant soles.

To me, he looks like a lawyer on a day off. He stops in the entrance and surveys the place, going left to right until he sees me. I take my hand off the chair beside me.

"You made it," he says, like he's surprised or something.

I just nod. "How'd you even pick this?"

"This place?" He's got one of those smiles on that tells anybody seeing it how smart he thinks he is. "My grandmother used to take me and my sister for breakfasts when we were growing up. We saw Cary Grant in here once. He was older but still Cary Grant, having an orange juice and a coffee right over there. That must've been midsixties. After *Charade*, I think."

He points to the side of the bar directly across from us where a woman in a T-shirt and a purple shawl around her shoulders is reading a book with one hand and holding a coffee cup in the other.

The name he said sounds familiar but I don't tell Collins that I don't know who that is, and I don't exactly want to hang around getting told old stories.

My pancakes show up. The chef serves them to me himself with a *Buen appetito*. I tell him thanks very much.

"Look at you making friends already." Collins says it smug.

Sure, I want to tell Collins, everybody in L.A. that speaks Spanish is automatically friends, but I don't. I'm staring at the tiny glass syrup bottle that says BEVERLY HILLS HOTEL on it.

I open it and pour most of it on my pancakes. I move the strawberry off onto my napkin since I don't eat those, and I spread one of the little balls of butter out on top.

The waitress is back. She says to me, "Pancakes, huh? I knew I could trust you." Then she nods at Collins. "How about you, sweetie?"

"Let's start with coffee."

"You got it." She actually smiles when she says it.

That order comes quick since the coffee station's right in front of us, and then we're left alone as much as we can be.

I say as casual as I can, "Is the safecracker out yet?"

"I'll let him know it later today. You were right about calling his boss. Apparently, his employer thinks he has cancer again, which is news to me since I didn't know he had it before."

I'm just nodding. Cancer. Right.

A lot of things make sense for me at that moment, about why he'd take the risks he did since he didn't feel like he had nothing to lose. With him off the board, it helps me make my decision about giving Collins the list today. Right now.

"So," Collins says, "have we known each other long enough for me to ask about your eye?"

I turn to look at him better. My right eye's messed up. The bone around it, the eye orbit, is healed but permanently dented. Everybody can tell.

So if I can I'm always putting myself in a place where things can't come at me from that side. That's why I'm sitting in this corner right now.

I say to him, "You didn't look me up?"

He smiles. Of course he looked me up. For somebody in his position there's more than enough to read on me.

"But you just wanted to hear it from me?"

"Nothing better than hearing a man in his own words."

"No, thanks." I cut into my pancakes. They're good, not $15 good, but good.

I'm not about to give Collins the long version of what happened to me. He knows enough. I make some right-handed noise with my fork on the plate as I take a folded piece of paper out of my left pocket with my left hand and set it on his right leg real slick. He figures out what I'm doing and takes it.

I can tell he wants to look at it, but he don't. He puts it in his pocket and pats it in a way that makes me lose my appetite, since this right here is me betraying Rooster.

The DEA now has addresses to all his drugs houses that I know about. They know Rooster's name now too, his real name. They now officially know he exists.

This is the wedding party Collins has been so worried about planning. Rooster's the groom. I guess the idea is to give him a ball and chain.

Giving them this information was half the price for getting my family out and me too. The other half is my testimony. I still don't know if I can give them that, but I do have the logs I've been keeping with the phone numbers and all the calls.

Collins don't know I have it. It's my last bargaining chip. With that, my paralegal says they should be able to prosecute without me saying nothing.

This is me, in now. All the way in. It's done. I can't go back.

Collins knows this too. He has a look to him like he's a cat and he just killed a big bird all by himself, but he didn't. I handed him the bird. I clipped its wings too.

He sips some coffee. "That's good."

Maybe he's talking about the coffee, but prolly he's not.

For me, it's not good. It's not even close to good. I'm taking a father away from his daughter with this.

My stomach's starting to feel like maybe it won't let me keep the pancakes. My skin's getting hot on my face.

Rooster has always been there for me. I'd be nothing without him.

There's reasons. There's always reasons. Reasons I'm not gonna sit around and tell Collins about, so I get up and thank him for breakfast and I leave without saying goodbye to the chef.

On my way to the truck, I can't help checking BBY. It's $43.90 a share and climbing.

27

I'm back in my truck, taking the 405 to the 105 again, finally going the right way for traffic. The other side's a mess as people are trying to get to the Westside, but this way is pretty clear.

My right eye's itching but I've trained myself not to rub it. That started after my first surgery. I couldn't rub it after that since it'd damage it.

Now it can itch all day, but the most I'll ever do is dig the middle knuckle of my index finger in my cheekbone below it. What it don't do, is make it feel better, but it gives me something else to focus on.

I was seventeen years old when two L.A. County sheriffs busted my right eye orbit and put bone fragments in the white of my eye, just missing the retina, the doctor said.

I was a no-joke cautionary tale after that, a reason never to get caught. After, my eyesight in that eye was not great.

I can read close, but far is bad, and I struggle in lower light. I had to memorize the chart to pass my DMV vision test. The dawn and dusk hours are a nightmare for driving.

I get diamonds across my vision, like how some cameras do that lens-flare thing in movies. So that was me, coming up in Los Angeles every day, permanently seeing stars. That's what Rooster said anyways.

The special glasses I had to get afterward, with a thick-ass lens on the right, were a badge of respect. They changed how I see the world, but they also changed how people looked at me too.

I was this survivor after, sort of untouchable. That's what made Rooster notice me at first, since nobody wears glasses in the hood unless you go to school.

What happened was, I did something stupid. I did a lot of stupid things actually. It's not that we didn't have nothing growing up, it's that we didn't have enough of it.

That's how I seen it anyway. Mom worked nights cleaning. Dad did whatever jobs came up. He'd mow and do yard work.

He always got paid in cash and everybody knew it. He got robbed a lot coming home, sometimes even by some little punk-ass thirteen- and fourteen-year-old kids.

He was weak. I couldn't respect that. So I never listened to him and I never stayed home. Always tried to make up for what he never had. I started stealing a lot.

The word the assistant DA used to describe me in court after was "brazen." It just meant I thought I couldn't get caught. That I'd take these crazy risks.

I'd go even in broad daylight, with people around. Nothing mattered to me. I thought I could do it. And this one time, I ripped off the register at the Cork'n Bottle and the guy I held up called the sheriffs on me.

They came quicker than I thought too, so we had a good little chase and I got pretty far down Duncan, almost to Sanborn, before they caught me and took a couple billy clubs to my head like I was a piñata and they'd get some candy if they broke me.

I don't know how many times they hit me until I blacked out. One of the last white people left in the neighborhood, Mrs. Blankenstein, used to live over on that stretch of Duncan, and she said they went twelve swings past me going limp. She counted since she couldn't believe it, since she thought they were killing me.

After I had two surgeries and healed up, I did some time. It wasn't a big thing since people knew sheriffs were the ones that hurt me. I got left alone. I read a lot, mostly fantasy stuff like Robert Jordan's Wheel of Time series.

I got headaches doing all that reading, but I increased my vision stamina. I got through *The Shadow Rising* before they let me out.

We worked up a civil suit and everything when no criminal charges stuck on the sheriffs that hit me, but Mrs. B. was sixty-four when it happened and dead of having emphysema by the time we finally needed her to testify to it.

Her sworn statement wasn't considered strong enough. She got discredited for being old. She couldn't have seen it right, their defense said. I was a known gang member, they said.

They offered a settlement of $75,000, which seemed like a lot of money in 1993, but it was three years after they did me, and I'd had medical debt with interest in the twenties since I couldn't exactly make payments when I was locked up.

Wiping that out took over $56,000 just on its own. I ended up walking with $19,000, but it felt like even less after they admitted no fault, sealed up the records, and that was that.

I was broken but I had a reputation. Only a wannabe gangster before, I sure became one after. I remember how Rooster sent for me one day when they were having a party at his mom's house, back when she used to live off Martin Luther King.

I got taken through the house and then down some back steps and through the yard, past a laundry line still heavy with wet shirts on it, and to a garage in the back that wasn't attached.

Rooster was back there with some people, but they got quiet when I came in, and he asked me if I wanted to see something badass. I said sure, and Rooster opened up a big box of air filters for me, but that's not what was in there.

It was full of cocaine bricks instead. I mean, all the way up to the top.

I leaned forward and must have adjusted my glasses or something, since right then Rooster said, "Yeah, check your glasses!" After that, I was Glasses, and Rooster made it so nobody fucked with me.

I'm slowing down since everybody's slowing down, and a bunch of us on the right are getting ready to get onto the 105 interchange so we're separating into packs going east or west. Me, I'm going east.

I pull out the phone and check BBY. It's at $44.10, still climbing.

The real reason why I started working for Collins was the *narco-cocinas*. What those are, are narco-kitchens, the type that cartels use to disappear people.

I'd been hearing stories on these for a while, mostly from Baja, not believing them, but they kept going around, always saying how after people get prolly tortured and definitely killed, cartels try to disintegrate the bodies with high heat from fires.

But I didn't hear about how that worked until Hector came back from Mexico with stories about what he had to do, back before he had a big gut and smoked too much.

What happened was, he had to cut holes in big metal barrels, then drop whatever person deserved it in headfirst. That's if they're going in whole, he said. Otherwise, it's just parts.

After, he poured diesel. Five gallons is what it took to burn anybody off the planet when he lit it.

What Hector said was, when he first started, he wasn't able to eat meat for weeks and weeks. He said raw chicken smells exactly the same as human flesh when they cook.

Exactamente, that was the word Hector said to make sure I knew there was no difference, and he had this look in his eye as he was saying it, like the type a bird gets when it's wild and sick, when it can't fly but it's gonna try to.

What I felt when he said it that way, the word just got stuck down inside me. To do that to a wife, a mother? A daughter? It's unforgivable, completely. Just hearing that told me where the line for me was, you know? That, right there? That's too far.

There's a line in between that and where I was at, and if I crossed it, I knew I wouldn't be coming back. I'd be something else forever after that.

And right as I thought that, it just sort of crashed down on me that I was part of it. I guess I just put up a blind side to it until then, but I couldn't deny that dealing here was basically sending money there to do *that* to other Mexicans, man. Financing it.

I was basically making it so cartels had the capital to pay some monsters to put people in barrels so their families would never even know what happened to them. I couldn't take that idea.

It kept me up nights. It put that thing that's like psoriasis on my chest. But back in the day, it wasn't like this at all. There were rules.

What I'd say is, back then you were only killing somebody if you could guarantee that they're sources or snitches, or a rival that needs to be taken care of. Those were the only ways. Innocent people weren't ever involved.

I mean, the drive-bys in L.A. were bad when they were happening, but a stop got put to those. Down in Mexico, with the last couple years, like girls in Juárez disappearing, journalists disappearing, I feel like those old days are gone now, gone forever. There's not much honor on that side anymore.

What I remember about the day everything changed for me is, I got picked up about a week after I first heard about *narco-cocinas*. It was DEA. It was Collins.

They snatched me on a bullshit trafficking charge since they had someone in custody that said he'd dealt with me, and I guess they had his signed statement too, something about how I helped run things and took hold of the dope.

It was enough to do warrants on me and arrest me, and when that happened, Collins wanted to know right then, did I want to be helping them?

He played it pretty good. The best move was him freezing my assets. I still remember the day, May 24 of this year.

I wasn't doing everything in cash. I had a bank account from putting what was left of the settlement away since even I knew I couldn't be having that money on me in the neighborhood.

When I opened the account in '93, the banker said I should think stocks with some of it. I picked one from a list he printed out, Best Buy for the name, BBY, but also for the price, $1.01, like the freeway.

It was a sign, I thought. I went almost all in on it since I figured it didn't even matter. If I tried keeping the money at my parents' apartment, it just would've got stolen, so I figured, might as well spin the wheel.

I put $18,000 in and the trade cost $100. The guy thought I was crazy, but he sure took my money.

I left it there too. All that clean money has sat for fifteen years and change. On the day Collins froze it, it was worth about $635,000.

Nothing smart about it. I got lucky. I'd been kicking myself for not selling in December the year before for $766,000, but I just kept thinking it'd go up and up like it pretty much always had.

I got greedy. I hadn't looked at the thing for months sometimes, being busy running things for Rooster, but the second it got frozen, I wanted out every day. Every day was a loss.

I checked the price a lot. Sometimes ten, twenty times a day. That's all I could do, just look. Couldn't move it to cash. Couldn't run. I was stuck good and Collins knew it.

What he said that day, I guess it would've been persuasive for some people. They didn't know I was thinking about something other than money then. What I was thinking about was how I didn't want some guy like Hector smelling me cook like chicken in a barrel. Didn't ever want Leya or my little boy to be that way either.

But more than that, I didn't want anyone else ever having that happen to them on my account. I didn't want to feel responsible anymore. That shocked me the most.

Rooster knows about Collins since I got scooped up. I couldn't hide being arrested and held. It was Rooster's idea after that for me to be a double agent for him, to tell Collins I'd do it and then feed him bad information, or good stuff too late.

Rooster didn't know I'd already said yes, and he wasn't going to know. That's why Collins puts up with me doing that so Rooster don't think I'm a narc. Collins must think all this trouble's worth it if it gets him busts all down the Southland and takes a real player off the streets.

So I said yes to snitching, but then what I said was, it's got to be worth it to me. You have to unfreeze that money. You have to protect my family.

When it's done, you have to let us leave California. Send us anywhere but help us go, I said. You have to make us new people.

Collins didn't exactly say yes to any of that, but he didn't say no to me either. He made it seem like the result that I wanted was up to me.

The more incriminating stuff I came to him with, the more high-up people I put in their sights, then the more likely it was that my family would be safe. It got clear real quick that the only thing that was gonna save us was trading Rooster.

So that was that, him, or me, Leya, and Felix. It was one weighed against three. Or more like two against three. Counting Jennifer. But that still don't balance out. Not with my family.

Me catching a conscience, that's how this whole thing started. I guess it's still a toss-up on whether that's gonna kill me or not. *If it does, I deserve it, but even if it only gets Leya and Felix out, lets them get at that stock money, it's worth it.*

That's what I'm thinking anyway when I'm on the 105 and passing the tall sign for Plaza Mexico with its little dome on top. There's the feeling again coming up in my stomach that I'm a traitor.

It's true too. I don't deny it.

It's just that I think there's worse things than being a traitor. Being a monster with no rules, that's worse. *You can make a choice,* I think.

And I'd rather risk being dead than being that.

Ghost

28

At night, Downtown feels like somebody opened a trapdoor and dropped all the people out. During the day, it's Commuterville. That's a Frank word. You got all these people driving in from everywhere else to work at the courthouse or banks or wherever, and then the workday's over and they're gone. Big buildings, empty. Parking lots with six stories, empty. Streets with a few cars only, and no semis. There's the rattle of a dude pushing a shopping cart to trash cans and raiding them for bottles.

I'm early, and there's parking spots on South Main because there's always spots on South Main after eight. Meters are free after six. Not that it matters. I roll into a spot right before Winston dead-ends into Main, and the pole for the meter is still there, but the top has been sawed off. That means it's due for a replacement, but when that's coming, not even the meter maid knows.

I eject Rose's tape, put it in its case, put the case in my jacket pocket, button it closed, and lock up the Jeep.

Seems like every time I come to Downtown these days, something's changed. More, and different, graffiti all up and down

Winston since that Crewest gallery opened. The Regent Theater's still a busted-up old mess, though. The art supply shop's closed and gated and dark. Three people are eating at the Vietnamese spot on the corner, chopsticks up, hunched over wide-mouthed white bowls.

I turn and walk up Main to Fifth, just to see how Skid Row's doing.

It's been a while since we saw each other. I did my time up and around here in the nineties, doing things nobody sane and sober would ever be proud of. It was way worse then. It was bad all the way to both bridges: Fifth over the 110, and the other way, over the river, but the Row has been the Row since forever.

The problem with Downtown in general, and Skid Row in particular, is people can smell it on you when you're *susceptible*.

That's a word that stuck in me because of NA. "Open to influences," it means. Mostly bad ones. And you don't even have to be down near the missions to see it. All you have to do is walk past the Rite Aid on Fifth and Broadway and you got people not looking you in your eyes, putting that hustle whisper on you: "Oxy, Oxy, Oxy . . ."

Or, "Any kind of smoke," and just in case you didn't catch it, "*any* kind."

And it's shit like this, promises honed, calculated, and damn near guaranteed to get that addict inside you going.

Making that voice inside me rev up and start telling me how it wouldn't be so bad if I did walk a couple blocks down, to Los Angeles Street, to San Pedro—just to see if I knew anyone around there still, if they made it this long. It tells me how I've been doing so good for so long that I can totally kick back.

That I've earned it. Shit. I *deserve* it.

And that's the thing about living with addiction that I can't explain to anybody except people living it. That having it is like practicing every day on which thoughts to listen to, and which to keep in the background. Not ignore it, not all the way, because that's how it gets strong over time and one day just smashes into you because it's been growing in your shadows and you thought you were stronger than it. So, this is me, just like every day, trying to tune in just enough to that addiction radio I got going inside me that I know what it sounds like, to know that it'll always be inside me, and that it's strong, but it doesn't own me so long as I'm aware it's there. So long as I just keep it in the background, you know? Like, white noise.

I can't ever go down to the Row again.

But that doesn't mean I can't look at it.

I stand on that corner and tell myself it's a beach. I tell myself that everything past this here curb is water. Main Street's nothing but water. The building on the opposite corner is nothing more than a beige tugboat with its anchor down. And everything past its ass end—the bow?—everything down that slope of Fifth Street is a river, and I can't go down there because I won't come back up.

Not for a week, or maybe more. Not if I'm honest.

That place has a current to it that's too strong for me. Too strong for what I got inside me. So I stand on the shore and I look at a pair of hypes going by and away, at the street folks coming up and out like they forgot what land looked like, and I get lost for a minute, because thoughts of Laura and Frank cutting me out are creeping up inside me, and I'm thinking about swimming a little, about how I really used to like doing that back before I discovered what consequences were and what permanent meant, so I just listen.

I listen to the night, to two seagulls fighting over trash, to a car horn punching the air a few blocks away, but my feet don't move, I don't go towards it, and I sure as shit don't get anywhere near wet.

I turn my back on that water and walk up the block, not looking back, and for me, right now, that's enough.

Being inside Pete's Café is like being warm without there being a fire going. Lamps hang from ceiling poles like yellow cake donuts about to get glazed. I tell the hostess that's reading some thick book that I'll seat myself in the bar, and she doesn't even look up, which is fine.

Sometimes you can tell when a place is trying too hard, but this place tries just right. High white ceiling. Tile from the early twentieth century that got restored. It's not like this place shuts the world out, because you can still see out the big front windows to the night people walking past. You know you're still in Downtown. You know people a block or two away are still out sleeping rough.

Pete's has been on Fourth and Main for a long time—I want to say from '02, which was still back when Downtown was all kinds of bad news. Raves. Junkies. Stabbings. All that. After the Hippodrome got itself knocked down in the eighties and it was just a parking lot for a long time, there was a Porta Potti across the street from Pete's, and I'll never forget how this one time I went to go use it and I opened the door on a passed-out junkie getting head with a needle stuck in his arm.

You can't unsee that, and believe it or not, I wouldn't want to. It was a warning. See, that could've been me. Shit. It still could.

I'm still only one full needle away from bad decisions like that.

Walking past the bar, I nod at the bartender and he nods back. We don't know each other or anything, it's just the polite thing to do. Janine's sitting at one of the bar tables, a tall circular thing. I take the red leather booth behind it because there's no one wanting it.

Janine's got her nighttime, going-out glasses on—the black rims with the sparkly bits down the temples. Long-sleeve red blouse. Black jeans. Blacker boots. You'd never know she had about ten tattoos, or that I steered her to tattooers I know for most of them. She's the clerk for Judge Warren F. Olney in the federal court. Olney's the conservative everybody knows has a soft spot for drugs warrants so he gets hit up a lot, and anything that crosses his desk, she sees, and whatever she sees, she remembers.

Janine's good to me. Always has been. Always will be. We got history.

See, she was divorcing her cheating husband and he'd squirreled away a bunch of money in a safe that only he had the combination to. Even though the court ruled that she was entitled to it, they wouldn't do anything about him refusing to open it for her, so I went in there and popped it when he was at work, called her, and had her

121

come over with a bag and we filled it all up. After, I got Mira to do a safety-deposit box for her. The husband could've given her half, but didn't, so he got none. That's a life lesson, man. Don't be greedy. Don't tempt someone out there to come take what you got. Because somebody will. And that somebody might be me.

I order a water and a plate of nachos that will come out too hot on blue-corn chips, with cheese, black beans, and sour cream mounded up higher than my head. I watch Janine finish her drink without looking like I'm watching. She checks her phone. She texts somebody that isn't me, then grabs her purse and walks to the stairs, the ones that lead down to the little lounge where the bathrooms are.

I watch her go and count thirty while the TV above the window looking out at a cheese shop in the building next door shows highlights of the Dodgers beating the Pirates, 8 to 2.

When they're over, I get up, adjust my belt, and go downstairs like I don't need anything from anybody.

There's a half flight, and then a landing before you take another half flight of stairs down into the basement. All along the way, the staircase walls are full of old black-and-white photos, all of them showing what the neighborhood used to be like in the 1920s and '30s, showing how this was a banking district before Bunker Hill got snatched and turned into skyscrapers.

There's a couch downstairs and Janine's waiting for me on it.

She's careful as all hell. I know this isn't even going to take three minutes.

I start. "I need search warrant addresses for upcoming DEA spots."

She takes a small piece of paper out of her purse. It's square and has an advertisement on it for high-blood-pressure medication. She writes one address fast, then two, then three.

I don't want to stop her, but I have to know. I say, "All of these have safes?"

It's not a photographic memory, she has. It's *better*.

She says she just remembers things. She doesn't have to picture it. You ask her and it's there. Like an Internet you can talk to.

"Paperwork mentions it, but you'll never know until you're in there." She writes a fourth address and then looks up. "You don't need more than this, do you?"

She's holding my stare with her own, and a whole lot goes back and forth between us. Twelve years she's known me, and she knows I'd never be asking about this unless I was about to do some of the stupidest shit I ever done in my life. She knows that can't last long. And I know she wrote down the best ones, the closest to yeses, and none of the maybes. That's who Janine is.

I look at the paper in her hand. "How many of these are acted on?"

What I mean is, how many have already been served by law enforcement?

"That I know of? None."

"You know any time frames?"

She gives me a look like I'm asking a stupid question, but then she says, "They all came in today, late afternoon. Judge signed off on them before the end of the day. I don't know what all they need to make these—if it's SWAT or what—but you know as well as I do that they go when they're ready, couldn't care less about business hours."

I do know. "Is this Nayarit stuff or what? Xalisco Boys? The dudes that got caught up in Operation Tar Pit way back?"

Janine covers her mouth so she won't laugh in my face. When she's done, she says, "Oh, honey, it's not been like that in a while."

That's when I know all this is about to take a turn. And I'm thinking about that bad feeling I had when I saw that white boy driving up to pick something up *himself* in those Rancho San Pedro Projects. I mean, that shit just doesn't happen when it's Nayarits running things. It bugged me then, but I was focused on other things. Too focused. It's a fire in me now. Already, I'm sweating and the back of my neck's hot.

See, Nayarits, they come to you. You call a number, get given a meet point, and a driver comes out with the stuff and spits balloons in your hand. And for a while, that worked real good. But then the gangs caught on and jumped right in the middle. *They'd* buy the black tar from the Nayarits and then sell for triple.

I heard shit like this was going down. Street gangs coming in hard, buying from Nayarits and marking up prices. A cold feeling balls up on either side of my jaw, and I feel it, and I know it's true: that much money in the safe meant this was always some hardcore L.A. gangster shit, not Nayarit-style Mexican-capitalist street selling out of little cells with drivers and cell phones.

Worst part is, I should've seen this coming from miles away. I should've known as soon as I saw that white boy driving his Mercedes up the block, looking to buy. I should've known. Shit.

I punch my thigh, hard. I should've *known*!

Janine blinks and turns her head to side-eye me.

My mouth's dry. I don't want to ask her, but I have to. "So who is it?"

She tells me the name of the gang and it's like I don't hear it at first. My ears are already ringing and I lean in, mad because I thought I missed it. But I didn't miss it. My brain just took a couple seconds to process it, and it's there now, hot and white at the front of my face. Like a flash knockdown in boxing, I just didn't see this punch coming. It buzzed me. It buzzed me good.

See, the problem is, this crew is a Lynwood crew. It's made up of homeboys from the area I grew up in. Old-schoolers that might know me by my face, that would kill me without even blinking because years ago I got told to lose myself and never come back. That if I ever showed again, there'd be no questions, only bad things.

And hearing that gang name, it's like I'm eighteen all over again. I'm feeling all the old feelings from when they first told me if I ever popped my junkie face up again, they'd shoot it, stuff what was left of me in an oil-drum trash can in Little Tijuana, throw some lighter fluid in, flick a match, and let it burn till there was nothing left to find. Homeboy cremation, they called it.

And they meant it. Every word.

These fools are nuts for real.

I shake my head. I try to get my bearings back. "On which of these addresses?"

Easy, I'm thinking, *I'll just avoid whichever one is theirs.* Like, no problem.

"All of them," she says. "DEA don't play."

This is *no bueno.*

All of it is like stepping through hell and *knowing* it. And even that's okay, but the worst part is feeling like there's no way to get out of this without hurting people. Last, do no harm. I mean, I can forget about that because if I'm going at this crew, I need to let that shit go. And I might have to let it go *quick.*

Because they'll be *about it.*

And I'm sweating that, but I can't shake the feeling that good people need more. It's burning inside me. And that's rough because taking when DEA had my back was one thing. Taking when I'm solo is something else altogether.

And that's how I make my decision.

It'll cost me my life. Of course it will.

But I knew that going in. It was always going to end. That's how life works.

So, I look up at the ceiling, at its dimples and paint scratches and scuffs.

And I decide I'm doing this.

I'm fucking *doing* this.

I nod at that ceiling, just so it knows too. Janine's got big, worried eyes when she grabs my shoulder. Like she's trying to steady me or something. But she doesn't know that walking into this kind of thing is guaranteed lights-out in a real bad way.

"Thanks, Janine," I say, but it comes out weak, like I still can't catch my breath when I slide out of her grip and get up off the couch to go to the bathroom.

When I'm done throwing up, when I've flushed and rinsed my mouth out, I make a call I promised myself I'd never make again as long as I lived.

Glasses

Monday, September 15, 2008
Early Afternoon

A name came in, Ricky Mendoza. Junior. What that gives us is a address, and a reason for me and Lonely to head to Hawthorne even when we're super sure that he's not there anymore. We go anyway.

The market's dumping like crazy, so I'm trying not to trip out with checking the phone, but when I see the BBY stock price as we drive, I see it's not so bad at all.

At 10:00 a.m., it peaked at $45 a share, then dipped down to the opening before settling fifty cents higher for $43.70.

Thanks to Collins, I have 17,800 shares I can't touch. DEA knows it's not illegal money. The only reason why they're holding it is to make sure I don't use it in a criminal enterprise, but that's a BS reason.

It hasn't been touched in years and they know it. Collins says he has discretion. It can be unfrozen on his say-so. He knows I need it. Cashing out and paying taxes on it is the only way to start a new life clean.

The Durango apartment building on Doty is basically a giant

stucco box the color of cat litter that only goes up three stories, but stretches back into the block about six. We drive by it first.

We check five blocks in both directions, but no white Jeep with black plates. There's a park next to the apartment building with a parking lot. We check that, but get nothing. On the front side of the Durango there's parking, but it's gated.

There's a buzz box up front with a video camera hanging off the roof pointing right at it and the front double doors. One of the things we found searching for this place online is that there's this apartment for rent inside, so we walk up like we're interested and buzz the button that says PROPERTY MANAGER.

After a second, it's either a crackly voice or a crackly speaker that says, "Yes?"

"Good morning," I say, "is the apartment still for rent?"

"Sure is," he says, like he's sighing into the phone. "Three oh six. Corner unit. Come on up."

On the way there, I send Lonely into the garage while I hold the door open and he checks for the Jeep. When he comes back shaking his head, we go up to the second floor and take a detour to Ricky's apartment to see what we can see.

What we find isn't good. There's this badass-looking handle on the door of 203, one with a big key lock anchored to the door. It looks like a little square unit with decent bolts on it.

I look down the rest of the hallway. I walk to another door, 202. That one has a different handle and lock set.

I walk to another, where it's the same cheap thing, and it's obvious Ricky didn't like the standard version. Lonely looks at me.

"He's a safecracker and a locksmith," I say to him. "It figures he did up a good one for himself."

We go to the manager's apartment after that. Lonely knocks, and a mayonnaise-colored white guy with wispy long hair going gray on the sides answers the door.

He's got a flannel shirt on that could be a type of pajama top, I'm not sure. He's got shorts on, and double-Velcro sandals for house shoes.

"Took you long enough," he says. "I thought you got lost or changed your mind." He forces a laugh.

I smile. Without a crackly connection between us, he sounds Texan. He also sounds a little scared.

Prolly he's even kicking himself for opening the door when he says, "You mind taking your sunglasses off? I like seeing the eyes of folks I'm dealing with. I'm old-fashioned like that."

I'm still wearing my sunglasses, left my glasses in the car on purpose, since these are bigger and it's harder to see how bad my right eye looks around them.

"I'm afraid I do," I say. "I just went to the optometrist and had the drops."

"Oh, well, that makes sense then. I'm Arlen, by the way."

"Arlen," I say back to him, and shake his hand in a way that lets him know I'll do things I say I'll do. "Good to meet you. Nice place you have."

It's not a nice place, the walls are yellow and the mismatched chairs at the card table off the kitchen look like they had a fight that none of them won, but it's the type of thing you say to a Texan. I've learned that much.

We deal with them a lot. Not all our product comes through Baja. Sometimes it comes through Arizona, but mostly it's from South Texas, especially the meth.

"I'm Bill," I say. "This is Ted."

When Arlen makes a face, I also say, "Not our real names, and I know you figured that out pretty quick since you're smart. I tell you that so you'll know that we're not here to lie to you."

I give him some space to nod, but he don't. He's stiffening where he's standing. An old dog wanders over with a clinking collar and tag.

It's a lowrider dog, a corgi with little legs, and the thing's eyes are that type of blue-white color that happens when animals go blind. She sniffs Lonely's knee.

"I love dogs," Lonely says as he bends down to pet the old thing.

"He does," I say to Arlen. "He loves dogs."

Hey, getting what you want from a stranger isn't about doing something to somebody. It's about planting a thought and letting it grow. Most people are reasonable.

128

They don't like pain. They don't like thinking about it happening to them or nothing else they love, and that goes for how Arlen's staring at his dog right now, looking nervous.

He's patting his thigh even, saying, "Petunia, come here now, girl. Let the nice man alone," but there's worry in his voice.

To him, I say, "Is two zero three owned or rented?"

The odds are that it's rented if it's in a building with other units for rent, but I need to know.

"Oh," Arlen says, playing it off like a misunderstanding, "that's not the one for rent. Uh, the one for rent is—"

"I'm aware," I say, before smiling and adding a nod to it. "Owned, or rented?"

Lonely picks the dog up in his arms and the dog lets him. You can tell she likes the attention. She looks heavy, maybe thirty-five, forty pounds, but nothing's heavy to Lonely. He picks her up like he's picking up a stuffed animal. Easy.

"Hey, now!" Arlen's turning red.

I take a step forward before he shouts more.

He flinches. "It's rented."

"Good, then I need the key."

"Now I don't actually have that." What Arlen's doing right now is squinting.

"You do," Lonely says, not taking his eyes off Petunia, still rubbing her tall ears. "State law requires a property manager or management office to be able to access all units in the event of fire or disturbance at the behest of the police or fire departments."

"Give us the key," I say, "and we'll bring it right back with Petunia before we go."

Arlen gets a look on his face then like I just punched his mother in her sleep, but he goes and he gets the key out of a special drawer where it's sitting all by itself next to a larger key ring, and when he puts it in my hand, I say, "Thank you."

Ghost

Monday, September 15, 2008
Evening

3 2

Here's why I promised myself never to call him again: Henry has shot people and gloated in their faces when they faded out of this life. He's stabbed people for no good reason. Shit. He even did it to me once when he was losing on a video game at Sega Genesis. Still got the scar on my left thigh from where the knife went in, and he was looking me in my eyes the whole time. He took me to the hospital after, but don't get it twisted, Henry Williams, a.k.a. Blanco, is nobody to spend any kind of time with.

Unless you're desperate. Unless you got no one else you can turn to. Unless you know someone else actually willing to roll up in a house with a gat and watch out while I crack a safe. And it's at least worth knowing that if he's going to stab me, it's not going to be in the back.

It's almost ten o'clock when Blanco shakes his fork at me like he can't believe I'd ever be sitting across from him again, much less at his own kitchen table. There's white lace cloth on it, like grandma cloth, and I can't keep myself from pushing a fingertip through one of the bigger crochet holes to rub waxed wood underneath. With my other hand, I'm forking up food, just like Blanco.

With his mouth almost full, he says, "When you called, I thought someone was playing pranks."

"You never changed your number."

He shoots back, "Why would I have to?"

He hasn't changed. Still the same dirty-blond hair, but slicked back now. Still got that purple scar down his chin, hiding in stubble. Perfect bony forehead for boxing, big and solid and hanging low over his eyes so gloves can't get in there and tear his lids up.

He sees me watching him and nods at me. I nod back.

Out of the corners of my eyes, I watch his knife sit still next to his plate.

I've known Henry since forever. After the Piñedas left for Arizona when their dad got a mechanic job at a semi-truck garage and my mom never really came back, Mr. Jimenez next door ratted me out to Family Services, and I went in the system. Was only two years of foster care, but it felt like longer. That's where I met Blanco. He was just Henry then, and me and him were family once. We still are, kind of. Even now.

Far as South Central's concerned, Henry never fit in nowhere. Growing up, he was always getting called out for being white, and having to fight black kids, *raza* kids, *guatemaltecos*, Thai kids—fuck, even Samoans. Sometimes you hear how what makes people is nature or nurture. With Henry, it was both. He loved socking fools up. That's who he is, but coming up in Lynwood just meant he had to do a lot more of it. Sometimes two or even three times a day. Didn't matter if he was tired or already busted up, he'd still do it.

And that's the kind of daily bullshit that either puts you in a bottle or slings you at a gang real early. For him, it was both. Me, I was never more than part-time in that gang life, mostly stealing, getting things for people that needed them. That's mainly because you can't be a full-time anything when you're a full-time addict. Me and Henry used to jack cars together and rob *paisas* for their payday sock stashes.

So many nicknames around here come from some obvious

shit. Dude looks like a big chubby bear? That's you, Oso. Dude's skinny? Flaco it is. For Henry, most people think he got named for his skin, because it's white as clouds and letters on street signs. But that's not how he got it.

One time early on, before he had a name, this dude named Lil Corners hated Henry and tried to get everybody to call him Güero for his nickname. That next day, L.C. got a visit in his front yard when three of his homies were there playing catch. Henry rolled up solo with a bat and broke ribs, but when he got to L.C. last, he damn near took the kid's jaw off. Broke it in seven places, I heard. L.C. had to get it wired up afterwards, and he's talked funny ever since, makes this sucking sound on his *s*'s and *f*'s. His mom's boyfriend at the time saw the whole thing go down, and he never liked L.C. This boyfriend was involved himself and impressed by the balls it took to come at somebody like that in broad daylight. Outnumbered. Not giving a fuck.

The boyfriend spread the word pretty good about what went down. "You should've seen them knuckles on that bat, holmes. They were whiter than white!"

And that's Henry now. *Nudillos blancos.* White knuckles.

Blanco for short. Named for his fucking grip.

To this day, you drop Henry's street name anywhere south of the 10 and people with enough sense and time in the game will close down right there and walk away. It's a name that people just can't have anything to do with. And that's because everybody knows Blanco will do whatever to whoever, whenever—that the dude has no limits.

When I walked in tonight, I looked him in his eyes. I gave him that respect. And I came with *cariño*: an envelope with $1,000 of my own money, my daily ATM max that I pulled out of my account on the way down. We do the dance right after I give it to him. He says no, he can't take it. And I insist, telling him it's for his kids, for their education, and then he can't say no.

Blanco offered me food straight off, and I said no because I could see his wife was pregnant again and had been sleeping on the couch right before he shook her awake. When she came over into the kitchen, blinking, I told her I was good, that I didn't need any food even though I'd thrown everything up before coming over and couldn't bring myself to eat the nachos after either, but her and her ma got up anyways.

Now there's chicken thighs in *mole amarillo* in front of us, and it's fancy as hell, loaded up with green beans and potatoes. Chayote too. On the side is a little plate of chopped white onion and lime slices next to some reheated rice and beans.

I bet it smells amazing, but all's I'm smelling is glue right now. Glue like they used to have in my elementary school classroom. I feel chilies, though. Heat. On my tongue.

"She didn't make the sauce," Blanco says, talking about his wife, "so you know."

He explains how it came from the market inside Lynwood's Plaza Mexico, that one development the Koreans from Mexico put together.

"They built it around the old swap meet, and the thing is," Blanco says, "it looks all nice and shiny and new on the outside, but inside? It's the same old."

He takes a bite, looking at me hard right then too, like he's trying to say I might look different on the outside, but I'm still the same inside.

That I never changed. That I can't. That he sees me. He *knows* me. All that is what his look puts across while he's chewing.

He swallows and says, "What do you call that, anyways?"

He knows what it's called. Blanco's no dummy. Like a lot of powerful men, he just loves asking questions he already knows the answer to so he can see what you'll come back with. Collins is the same way. Frank too, sometimes.

I come back with the same look he's giving me. The same look I would've given from a lifetime ago, because you can't let people like Blanco front you or they own you. And this is him testing me, seeing if I'm still worth his time.

"A metaphor," I say.

"Right." He's still eyeing me hard.

Blanco's got a smile and a disbelieving shake of his head on top of it too. He's got my old name in his mouth, and I can see how he's about to spit it, so I stop him because I don't need to hear the name I left behind here.

"I'm going by Ghost now."

He leans back at that, and the look in his eyes tells me how that's *perfect*, how he just nailed me down with the bit about the swap meet still being the same thing just under a different name, how he knew it was the same for me too. He's proud of himself for that. He goes back to smiling and nodding.

"Fits you," he says, and then turns to his wife. "Don't it fit him?"

I never really knew Esmerelda back in the day, but she's from the neighborhood. She's got that cinnamon-red Mexican hair. I mean, we got drunk together once and fucked at the old Casino House that Millionaire used to run, but nobody else knows and neither of us is going to tell Blanco that. Not ever.

She doesn't look up from whatever it is she's doing with dessert. "Fits him if he wants it to."

"Yeah." Blanco says it like he didn't even hear what she said.

That's Blanco. In his own world. Always has been. Always will be.

He comes back with "Some folks thought you was dead anyways. Coming back here, it's like you really are a ghost, *Ghost*."

I'm about to be one soon too, I think. People have a tendency to die around Blanco. Sometimes on accident. Mostly on purpose.

Right then, he laughs a late laugh that wobbles on the line between fake and real. It's just awkward enough to remind you that his crazy is in there, lurking under his skin. That he has control of it. For now.

"This dude, man," he says. "*This* dude. It's good to see you, *cabrón*!"

He throws a little check hook my way to catch me in the shoulder, but I dip an inch and slip it. That was a test too. How slow was I now? It's funny sometimes how much gangsters are like boxers, just physical. Always touching you, putting an arm around your shoulders, poking at you. What they're doing is trying to see who you are underneath everything. Trying to find weak spots.

Me and him used to scrap. He never beat me when I was sober, when we were evens, he called it. To this day, apparently, I'm the only one that never lost to him fair. And to Blanco, that means something.

See, he doesn't ask me what I want, or what I need. He just leans forward and says, "You know it's been boring around here lately though, huh? It's not like it used to be, not like that Wild West shit. None of the little-ass homies get that. Damn, man, nobody even gets tattooed anymore!"

He's got that look in his eyes. *La luz*, we used to call it. The light.

Not many people on earth enjoy going out and getting wild for no damn reason, but Blanco's one of them. Thirty-two years old. Wife. Two kids. One more on the way. Seen the inside of county jail plenty, even been tried, but never once convicted because witnesses had the habit of getting noncooperative at trial.

But that light's blazing now. I can see it.

And like all fires, it's got to be fed.

He takes a bite, chews, smiles, and says, "So what kind of trouble you gonna make for me?"

His wife flinches and that makes me hesitate, but Blanco's making a face you can't say no to, so I tell him I got an address. He makes me tell him what it is, and where it is, and I watch as he does that mental math about whose click owns it and if he can fuck with it or not. It must be a yes, because next he wants to know what it is about this particular address, so I tell him that maybe there's a safe inside, but we won't know till we get there tomorrow.

He scoffs at that. "Tomorrow? We're going *tonight*, fool."

Behind him, in the kitchen, I see his wife's shoulders sag. She turns and shares a look with her mother that I'm no good. That I'm taking her husband away. That I'm putting him in a position to do dangerous shit like he probably hasn't done in years. That I'm bringing the past back. That I'm reminding Blanco about what's bad inside him, not about what's good.

"Tomorrow's better," I say, as if anyone could ever tell Blanco when to do anything.

He doesn't like that. "We're rolling through, seeing what there is to see. You fixing to bust in somewhere without ever putting eyes on it first, dick?" He scoffs again, harder this time. "You been gone *way* too long, seeing things from that other side. It's a good thing you called me, man. These streets would've swallowed you up otherwise."

Blanco pushes his plate away and gets up to put kisses on his wife and mother-in-law. *"¡Riquísimo, señoras! Mil gracias."*

With them feeling worried right now, they don't want to accept these, but they lean forward, hesitantly, with their arms up, so he doesn't come too close. He crushes them in hugs anyways. And all's I can think about is how I'm about to know that feeling. The smothered part.

My whole life since I got clean I've had control till now.

But it's Blanco's show from here on out.

I'm driving, but the truth is, I'm just along for the scary-ass ride.

Glasses

Monday, September 15, 2008

Early Afternoon

34

The key to Ricky's apartment is an inch long but it's heavy for how small it is. It's thicker than a regular door key too. I never seen something exactly like it before. It has little round holes on the top, bottom, and sides in random sort of patterns.

It looks like braille but it's sunken in, not raised up. It fits the lock and it makes a double-clicking sound when I turn it, grab the handle, and push into a one-bedroom apartment that's mostly living room.

I look to my right, thinking I might see some type of alarm system, but there isn't one. I guess he trusted the lock. It's warm in here. Stale. I check the thermostat and it's set to off. How long it's been that way, I don't know. A few days at least.

The floor's wood in here, nice wood, different from the brown carpet in the hall. Petunia's claws tap on it as Lonely sets her down to roam.

What me and Lonely do is look for a safe first. We open closets and cabinets. We don't find one and we don't find anything else either, not even pots or plates.

Either he never had them or he got rid of them. The fridge is empty too, and clean. There's no bed in the bedroom, just dents in the floor for four legs where it used to be.

"This guy was always ready to run," I say.

Lonely nods at me and I move into the living room. There are white shelves built into white walls, but there aren't any books or magazines on them.

There used to be some posters on the walls, but now there's only empty rectangular shapes where the paint's lighter.

Closest to a small green couch in one corner are two boxes taped up nice and tight. They both say FRANK on them in black Sharpie letters.

"Hey," I say to Lonely, "open this."

Lonely always has a knife on him. This one he pulls from his calf sheath and locks it open with a snap.

He's super careful the way he cuts down the middle of the box seam, making sure not to go too deep. When he's done that, he does the sides and pulls the box open like he's revealing a Christmas present.

What's inside the boxes is a bunch of books about locksmithing, historical books about safes, books about collecting safes, books about how drills work, all types of stuff. I put them back the way they were stacked since none of it's helpful.

Beside the boxes is a tall table with a TV on it. It's unplugged. Next to that is a turntable, also unplugged.

What this makes me notice is how nothing's plugged in here, not the toaster, not even the fridge. It's like he was making it easy on whoever was gonna come in here after him, like he was being super respectful.

On the record player is a sticky note with one word on it. *Laura*. It's still stuck so maybe he didn't leave it all that long ago. There's another note for her under the table on a set of super nice speakers.

Next to them is a big black box with stainless steel buckles on it. On the top of it is a handle with a little tag on it. *For Laura,* it says, *from your sister.*

I'm wondering what that even means when I open it. It's not

locked or nothing, just latched. Inside are record albums, a lot of them.

The first one's purple with a picture on it of three girls that are only wearing these little white towels over their privates. They're naked above the waist but covered in mud so you can't see nipples. Above that, there's words.

Cut, it says in black on the upper right, and in the lower left above the picture, *the slits.*

Lonely looks over my shoulder. "I don't know of them."

"Me neither," I say.

I open it. I try pulling the record out, but before I get it even halfway with its white sleeve, an old photo falls out and hits the floor facedown with a note. Petunia walks over and sniffs them. I pick them up from under her nose.

The photo looks like the kind taken with one of those disposable cameras that used to be popular in the nineties. It's of two teenage kids, a white girl pulling a Mexican kid close to her with a arm that's so skinny it's gross. With her other arm, she's holding the camera.

She's smiling but her cheeks are all hollowed out. Just looking at her I can feel in my stomach that she's sick, and that there's almost a 100 percent chance of her being dead by now. Her hair's sort of hacked and sprayed up like the mud girls' on the record cover.

She's got a black T-shirt on inside out with the sleeves gone. The collar of it has white stitches where it got torn and put back together. What the boy's doing is squinting and smiling pretty hard. She's leaning forward and blocking the bottom part of his face with her head, but I know it's him.

He's our boy, our Ricky. Twentysomething years ago maybe. But it's him. It's got to be. There's a pier behind them and a little water, and two real smiles on both of them like it's their last good day. Hers, at least.

I put the photo in my pocket and then I pick up the note. It says, *Laura, meet Rose. This was her favorite album. I know she would've wanted you to at least listen to it.* It's not signed.

I put that back in with the purple record before I flip through the rest, checking the jackets for notes or pictures. There's nothing else in them and I don't recognize any familiar bands. They look pretty old but in good condition, like he loved them and was keeping them for this Laura.

I don't share it with Lonely, but everything I'm seeing in here fits up with what Collins said about him having cancer. This whole place is just depressing, like a storage space for things to be given away in a will.

I tell Lonely I'm done looking, and we go back up to see Arlen. He's holding back tears when he opens the door and sees Petunia is just fine, happy to see him even. Well, not see him but smell him and know he's there.

When I'm putting the key back in his hand, I get an idea, so I say, "Do you own this building?"

"I'm not the landlord. I'm just the property manager."

"Who's the landlord?"

"Frank." He whispers it, almost like he's betraying the guy. "Frank Stenberg."

Ghost

Monday, September 15, 2008
Evening

35

When I turn on the Jeep, the tape player kicks back in, and it's "Hey Holmes!" by the Vandals, all loud and fierce with its guitars right near the end of the track, and my cheeks burn as I curse myself for not turning it off and taking it out before, like I always do, but didn't because I was too focused on how meeting Blanco was going to go down.

He's laughing now though. "Oh, what? Is that for real?"

I just hit EJECT and pop it out.

"It's from Rose," I say.

"Like, *Rose* Rose?" He's surprised. "'We're going to the beach'? *That* girl?"

Blanco is the only person from the old neighborhood that ever met her. The time Rose picked me up in her Jeep to go to San Pedro, and to the beach. That was back when he was still at the foster house but I wasn't anymore. But that's where I was standing, waiting on that $68 he owed me, and there he was coming back with a bloody bat in his hand that he had to hide behind his back when

141

Rose rolled up, flashed a smile, and said, "We're going to the beach. You don't mind that I'm taking him, do you?"

Blanco didn't mind. It meant he didn't have to pay me. He watched me go.

And he knows she died from the cancer. He watched me go crazy.

Real easy, Blanco pushes the tape back in the player and the guitars jump back on. He stays quiet, and we drive.

The first time I ever heard this song, I couldn't believe how some Huntington Beach fuckers had any idea about my life, about walking that line between clicks and how the dumbest shit could pop off at any time. That was the nineties, though. I mean, the language in the lyrics isn't quite right, talking about sets getting fronted on, but it was close enough to my experience that it shocked the hell out of me back when Rose first played it. That they even mentioned Bellflower in it was crazy. I knew some heavy hitters from out that way even though I'd never been there before.

"You got the case for this?" Blanco wants to know.

It only takes a little rummaging in the glove box for him to find it.

He reads it out all slow, *"Fuck Dying, A Mix by Rose G. Sternberg."*

I correct him in my head, *Stenberg.*

It means "stone mountain" in Swedish. I looked it up.

When Blanco opens the case, I feel sickness working its way around my stomach. Under. Around. Over. Trying to crawl up into my throat, but I've got to eat it, so I do. Because words from me don't matter. Blanco's going to do whatever he wants anyways. Whenever. However.

My hands are sweaty on the wheel. It's from being back in the neighborhood. It's from Blanco. It's what we're about to do. It's everything.

A thought pops into my head: *Maybe I should score something, take this edge off. Doesn't have to be* chiva. *Just weed. Maybe a little beer.*

I could take all my edges off if it's going to be that kind of night, I'm thinking.

Doesn't take me but a few seconds to dismiss it. That's just my frustration talking. My fear. I know that. And I know I got an anchor inside me, deeper than anything: I can give up my life, but I can't give up being clean.

When I go out, I'm going out clean.

For me. For Rose.

When I first kicked, I was angry all the time. I didn't have any coping skills. It was like I Rip Van Winkle'd my own life. I mean, my body was older but my brain was still the same age as when I first started using heavy, thirteen. And I had to learn everything I should've learned by failing and struggling during the years I was caught up. But the drugs took that away from me, insulated me from everyday pains of living, put me in a room inside myself where nothing touched me. A place where the world turned outside but inside I stayed the same.

Outside's tougher now. But at least it's on my terms. Not some mindless, soulless drug's.

As we're passing by streetlamps, skinny rectangles of yellow light swipe over Blanco's darkened face while he concentrates on the track listing that Rose wrote by hand on the back side of the cover. I know every line, every letter, every stroke of her pen. Like, how her *r*'s almost look like *n*'s. Her writing's faded from where I rubbed my thumb over it so much. Even that BASF logo's looking sad as hell on the tape label.

The Vandals finish up and I count five silently with Rose, and then Poison Idea comes on. "Just to Get Away."

This, Blanco also finds funny.

"If you were trying to get away," he says it all deadpan without even looking at me, "you sure didn't get far."

I don't say anything. I turn on Imperial. I get a red on MLK as I pull into the left turn lane and we stop in front of the hospital. I stare at Tom's Burgers across from us, at the people I can see inside, through the blinds. An old woman holding a fry in the air, paused. People with their mouths at straws, sucking.

The light's still red ahead when I hear sirens. I look left. But they're behind us. I stay put even though the light goes green and the dude next to me peels out. An ambulance comes along soon enough, straight up behind me before turning to go into the hospital. But the light's back to red again, so we sit.

I can feel the adrenaline in me, washing back and forth, when "Big City" comes on. Op Ivy. The last track on the side that Rose said is supposed to be about me. Motivating me. Teaching me. Seeing me. Showing me, forever, how she feels.

"I like this dude's voice. How it's just"—Blanco searches his brain for the word before finally landing on one—"anger."

He folds up the liner notes, swipes them off with a sleeve, and puts them back in the case all gentle, closes it, and puts the thing back in the glove box.

At first I'm thinking, *That's good of him.*

And then I'm thinking, *He doesn't want to be tied to this Jeep, smart motherfucker that he is.*

And this little alarm bell I got inside me goes off when he pulls sleeves down over his fingers and scrubs at the tape case, closes the glove box, then swipes at its front and at the door handle and at the seat belt and its buckle.

He's getting ready to go for real, I'm thinking. *Tonight.*

And I got to take a breath at the thought of it.

Blanco's not even looking at the road when he tells me to bang a right on Norton, swoop two blocks, and turn left into the neighborhood.

"Right here," he says, squinting now, into the night.

"Like, turn right, or one of these houses?"

"Next turn, dick."

I turn.

We go three houses.

"Stop here," Blanco says. "Lights all the way off. Engine on. Unlock the doors."

I do as he says as Operation Ivy finishes up and the speakers go quiet. I reach down and stop the tape so it doesn't switch over to Rose's side.

I don't want to share that one. I can't.

The door behind Blanco opens and a little homie slides into the backseat. He couldn't be more than thirteen. At most.

He says, "What can I be getting you, Mister Blanco?"

He's young, this kid, and nervous. You can hear it in his voice, the way he cracked on "getting."

"I need a two-piece. Box of them doctor *guantes*. Candy. And, uh, one of them mag bags." Blanco turns to me. "Need anything?"

I got my tools, so I say, "I'm good."

But then I'm thinking, *If by "candy" maybe he means coke, then that's no good.* A sober Blanco is bad enough, but a high one? Game over. On top of that, I got no idea what a mag bag is. All's I can come up with is a bag of magazines, like, fashion, or for bullet cartridges. And gloves, well, that's for leaving no prints anywhere.

Shit is piling up, getting heavy inside me. Like, the food I just ate is turning to a wet chunk of concrete in my stomach.

And all of it is triggering something else, I'm realizing.

Because Blanco's way more involved than he says he is. Way more important too. This is some boss-level shit. Rolling up like this and getting whatever the hell he wants tells me he's not bored, just sitting around the house these days. He's *active.*

My words take a second to form up, but when they do, I say to him, "You sure seem bigger than you used to be."

"Me? Same size I always been." He grabs his belt and says it like I'm talking about his weight, like it's a joke, and that's how I know it's not.

I know right then, clearer than I ever knew anything, that this is happening tonight. We're not just scouting. We're going up in that drugs house no matter what. Fast and reckless. Because Blanco never changed one bit. It's who he was at seventeen when we were out robbing. It's who he is now.

There's no question in my mind.

And that's sinking me. The concrete's just pulling my whole body down with it. Into the Jeep's carpet. I'm trying to convince myself it's good though, that if we go now, we beat the DEA.

Soon as the kid goes and the door's shut behind him, Blanco turns to me all cool and says, "I know you fucked Esmerelda."

Inside, my concrete whips up to around hurricane speed.

But outside, I don't hesitate. Not even a millisecond. The addict inside me, the one always ready to get over on anybody, jumps up and fields this one.

"Ha! And she was good too! Hit that from behind while playing connect the dots with all them hairy moles on her back."

Esmerelda has no moles on her back. She has a birthmark on her thigh kind of in the shape of a melted Africa. But no moles. Not even one.

I don't say that, though. I laugh instead. I laugh hard. Not so hard that it's awkward, but just enough.

Even in the dimness, even with his hood pulled up, I see Blanco smile at me.

"There he is! There's my fucking *vato*! Driving around all serious. That's no way to pull a job. You gotta get loose." He's pushing his finger in my face now, wagging it. "I *almost* had you!"

"Keep telling yourself that." I ape the kid's voice: *"Mister Blanco."*

Now it's Blanco's turn to laugh, and he does.

Almost as hard as he should.

When the little homie comes back, he's got everything Mr. Blanco asked for. The two guns he puts on the floor at Blanco's feet. Full clips. The mag bag is—I don't know what. It's a heavy-sounding sack when it hits the floor by his feet. Sounds like metal, or weights. The doctor *guantes* are just rubber gloves, same as I got, but white and not blue.

"Open that box and get a pair on me," Blanco says to the kid, holding hands out towards him.

And the kid leans forward from the backseat and does it, careful to pull the elastic openings up past the sweatshirt cuffs so they sit on the seam.

The ease of this routine for Blanco doesn't sit right with me. The hurricane's gone for the moment but the concrete's settling again. Under my skin. I'm imagining it filling in between organs, taking all my empty spaces.

Back in the day, you were lucky if you got a good stolen gun and a full clip before you did work.

Nowadays, it's a goddamn one-stop drive-thru with little homie curb service.

And it turns out the candy is just that. A damn chocolate bar.

This, Blanco tears into right away and starts munching. From the crunches, I can hear it has nuts in it. I must give him a look for this because he scowls at me.

"What? Got to get my blood sugars up!"

"We just ate twenty minutes ago, man."

It's like old times.

"I got good metabolism. Shit. Trying to find my balance. You don't want me hungry when it's time to—"

Blanco stops, remembers the kid's still inside, and turns to the backseat. "What's your name?"

The kid freezes. He wasn't ready for this one.

Blanco switches it up. "*¿Como te llamas?*"

The kid struggles to come out with "Uriel."

"Uriel, that's a good name. *Fuerte*. But I need you to do me a favor from now on, okay? Because maybe nobody's told you this yet."

Uriel nods.

"Don't ever tell anyone your fucking real name again. *¿Entiendes?*"

The kid's got a hard look in his eye, like he got slapped. And he kind of just did.

Blanco says, "Get the fuck out, little *vato*. You didn't see shit tonight."

The door opens and closes quick. I get the engine going again and that's that. We're only about a half mile off. Blanco's got me going the back way. He's all over it.

"Turn right here, then left. Nope. Don't go there. Roll through that alley. No—wait. Turn here."

I recognize the sign as we pass it. This's the street, the same one from Janine's piece of paper. It's clogged, though. Cars everywhere, out in front of one-level houses with trees in their dried-up front yards. There's two streetlights out on this block. Even with our windows up, I hear music. Some sort of club shit. Bass like crazy.

"Yes," Blanco says, and he's getting amped now, seeing this party.

I can feel the wheels running in his head. It's big. It's loud. It's the best possible distraction.

"Turn up in there," he says.

"No."

"Dick, we're rolling through like we're normal party people, okay? *Go.*"

I go.

If there was the slightest chance it wasn't real before, it's real now.

We cruise by just fast enough for nobody to put eyes on us. The good news: nobody cares. They're all rolling up to the party. The even better news: the drugs house is right next door and its lights are all out. All but one. So we keep going, down to the end of the block, hang a left, and come back on it from the alley behind.

We have to count houses as we go backwards. Eight, seven, six, five, four.

Four.

"This's it," Blanco says, and takes up the black sack that he called a mag bag from the floor, opens it, and nods his chin up at me like he wants me to put something in it.

I'm not liking this. But it's not like I got a choice either.

I say, "What is it?"

"Fucking magnets. The game's changed since you been gone. Just put your shit in the bag."

The concrete I got inside is telling me not to do it, but my head's telling me I got no choice. That I stopped having choices the moment I called Blanco. And I'm no tech dude, but I've been around federal agents enough to know that magnets don't do shit to smartphones or data stored on servers or phone company records. But none of that matters now. All's I know is, I need to keep my prepaid and its numbers intact.

So I hand my regular phone to Blanco instead. The one I got as a Stenberg Locksmithing employee. *Because fuck it,* I think. *Why not?* It's no good to me now anyways.

"That's good. I'm glad you did that." Not taking any chances, Blanco puts his own prepaid in the bag too. "Because you need to quit living in the past, homie."

There's no going back now. I'll never see that phone again because this is him closing the loop, trying to destroy evidence before the fact. Like a pro. This is him trying to cover his tracks before he does anything.

It's so dark that I can't see the bottom of the bag as he zips it up, which feels about right. Like, it's a tiny black hole, sucking up everything.

And I'm thinking about how since this is definitely going down tonight, I still need to get the money to Mira, and I'm not seeing how that's happening yet.

I got to be patient for that. I got to wait.

"Hey." Blanco's punch to the shoulder brings me back to the surface. "Did you hear what I said or what?"

"Sorry. What?"

"Quit living in the past! You got that tape. You're driving the same style of Jeep that Rose drove—that's creepy, dude. What the fuck you think you're doing? For real, has nobody ever gave it to you like this? Straight up?"

The answer to that is no. Nobody ever has.

Because not many people in my new life know about Rose, and those that do, don't know how much I hang on to everything of hers I possibly can. They suspect, maybe.

But they don't *know*.

They don't know I needed her every day just to make it this far.

That certain-doom type of feeling in my stomach isn't shrinking. It mushrooms when Blanco confirms everything I've been thinking.

He's staring at the back door of the house when he says, "So you know, we're about to do this."

The only thing I can do now is check him a little, insinuate he doesn't know his own business.

I say, "You sure this isn't going to come back on you?"

"Dick." Blanco rolls down the window and spits out of it.

"Quit talking like we're about to get caught. You *trying* to jinx this shit?"

I've been hearing rumors, here and there over the years, that Blanco made some connects with the Soviet Armenians that seem to be running all the Medicare and credit fraud around, and the Russians too, the ones moving girls on the Westside and in the Valley.

Maybe both. It never got made clear to me and I didn't ask.

I didn't need to know.

I got to get one last needle in though. "Well, just checking."

"Oh, thanks for 'checking.' I been above the street for a long time, *Ghost*." The way he says it, he's reminding me that I used to be somebody else and that I've been away a real long time, and even when I was up in it, I was nothing. A nobody. This is him saying it's a new game now. *His* game. "If they're slipping, we're doing them a favor. Better than *la DEA* coming through tomorrow or whenever, right? We blow their spot now and it's like a practice run for them to tighten it up because none of their dumb fuckers go to jail, right? That's worth something. That's leverage, holmes. You're welcome."

There's only one last thing to handle.

"*If* there's a safe," I say, "you get the drugs and I get the cash."

He knows as well as I do that the odds are in his favor there, so it makes sense that he doesn't hesitate or try to sweeten it on his side.

"Deal, *puto*," he says as he slides out of the Jeep and soft-closes the door so it doesn't bang, only half latches.

He's on the other side and next to me before I do the same.

"Now let's go see who's slipping."

It's dark, and I can't see shit, but I know the sound of *la luz* sparking up in his voice when I hear it.

I'm in and out of the back of the Jeep quick to get my cases. We cross a dead-grass backyard and then it's three little concrete steps to the back door. The light's out in the kitchen, but Blanco puts his nose right up near the glass anyways.

He mouths at me, "We good."

I set both my toolboxes down on the stoop.

From the next house over, I'm hearing the beat transition into something else, into a party track of some kind, and my heart's thumping like it's about to pop.

Slow down, I think. *Slow. Down.*

And I don't know if I'm trying to talk to my heart or to the concrete inside me or to my hands.

But it may as well be all of them because my palms are sweating inside my gloves as I grab a bump key from my pocket and do the doorknob lock. It gives about as easy as a plastic Easter egg. But then, when I go to grab a new shark and do the same to the dead bolt above, I find the thing is not even done up, so I turn the knob and the door opens just enough to see a dirty rag on brown tile in a kitchen.

Blanco mouths it at me like he's screaming, *"Motherfuckers be slipping!"*

I crack one of my cases, grab some WD, and wet up the hinges. Just in case.

When I put it back down, Blanco hands me one of the pistols before pushing the door open enough for both of us to go in.

It goes wide without a sound.

Glasses

37

When this leathery white guy Frank Stenberg goes into a Mexican minimarket by his work called La Chelita, I follow him in and Lonely backs me up but at a little distance.

The second I saw Stenberg Locksmithing I knew. This is Ricky's boss, or it was. Boss and landlord, making it even more complicated.

This Frank goes left. I'm in behind him but it takes a second for my eyes to adjust, and when they do, I can tell how this isn't a typical minimarket.

I mean, the tiny market is on my right, with toilet paper and cereals and all that, but in front of me is a whole kitchen setup with a menu board talking about fried shrimp and *hamburguesas*. Beside all that is a freezer for ice cream.

To my left is the register with a guy behind it flipping through a *Hot Rod*. He looks in his forties. What my guess is, is he's Guatemalan. On the wall to his left are coolers. That's where Frank is, standing in front of the rack for sodas.

As he opens a door and leans in while a little cloud comes out, I get close to him and say, "Do you know a Ricky Mendoza?"

He turns and looks at me. "Nope." He don't blink, but he's lying.

I take the photo out of my pocket, thinking I'll just show it to him so I can get a reaction and he'll know I know he's lying, but I don't even get my arm halfway up before his eyes are following it and going big and wild.

He lunges at me, snatching the photo straight out of my hand. I take a step back to keep the right distance between us in case I need to swing.

Lonely's inching in behind Frank, getting close enough to do something and I'm about to let him loose, but then this guy Frank brings his face up from the photo and he's crying.

Red angry eyes filled up with tears he's not even trying to control. What it is, is crazy. This hard-looking old man cracks in half right in front of me and I don't even know what to do.

I'm just standing there stunned until he shouts at me, "*Where* did you get this?"

His voice's loud, so loud it snaps the Guatemalan register guy out of looking at his magazine.

"Hey!" the guy says. "What the fuck is up?"

I give Lonely a look that says it's time for him to handle this, and he's about to, but right as he's stepping up, the old man turns and stomps on his toes.

Lonely don't go down from that, but the old man does. He goes down and comes back up with a little pistol in his hand. Super slick. On purpose.

He's not pointing it at me, just showing me he has one, and if I'm thinking of doing something stupid in a room full of cameras, I may as well not bother.

Frank shouts, "Why are you looking for Ricky? Are you threatening him with something?"

Register guy's chiming in at me and Lonely, "You think you pulling something? You ain't pulling shit, fuckers!"

I put my hands down in front of me, to show how I'm not a threat to either one of them.

"I would never do that," I say to Frank, then add, "sir."

"No?"

He's eyeing me. He's getting smart, memorizing what I look like and then what Lonely looks like, what we're wearing down to the cut and the colors. The kinds of things that go in police reports.

This's a problem and it's my fault. I never should've followed him in here. I'm kicking myself for it now. That's what I get for thinking being in public makes little things like asking if somebody knows somebody easier.

The whole situation gets one push further in the wrong direction when the guy behind the register says to Frank, "What's up with Ghost? He in trouble?"

I circle a little bit where I am to see the guy bringing his hands up from underneath the counter to show me just the butt of a gun, either a rifle or a shotgun, and that's our sign not to push this anymore or somebody's liable to get shot.

"Not yet," Frank says, but he's keeping his eyes on me.

I need to take some heat out of this quick, so I step back. Lonely follows my lead.

"Sorry to upset your day, Mister Stenberg." I say it like that so he knows I know who he is, that he'll for sure be seeing me again but under better circumstances next time.

Me and Lonely back ourselves out of the front doors and turn and walk down the block. I'm deciding whether we should walk by the car, disappear somewhere, and come back to it.

I ditch the idea when I see Frank's not following us. He's watching us but not following us, so I turn on 142nd and head for the car. As we get in, I don't see nobody coming after us, so we go.

"That got crazy," Lonely says.

"Yeah."

"I don't think he knows where Ghost is," Lonely says about Stenberg.

"I know he don't."

Since we're far enough away, Lonely takes it down to the speed limit as I'm thinking about how maybe Ghost is ashamed of what he did, that he don't even want Frank to know about it or be involved, but I feel pretty sure Ricky took that safe for a reason bigger than himself.

This isn't something to share with Lonely, or Rooster either, but it hits me pretty hard, since I understand the motivation to doing something like that. I got it inside me too.

Lonely's not saying nothing, but I know he's thinking about how we might need Frank to get to this Ghost.

"We know who this Frank is and where he is," I say. "We can get him later if we need to use it like that. First, we tell Rooster."

Even as I'm saying this, I'm getting the feeling this isn't over, that it's not even close. A guy like this, does he cut ties with the closest people in his life over one safe? Prolly if he's in a tight spot, but I don't buy that.

What I'm thinking is *He's acting like his life's already done.* I can't get over how he left everything behind, all ordered or sold. That commitment's crazy.

I feel like it's a lesson to me, that if I want to get out, this is what I have to be prepared to do. But something isn't sitting right with me. Maybe it's thoughts or maybe it's my stomach.

I pop a couple more antacids, lime this time. What I'm worried about is, I don't know that anybody goes this far for just one rip, not that almost nine hundred gees is little, but it sure don't seem like he's the type to act on a gut feeling now.

It seems like he was waiting for it, getting ready. I could be wrong but I think he cleaned that place out before he even took what he took.

I mean, are you gonna go home and junk your bed after you put that much money in your pockets like that? No. You got your bug-out bag with you, and you just go. You run.

"Hey," I say to Lonely, "go right up here on El Segundo and then right on Crenshaw when we get to it."

Lonely changes lanes. He don't know where I'm taking us and don't ask why, he just does it. He's a good soldier. Prolly he's exactly the one they send to get me if they find out I done what I done.

It don't take long for us to roll by El Camino College. I was a student there. Twice. After the settlement was the first time. I thought I could go right and do something, so I signed up for an economics class and a business class too.

That was it, not a full schedule or nothing. I didn't go so far before dropping out, but it was a good year before Rooster swooped me up. I met a South Gate girl there. Well, she met me when she was working circulations at the library.

Leya was doing her A.A. in paralegal studies and sort of minoring in avoiding me. That's what she calls it to this day, but she said yes the first time I ever asked her out. Just a few years ago, I went back there for some sign-language classes, interpreter training they call it.

It was just to give me a jump off. After, Rooster taught me the rest.

As we're going by the campus, it feels like I'm waving at what I could've been without even moving my hand. But when we're past it, we're past it, and my mind's on more serious things than could haves or should haves.

"Left on Artesia," I tell Lonely.

I don't have to say it becomes the 91, that it's the fastest way back to Lynwood from here. He knows it.

When we turn, I'm thinking over the best way to tell Rooster that somebody going by Ghost took his money and that I don't know why exactly now, but I'm wondering if it's so simple as greed.

That worries me, since as I'm trying to figure out exactly how dangerous this Ghost is, I need to know if he can even mess up these plans I put into place. It's maybe a paranoid feeling hitting me but I'm feeling like if we have sources in the DEA, then this Ghost does too.

I'm worrying about the addresses I gave Collins this morning over pancakes. I shouldn't, since that's stupid, but I am. I'm thinking those spots aren't safe.

III

LAST, DO NO HARM

Ricky Mendoza, Junior, a.k.a. Ghost

Monday, September 15, 2008
Evening

38

There's a TV on somewhere, maybe the front room. It's two white people talking. A man and a woman. Clipped. Proper. And under their voices is piano music. There's somebody here. Watching it. Most likely *somebodies*. Chances of there being less than three dudes here, all with some kind of gun: pretty much zero.

I'm sweating already. And I'm telling my heart to slow down, to be cool.

I tell it we can do this. While I'm at it, I tell whatever part there is inside me that's making me feel helpless to shut the fuck up. Because I'm not helpless.

I got my mouth. I got my guts. I got a way of talking myself out of anything.

Shit.

I could've been dead in my Jeep if I didn't pass Blanco's Esmerelda test.

I'm going to make this worth it, I tell myself. All the way worth it.

But my heart's still pounding up in my ears as Blanco goes first and I follow him up. Moving slow-slow over dirty tiles that stick to the bottoms of our shoes. The kitchen's dark, but not so dark we can't see. On the counter by the sink is a hot plate with a pan sitting on it, and some sort of melted pasta stuck to it. A minifridge is in the hole where a big fridge should be. Next to it is a trash corner piled up with empty beer-case boxes, tissues, and fast-food containers.

To the right of that mountain is an open doorway into a hall that has blue and orange colors alternating in it. Flashing TV shadows paint white walls nobody ever bothered to do anything with.

Above the doorway, stuck to the cottage cheese of the ceiling, are beer-bottle caps. There must be a couple hundred of them, all pressed in by hands. This whole place smells like stale beer.

And it hits me then, I can *actually* smell it.

My nose is mine again. For a minute at least. Not buried in memories.

And that's a weird feeling. Because it makes all this more real. More worrying. But also better somehow too.

I mean, I haven't gone in wild like this in I don't know how long. For sure this isn't a well-organized way to go in. It's hit and hope. First time in years I haven't gone in safe. But I kind of like it. That's the crazy part. I'm getting back into it. Like finding an old rhythm I still know how to dance to.

And there's that old buzz of getting over, of being some place I'm not supposed to be, pumping up inside me. Running, no, *stomping* in my veins, getting pushed all the way down to my toes and back up. Hitting that sinking feeling I been having and wrestling it to see which one wins.

I even smile a little when we step into the hall, Blanco and me. I look left and see a little room with only a chair, an almost-empty bookcase, and a monitor on top of that showing four outside angles of the house. My Jeep's parked in the lower left one, just the nose of it peeking out. If someone had been sitting in that chair, that would've been it for us.

Next door, the bass is getting louder. It's shaking the nearest wall. And in the front room, the volume on the TV's getting louder as we get closer. We can hear words from it now, two white people having an argument about some kind of stupid misunderstanding about coffee. A laugh track comes in right after.

And it's luck like this that's making me feel like the old me. Like I already got everything inside that it takes to pull this. I just got to keep reaching down and keep bringing it up.

This is me settling. Breathing. Getting balanced.

Fuck sinking, I want to say. I don't have time for that.

But I still got these bees at the back of my brain, buzzing around, bumping into my skull, into each other. Doubts. And I'm hoping that I still got this nasty know-how in me somewhere. Buried, maybe, but still there. Because if I don't, I got no ideas how I'm pulling this off.

This is me, teeter-tottering. Up one moment. Then down. Thinking I can do it. Then sure I can't. But maybe the thing is, I'm just scared that it is all still inside me. That flipping that switch means it can't be unflipped. And the weirdest thing is what's steadying my heart right now is that I'm looking at the back of Blanco's bumpy head and thinking, *I know he's going to screw me.* The second this goes bad for him, he's throwing me under the bus.

And it's cool. Better to know it now and see it coming.

Doesn't mean I won't go down swinging, always trying to get that *more* for the people Mira can help. That's the anxiety that's not going away. How to get that money to her. It's the only goal I got now.

The only one.

We check the back room, the bathroom next to it, the bedroom with a closet and a safe inside it, but we leave it till we lock everything down first.

At the end of the hall, we come to the front room. For me and him, there's no point wearing masks. This's my last ride, and Blanco is Blanco. Terrifying people is half the fun of it when you're him.

Blanco gets his body behind the near wall and pokes just a little bit of his head out so he can see. I'm blocked off. Unable to see what he's seeing because I'm behind him, but this is exactly what he's here for. Crowd control. And nobody's ever done that better. I tense up when he whistles two quick notes. Like a *bap-bap* on a trumpet. Like he's trying to get a parrot's attention.

Even with the bass and the TV, it's just loud enough to be a distraction. And that's all Blanco needs. He steams right into the room after that, gun up and ready.

I hear somebody say, "Oh, shit!"

And then a girl's screaming and I'm running in behind with my gat up, and it's obvious what my move is, because Blanco's already got a young dude cornered and the kid's holding his hands up in front of him, but there's a girl in there too and she's up, trying to bolt past me.

That's when I surprise myself.

When old reflexes jump into me and I just react.

Grabbing her by the throat and slamming her into the nearest wall, I hold the end of the gun flat against her ear so it's not pointing at her skull, but out, to where her eyes are looking, up the hallway, out the kitchen, out the door, to freedom that's just not coming now.

This is me and not me, I'm thinking. *Don't hurt nobody smart enough to avoid it.*

John's words are still in me too. Last, do no harm. And that means none. To anybody. And definitely not this girl.

She's got hair for days, thick and curly.

I mash my face into it, smelling leafy shampoo and sweat. I whisper, "You cool it down and I can keep him from shooting you. You don't, and you're on your own."

I pull my face back and give her a look.

I watch my words land and her eyes get big.

Her mouth's all knotted up and her brow's furrowed as fuck but she nods at me.

She's tough, this one. And smart.

Good.

But I'm not worried about that. I'm worried if she's going to stay that way.

I let go of her throat. My gloves make a little noise when I do. I breathe out and realize when I step back that I've been holding my breath. I got the gun pointing at her chest now, and I point to the floor with my free hand. Like, *Get down.*

She goes down flat real quick, with hands behind her head like she's been asked to do this before.

I turn and see Blanco's got the kid facedown on the carpet. Ankles tied. Hands tied behind his back. A knee on his neck just because. I see Blanco's look, how he's doing this kid a favor catching him slipping like this. How if he doesn't end up killing him, he's saving his life. And that's right about when I'm guessing that Blanco brought those zip cuffs from home since he didn't have to ask for them at the pit stop. And when I'm trying to figure out how I feel about that, I follow Blanco's eyes to the TV, and how it's a rerun of that show *Friends*, and seeing that?

Even I got to laugh.

And Blanco's nodding at me.

"That's right," he says. "Get fucking loose!"

39

After that, it's all business. The TV stays on, but gets muted. We don't turn lights on. Can't afford to. I go through the kid's pockets and grab keys and a cell. The keys I hang on to. The cell I toss to Blanco and it goes in the mag bag. I'm about to do the same to the girl but I notice how she doesn't have her jeans on. And I have to walk over to where the couch is and grab them off the floor. There's nothing in the pockets but a mascara tube, though.

It's like I got my rhythm now. I'm in the moment. Not overthinking things. Just acting. Trying to take it one step at a time.

I step back over to the girl, about to offer her pants back, but Blanco's got her wrists and ankles tied already, so I just lay her pants down over her legs lengthwise to cover her up in case Blanco gets any ideas he can't shake.

To her, I say, "Where's your purse?"

She moves her head away from me, talks toward the wall. "I locked my shit in my trunk."

I knew she was smart.

Right about then is when the kid decides to be the exact opposite and run his mouth. "We don't got nothing."

Blanco's response is another knee on the back of the kid's neck. It gets kept there, just grinding, for so long that the kid's drooling and kind of sputtering and coughing into the carpet.

That shit is hard to watch, so I don't.

I'm grabbing my tools from the outside stoop and locking the back door with the deadbolt since the knob lock's useless now. I drop my gear in the bedroom closet, next to the light gray box of a safe.

It's a Fire Fyter. About as tall as my knees. Combination lock. And I know the kid doesn't have numbers to open it. That's just not how this game works. Nobody guarding safes ever has the know-how to open them. Lowers the risk of stealing so much better that way.

I'm about to get cracking, but I need Blanco's help first, so I roll back to the front room to find him looking out the window. Up the street. Down the street. Checking. Being wary.

"Hey," I say to him, "you've got to help me flip this real quick."

He knows I mean the safe, but he needs two things from me first. We do one more sweep of the house. We find another cell in the bathroom, on the counter. It goes in the mag bag too. Shit, even a wireless router goes in the bag, just because Blanco wants it to. There's no recording device connected to the outside cameras. We know because we looked for a solid two minutes for a VCR or for a computer it was hooked up to, but then I checked the back of the monitor and it was just four little cables running from a hole in the wall into a splitter in the back like it was 1988 or something.

After that's done, we walk the safe forward on the closet floor and then tip it onto its back. These kinds of safes, they're meant for staying in one piece through fires. They're not meant to protect against sincere force to the mechanism behind the combo wheel. Frank says it was a big oops in the overall design of these models. Almost like they'd never even talked to a safecracker before.

Some rap is starting up next door, popular enough that you can hear drunk people shouting the lyrics too loud from the backyard.

"One last thing," Blanco says.

I follow him back to the front room, where we lift the girl up onto the couch and lay her flat facing up. I put her pants over her again, and then we lift the kid on top of her. When we let him go, she makes a sound like he's crushing her, but it's not our problem. The dirty towel from the kitchen floor goes in the kid's mouth after that. The girl has to deal with chewing on part of her sweatshirt.

We cover them in the blanket they must've been under before and move the chair from the study room into the front room so Blanco can sit out of sight with a gun on the door.

It's a setup. We know we caught these fuckers on a break of some sort. No other way to explain it. That, honestly and most likely, the other one or two supposed to watch the house are next door drinking and being stupid, and in case they decide to come back over before we're done, they'll just think these two are doing it, and that'll give Blanco all the time he needs to do what he does.

This closet smells like mothballs and it reminds me of how Mrs. Piñeda's mother's room in their apartment used to smell— just, *chemically*.

But I don't mind it.

I crack the combo wheel housing with a chisel and my baby sledgehammer. It comes off the face of the safe in two pieces. After that, I take a wide stance standing over the safe and drill in bursts, straight down through the wheel. I chew up one diamond tip, then I go again. This's my thinking time, and my first thought is *If I can do this fast enough, I can maybe grab what's inside and be out the back door before Blanco even notices. I can leave him here, drive, and go meet Mira with whatever I pull out.* It's not the worst idea I ever had, but it's not great. Just carrying my tools takes both hands, and even if I can stuff the money in the spaces I carved out of the cases, I know I'll be making noise on the way out, it's just a matter of whether he hears it or not, over the party music.

I drill again. The housing's getting eaten, but that doesn't matter.

All's I need is a hole big enough to punch the mechanism off its track. And for that, I've got a half-inch-thick bit of rebar. I drill once more and try to widen the hole. But the rebar won't fit. I go again, but I'm hearing something, so I stop.

It's voices.

Voices close to the house.

Coming closer, getting louder, voices passing by the bedroom window a few feet away from me. So fucking close.

I stop dead.

The voices fade a little as they go away from me, towards the front of the house. I drop my drill, grab up the gun, and move to the hallway, where Blanco sees me and smiles before scrunching his face up and nodding me over to a place next to the front door.

We hear keys getting jingled on the other side, but I'm to where Blanco wants me in three quick steps, standing with the gun in my right, pointed towards the floor, and my left hand up, so the door doesn't hit me if it swings in hard.

No point unmuting the TV now.

The door opens. But not enough to hit my hand. The voices come in just before the people do.

As he's stepping in, one says, "Oh, please, that girl's nothing but a bitch, dude. Besides—"

And the other must see the couch first, because he jumps in with "What the fuck, *loco*? You getting down?"

Right then is when Blanco cocks his gun. For effect. Just letting them know they got *got*.

And I close and lock the door behind them.

Rudolfo "Rudy" Reyes, a.k.a. Glasses

Monday, September 15, 2008
Early Evening

40

I'm not allowed to even say where Rooster's house is, what it looks like, or what's really inside it. This one is his house when he's here anyway. He's got others.

I don't even know whose names they're all in. I'll never know. I can say Lonely drops me at the curb since he's not allowed in, and I go up the walk to the doorbell and ring it.

Inside, I know the light's flashing and I hear some running footsteps coming to the door before Jennifer opens it. She's out of breath like she ran all the way since her dad must've said I'd be coming, and then she turns into a blur and a real good hug before she steps back.

When she does, I can see how she got her hair cut a couple inches and there's a wave to it now. My eyes get big as I look at how much she chopped off.

She sees me staring at her hair and smiles since she's happy I noticed but also happy she put me off-balance. I make a show of blinking and looking off to the side like I'm uncomfortable even when I'm not. She's getting sick of me dragging it out, so she closes the door and locks it behind me.

Jennifer lip-reads real well but that type of thing is for the outside world, man. That takes energy and commitment. What I do when I come into her house is greet her in her native language. I bring that respect.

School, I sign, *how is it?*

She laughs. There's this breathy *tee-hee* type of sound that happens when she does it. It's how it's always been and I love it. It's hers.

I'm no type of expert, but deaf people are expressive with feelings in a way not so many hearing people are. I mean, I'm sure there's plenty of shy people inside the community and I'm not saying they're nothing other than human, with the same thoughts and problems and everything, but it's just that it's different when your whole body's your speaking tool.

It gets real important then to know yourself and represent yourself right, especially when most of the world isn't really seeing all of what you're about or even understanding a word of how you talk. Being an outsider is no joke. It shapes you.

She signs back, *My new haircut, you're not going to comment?*

On my face, I show her how shocked I am. I sign, *Haircut?!* Like I didn't know she had one until just that moment.

She slaps my arm in a way that says, *Okay, you can stop messing with me.* I smile and sign to her how pretty it looks, and I like how she's not trying to hide her hearing aids in her hair anymore.

She rolls her eyes, like, *Yeah, yeah, not this again.* She turns me around and leads me in through the foyer, past the big staircase, back towards the den.

I know that's where Rooster is, chilling in front of the big screen. The Dodgers must be on TV by now since he already told me they're playing on the East Coast.

I always told Jennifer be proud of yourself. Never hide. This has been our ongoing thing since she was about eight.

I think the reason Rooster likes me around her is I'm different too. I know what it's like for people to look at my eye and think there's something wrong with my brain or that I'm less of a person.

The school dance, I'm signing to her, *you going? Your haircut is for a boy to notice? True?*

She makes a face and I know I hit a nerve prolly. Right then, I get a serious thought. I sign, *Oh, I see, is he a* hearing *boy?!*

Jennifer don't go to a deaf school. Rooster refused to put her in a place that would be different from how the whole world might treat her.

She blushes all over and signs, *No!*

His name, I sign back, *what is it?*

She's not telling me. She's looking horrified and changing the subject, asking me if I want food. *Dad barbecued!*

I sign, *Yes, I love barbecue,* and she heads off to the kitchen on a mission. I already know I'm in trouble. She'll pile as much as she can fit on that plate.

The thing about Rooster's house is, there's lots of reflective surfaces up to help Jennifer notice when people are around or needing to talk to her.

I see him looking at me in one of the mirrors next to the TV that's showing an outfield so green it hurts my eye a little. I blink. I nod at him.

Rooster says, "How was the *quince*?"

That catches me a little off guard. With everything going on, I'd forgotten to talk about it. "Was good. A good night."

"The DJ was okay?" Rooster was the DJ *padrino*.

I shrug. "He was a DJ, you know. There was a lot of yelling."

There's not much more to say than that. I don't remember the names of everybody that came up to me, but nobody disrespected. Rooster knows I'd tell him if that had happened.

From his side of the couch Rooster gives me a good long look, like prolly he knows there's something I'm not telling him before he nods towards the TV. "Game started a while back. You need a beer?"

"I'm good."

Since it's a game where players can get hit in the head or face with a hundred-mile-per-hour fastball, baseball don't agree with me. Just seeing stuff like that gives me sympathy pains. But I have learned to always ask about the Dodgers' pitching.

True-blue Dodger fans always want to talk about it. I'm thinking it must be good tonight too, since it's the top of the sixth and the Dodgers are up 5–0 on the Pirates.

I say, "Who's pitching?"

"Kuroda. He's doing okay tonight. He's getting help."

I say, "From Manny?" He's the only Dodger I really know of, Manny Ramírez.

"Manny's earning that check, doubled and scored. He's making up for doing nothing last night against Colorado."

Jennifer saves me by coming back in with a plate. What it has on it, is six ribs, some mashed potatoes, and grilled carrots. She sets it up on a TV tray in front of me.

I sign, *Thank you!*

She's about to sit down next to me on the couch when Rooster signs, *No. Biology homework. Do it.*

Dad, she signs with some whiny hands, *lab logs are easy. Busywork. Writing down experiments we already did. Simple.*

Rooster's face makes it clear that he don't care what it is, she's not coming back downstairs until she's done with it.

Fine, she signs, *can I tell Uncle Rudy before going?*

He holds up an index finger for one.

She squeals and signs, *Archery! I'm doing it.*

I sign, *Archery? Wow! I want to watch!*

This kid's the coolest. Spending time with her made me want to have kids of my own. If Felix can grow up half as good a kid as her, I'll feel like I did something right for the world and I can go out with no regrets.

Maybe, she signs, then smiles. She's teasing me.

We sign goodbye just in case I don't see her before I go and she pops down onto the couch to give me a quick side-hug before jumping back up and speeding upstairs. The smile on that little woman, man, it could melt a whole city block.

And I should know, since that's how I feel right now, knowing I'm gonna break her heart, and that someday somebody's gonna tell her it's me that did it. So that's how I'm really feeling on this couch right now. Ground zero.

If it wasn't for her, I would've been out so much sooner. Always

I worry about what it'd do to her, me ratting. I been scared of ruining her life. But now there's Felix and I had to choose blood.

"All right," Rooster says. That means, report.

"I know it sounds crazy, but I think something's going down. A guy like Mendoza, he don't take once and quit."

Rooster gives me a look that says I should explain why.

"His whole apartment was packed up before he even took that safe, and I mean, bed gone, stuff in boxes for other people close to him to take."

Rooster nods. "So he's ready to die or what?"

On the screen the umpire calls a strike.

"He's already dying," I say.

For the first time, Rooster looks away from the game. He looks right at me when he says, "Dying how?"

"Cancer. Also, prolly just since it fits, he goes by Ghost."

"Ghost?" Rooster's looking thoughtful, but not sharing what he's thinking.

"Yup. I think he means to keep going. I don't know how he quits now. I can't see it at all. Over eight hundred gees might not be enough when you're acting like your life's already done."

I don't say nothing about Frank. I keep that in my pocket for later, like if we need some bargaining with this Ghost. If I'm wrong about this whole thing, I look paranoid, but this isn't exactly a bad thing with somebody like Rooster.

If I'm right, I look like I'm smart and careful, but I can definitely say I'm scared to be right on this, especially if it has a thing to do with those addresses I gave Collins. If that goes down, tonight, tomorrow, whenever, Rooster's gonna know something's not right and he'll ask me about it first.

"If something does go down," Rooster says, and leans forward as the count's full for the batter on the screen, "I got some things up my sleeve."

I don't know what that means exactly and I know he's not gonna tell me, but it don't sound good.

"I should leave you to it," I say.

His eyes are back on the screen. "You're not even done eating. Stay. Finish watching the game with me."

It's not a suggestion. So I fork some jalapeño cheddar mash into my mouth and have to remind myself how this nice house, this giant-screen TV, this good food, is all connected to burnt-up bones sitting in unmarked graves in Mexico.

Somebody's little kids and grandmas got disappeared somewhere on the other end of this transaction. Thinking that is the only way I can keep going with the plan, the only way I can keep doing any of it.

Ghost

Monday, September 15, 2008
Evening

41

When I grab the nearest dude that came through the door and kick the back of one of his knees out, the beer he was bringing back spills all over the floor and turns the ratty old carpet into a soggy sponge.

The rest's just easy.

Blanco's on them with the ties, and it's just zip, zip, zip, zip—done—none of this's going down how things do in movies, with people screaming at each other while the soundtrack's banging, getting your blood up, and everybody's shouting about how *You don't know who you're fucking with*, or this or that.

Here's the real: the only soundtrack here tonight is the muffled beat next door. It's gone slow jam on us. *Bwump, tump-tump.* Like everybody just collectively decided to calm down. This shit isn't personal.

It's business. And when it's like that, you do what you can to fight another day. You grit teeth. Keep it tight and take it. You keep your fucking dignity. Because Lynwood's still Lynwood. No use pushing anybody to shoot you. But if you're dying, you might as well die well. No tears. No begging. And if retribution's coming for those that did this to you, it'll be down the road, when your boys got the drop, when the numbers are better, and even then, only if they're big enough to take it.

That's never changed.

So this is all going down calm, in a way. So quiet you can hear people trying not to be too loud when they're breathing. They know what time it is. Not even champs win all the time. And these two that just came in obviously feel like living so they're not making any fusses. Not claiming anything. Just keeping mouths shut. Professional. And they're inspiring the other two to keep it together too.

And the forced calm of it all, I got to be honest, it's scaring me.

I look to Blanco, but he doesn't seem bothered as he's lining all four of them up in front of the couch, facing the wall behind it.

And I'm looking at the one that was on the couch with the girl before. He's got all the makings of a little knucklehead trying too hard to fit in. But these other two to his right? They're on another level. They're slicker, smarter. Like I said, scarier, but only if you know what you're looking at.

They're the kind that when something's going down, they put on blank faces and start memorizing everything they can about us, and about the situation around them. Which is why they were the first two facing the couch now.

They are the new gang members. Unrecognizable because there's no uniform anymore. No clean-shaved head. No tattoos, and I mean *none*. No Pendleton flannel buttoned only at the top button over a white wife-beater. No khakis with a perfect crease. They're new breed, these two. Built from a totally different mold to the one that spit out me and Blanco.

I mean, one of these fuckers even looks like he's college cut, got a black polo on and his hair combed with a part in the middle and everything. Hemmed fucking denim and black Cons with black laces.

Welcome to the new L.A. gangster. They blend in on purpose. They look just like everybody else. You'd never pick them out of crowds. That shit's by design.

The phones they got on them go in the mag bag. One, two. Neither has a gun. Or a knife. Which isn't crazy. We probably missed the stash spot in the house where everything is. But that puts an extra dash of worry in my mind too. Like, maybe they're not guarding much of anything if they're fucking up this bad.

And they are too, being bent over the couch like this. Faces in cushions. Knees in spilt beer. Having some time to think about failing. About maybe dying too.

Right now I'm glad Blanco doesn't have us wearing hairnets or something. Shows he's not worrying about that DNA, which is good. Means Blanco's at least not *planning* on killing anybody. No law enforcement wastes time on collecting, much less testing, tissue samples unless there's a body.

Blanco cuts my thoughts off with "So, you gonna see to it then?"

The safe, he means.

We have a moment right then, a silent conversation. Me looking at Blanco, shooting invisible thoughts his way about how he better not kill anybody while I'm in the next room. And he smiles at that. He dips his head, like, *C'mon, man!* I nod up. Like, *All right then.* Like, *You got a wife and kids and no threats in front of you, so don't be doing anything over some bullshit.* At this, he just cocks his head to tell me I'm stupid, to tell me he's more than got this situation under control, and the only thing keeping us here is my being slow.

He's not wrong.

I'm back in the closet, working the drill, feeling its vibrations all the way up into my shoulder.

The rattle, Frank calls it.

When the mechanism finally gives way below me, I lurch forward with it, right through the door. After that, I get going on widening the hole enough to put the rebar in. That takes a minute, if that. I punch with the metal rod and get nothing. So I turn the light on above me and close the door. I scope the hole. I can see the mechanism. I just have to get it off its line, and I need a little more room, so I drill once more. I rattle. Then I put the rebar in and I shove.

Once. Twice. Three times.

It gives on eight and I feel the handle.

It's completely loose in my hand. No resistance at all.

Yes. That's the feeling I've been looking for since the moment I stepped foot inside Blanco's house. It's a release for the lock, but it's a release for me too. It means I'm not tied to this place anymore.

And I got to take a huge breath before I pull the door wide-open. I shake my shoulders. I arch my neck. The door maybe weighs twenty pounds, but I prep like I'm about to do half my weight in a dead lift.

Then I just pull it open and look in.

42

There's watches in there. Lots of metal watches with fat faces. And chains too thick for their own good. It's all mostly silver. Some gold. And loose poker chips. And two packs of playing cards without boxes to put them in. There's a gold baby's rattle crammed in the top shelf on its own. Which makes no sense till I figure maybe someone won it gambling and didn't take it away with them for whatever reason.

There's black tar in there too, packed up in rolled tinfoil like tiny burritos in one-gallon Ziploc freezer bags. There's three of those. How much that is, I don't know. Five pounds each maybe, but that counts packaging. How much that's *worth*? No clue.

I pull them out, though. For Blanco. Because a deal's a deal.

But when they're coming out of there, I see something else, something underneath them, and just seeing it makes my heart skip and do happy things like it's supposed to. Like, fill me with adrenaline. With relief. With thinking that maybe this was worth it.

Cash. Three fat green rolls of it, done up with different colors of rubber bands. Red and yellow, mostly. One black. One long and brown and tied back together in a knot where it must've snapped.

I grab the nearest roll and undo it so I can flick a rubber-tipped finger over the bills and watch them flip at the air, doing a quick mental count. There's, I don't know, $16,000 or so here, which means, times three, about $48,000.

It's so good I almost shout something.

Like, *Hell ya, that's the* more *I'm talking about right there!*

But I don't. I keep it inside.

I knew it'd never have been $887,000 again. But forty-plus is something. A legit something. And I pack it away in the hollowed-out parts of my drill cases as I'm wrapping up cords and putting bits back in their little holder sockets. Doing my last check to make sure I have everything. And then checking again.

I tuck two tar bags into my armpits, loosen my belt and put another in my front waistband before grabbing up my cases. This's economical hauling right here. But before I turn to go, I think about the last safe. About being in that evidence lockup with Collins and getting lectured about how I could've blown up half the neighborhood.

And I lean over the safe far enough to see the top side of the door, the part of it that was hidden when it was closed.

There's nothing there.

No drilled and gummed-up giant Dracula holes. No dynamite powder, or whatever it was, hiding underneath.

Good, I think. *Normal. A safe just being a safe.*

I head out the door, and even though I'm carrying more weight now than when I came in this house, I'm feeling twenty pounds lighter.

Blanco must hear my case handles squeaking, because he meets me in the hall. I don't need to ask if we're leaving the kids in the living room like that. You know we are. I angle my body towards him to show him I got the Ziplocs tucked under arms and one in my waist. He grabs the ones from my arms. His eyes light up and stay lit up.

"Yup" is all he says, but it says a lot.

It says we did it. It was worth it.

Then we're out the back door, letting it bang as it shuts.

As I'm loading up the Jeep, looking every which direction for phantom fools that I'm expecting to run up on us, Blanco says, "Hold up."

And then he runs back into the house.

Back in the driver seat and starting it up, I got half a mind to leave him.

I look to the house. Nothing. No movement.

I check my mirrors. Nobody in the alley.

I'm thinking, *It's best if I drive off right now.* I'm thinking how that'd be smarter. Less risk. *It's not like I'll ever see him again if I—*

The shotgun door pops and Blanco comes in shaking that damn gold baby rattle with a wrist that's wearing four new watches loose, not even done up, and saying, "How were you about to leave these?"

The look on his face tells me I'm stupid, but it melts to a smile that he breaks with a laugh, like he's celebrating. Like he doesn't want it to end.

Like he won't let it.

The crazy light's still in Blanco's eyes when he says, "We still rolling, dick? I know you didn't drag me out to make me go one-and-done."

"I got another address."

We roll down the alley and out.

High on success.

High on getting over.

"Yup," he says, like he knew it the whole time. Like, he never would have come out tonight if he thought any different.

We're back out on Imperial, hospital in the rearview, heading towards Atlantic when Blanco gets it into his head to push Rose's tape back in. When it doesn't start playing immediately, I hope he'll give up. But that's not Blanco. He figures out that the side is done and pushes fast-forward. It hits the end and flips. My stomach turns with it because I know what the next track is. And I never wanted to share it, but now there's no stopping it.

Blanco says, "Hey, *brochacho*, fuck dying, right?"

I know he's feeling good. Feeling like we just pulled some crazy shit and it's good we're alive and all, but—

On the tape, there's this little "Yo," or "Yup," I'm not sure which. I've listened to it thousands of times. Sometimes I think it's one, convince myself, and then I'm certain it's the other. This time it's "Yo" before guitars ambush us through the speakers, like *bah-bah, bah-bah*. It's "Los Angeles" by X. And Blanco's all over it, shaking the baby rattle like it's maracas. Getting into it like a little kid.

How I feel is confusing. I mean, it's good to hear this song now. To feel Rose nearby with my heart still beating fast, but her side of the tape is personal. Between her and me. Not meant for other ears.

Sonic autobiography, she called it. She said I'd listen to it after she was gone and understand things better later. She wasn't wrong.

Rose started her side with X because of the first line, because Rose had to leave L.A. too, just for different reasons than the racist idiot girl the song's about. I mean, that wasn't Rose. She loved Los Angeles more than anybody. Even the bad parts, Rose loved. The bad people too. I'm proof of that. And she didn't want to leave. And she never would have left if cancer didn't make her.

There's other lines in the song like days changing to night in an instant. And that shit makes so much sense when you're chemoing. You get tired. You pass out. You wake up odd hours. Stay up odd hours. Time doesn't work the same when you're sick. And now I'm thinking of Rose with the tubes in her. Her grandmother's afghan over her. And I move to eject the tape, half leaning over to do it.

Blanco grabs my hand, looks straight at me, and says, "Remember when you made me stab you that one time?"

He's not letting go. He's fucking with me. But I give him the look. The one that says, *You're not allowed to fuck with me over this.* The one that says, *This means nothing to you, but everything to me, and I'll die for it if I have to. I'll drive this Jeep into a wall. I don't give a fuck.*

He lets go. I turn the tape off.

"You've changed a lot, you know." It's not a question. He says it like it's the furthest thing from a compliment. "You remember or what?"

The only thing I say is "Eli Gomez never forgets."

Which is my way of telling him, yes. I remember. I remember a lot.

Two days in a row we'd been partying. No sleep. Coke. Coffee. The other Coke. Whatever it took to stay awake. I was crazy. Really out of my head. And it was Blanco's dumbass idea to try to calm me down with video games. Like that would ever have worked. Because all it did was the opposite. All it did was trip me out. Hard. I got no recollection of this, but apparently I started screaming that I had a spider on me. On my leg. On my thigh. So that's where he drove the knife in, and after, he told me he got it. He killed the *araña*. I woke up alone in a St. Francis ER sitting bay with its white curtain pulled half-back. Name on my sheet said Eli Gomez, obviously something Blanco made up when he checked me in.

"Just never say I didn't pay you back," he says.

"This's you paying me back, right now?"

Blanco smiles and switches the subject. "Where's this other address, anyways?"

I tell him.

And when I do, a change hits his face. It goes from real to mask in a heartbeat.

His voice's flat when he says, "You sure about that?"

He doesn't need to ask. He knows I'm sure.

"That's Rooster's too."

He says it like the name is supposed to mean something to me, but he sees it doesn't, so he says, "Maybe we skip this one. You got others?"

I tell him those too.

Blanco nods through each one. "Fuck. They're all his. *La DEA*'s got his number, huh? Fucking good."

I say, "What's he to you?"

But I already have an idea. He's a lieutenant, maybe. A lot like

Blanco. Maybe they're even on the same level. Running different shows. Maybe they compete.

Blanco doesn't answer me. He's calculating, silently running figures to see how this might work for him. This is exactly what he's good at. Exactly why he's lasted this long. Knowing details. Knowing who owns what. Knowing what's vulnerable. And I see Blanco getting cocky again as he's moving through the mental math, and he's got a look like he's thinking how if Rooster's going down, it means he's coming up.

When he smiles, I know it's because he's unable to resist the chance to get over on a rival. It's the kind of thing that would give him rep forever. It's the kind of thing only Blanco is crazy enough to do.

"Clark Street," he says. "That's the one."

"It's Clark and what?"

"Atlantic," he says, "just off where Clark dead-ends into it."

"So I keep going then?"

"No, we're going somewhere else first."

44

We stop off at a pay phone and Blanco gets out to make a call that doesn't even take a minute. After that, we go to a little house on Wright Road. In the nineties, it would've been bugging at all hours. But it's quiet now. More and more families moving in these days. This place even has a big playground set in the side yard. One with a red plastic slide. I pull into its driveway and the front door opens behind a heavy metal security door. I see white lamps on inside, a silhouette looking out.

Blanco rolls his window down and nods at the figure.

From inside the house, we hear the television. Sounds like stand-up.

"I don't need no backing," Blanco says to me as he slides the watches off his wrist and sets the rattle down, "but, you know, just in case."

He hands me the other gun and gets out.

I follow.

When we get to the metal door, it gets opened by the finest chick I've seen in a long time. Magazine-cover fine. TV fine. So fine I got to stop for a second and check myself before I go into the living room, where there's one long L-shaped couch facing the TV, and behind it, sitting on top of a low table about two feet off the ground, is another couch. It's like stadium seating or something, so people behind the main couch can see too. Sitting up there is a little *abuelo*, fast asleep, threatening to lose control of a limp hand and spill his can of beer all over himself. But he hasn't. Not yet.

There's no doubt that she's the jewel of this house. Pictures of her at various ages are on two of four walls. In person is best though.

In her midtwenties, she's got long straight black hair pulled back. Eyes like faded jade with bits of brown in it. The kind of nose people get cut every day in Beverly Hills to try to have. Mayan lips. Some *café con leche* skin tone. Little tank top. Littler running shorts that she's clearly just lounging in. September's when it gets hottest in L.A. And right at that second, I'm grateful they've only got the one AC unit sticking out of the house.

Elvia, her name is. I know because Blanco calls her that.

"Elvia," he says it all sweet, "I need to get up with your man."

She takes a step back into the room like she knows what this means. She's got bare feet. Long and lean like a runner's. I see her bones tensing there, through skin.

Blanco sniffs as he closes the distance between them. "Don't play, now. If he's on Clark Street for tonight, I need you to say."

"I wouldn't know," she says.

She's looking away, to a room with a closed door. *Her kid's room*, I'm thinking.

On the TV, a dude in a suit is making a joke about women and hair dryers. How they both blow, or something. I don't recognize him. Somewhere far off, an audience laughs.

"His business is my business now," Blanco says as he puts his arms around her and hugs her.

I watch Blanco push his hip into her so she can feel the gun in his waistband.

The cold metal shape of it.

"If I wanted to get at you, you know there's nobody that could ever stop me, right? No walls, no doors neither."

The menace of it twists into me. And I'm thinking, *I don't need to be a party to this*. Because Blanco's tone carries a promise of pain in it. An *or else* if she doesn't do what he says. And she gets it as he steps back from her, and she stands there, waiting for him to say what he wants.

"Call him and tell him he's gonna open the garage and let us in."

The muscles in her neck strain like she's having to swallow something she doesn't want to.

"You do this," Blanco says, "and you're doing him a favor."

She doesn't ask how. Doesn't have to. Because Blanco makes it crystal.

He says, "You do this, and you won't have to *catrina* yourself up and carry his picture around on Día de los Muertos from now on."

She gets that he means killing. It's in his eyes too.

Elvia goes to an old green phone mounted to the kitchen wall, dials a number, has a little argument about how she's calling because she has to call, and yes, she knows she's not supposed to, but he has to know about this. She never raises her voice. She stays calm. Conveys the information. Tells the voice on the other end there are two of us. To expect us. Soon.

She puts the phone back on the cradle.

"It's done," she says without looking Blanco in the face.

And that's that.

At least, she must think it is, and I do too. Till Blanco leans back and opens the metal security door and a dude comes through. A skinny little homie. Maybe eighteen years old. Peach-fuzz mustache and a little shuffle-walk. He looks a little off, if you want the truth. Like, not all there.

"This's Snapper," Blanco says to Elvia. "Maybe you can cook

him something, because he's staying for a bit. Make sure your family's okay. When we get up out of Clark Street just fine, he'll be on his way."

So that was Blanco's call from the pay phone, I'm thinking. Calling this dude to come keep an eye on Elvia while we're knocking over the drugs house.

Pretty smart.

And that's the problem with Lynwood, what's always been the problem with Lynwood. See, everybody knows everybody, and when that happens, you know who's precious to who. And when you know that, you know weak spots. And when you know those, all you have to do is dig into them to make something happen.

Glasses

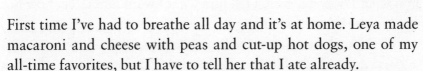

First time I've had to breathe all day and it's at home. Leya made macaroni and cheese with peas and cut-up hot dogs, one of my all-time favorites, but I have to tell her that I ate already.

She's cool with it, kissing me on the cheek and wrapping it up for the fridge. She knows something's up with me but she's not pushing.

She's got a divorce case to go over in the living room while the TV's babbling in the background. She can focus like that, just have noise around and be good. I'm in Felix's room down the hall, hearing her shuffle papers.

He's sleeping and I'm just staring at him holding the back of his right hand in front of his mouth like he's smelling it. I don't know why he does that. I don't think he even does. It's unconscious.

I tried undoing it once, just moving his little hand away from his mouth and putting his arm by his side and under some covers, but he woke up and screamed so I never did that again.

I learned that time. So, now, I just look at this little miracle baby, and the dog's chilling at my feet, putting her big old jaw on the top of my shoe.

I say miracle since we tried for years and then there was the umbilical thing with him. We had four miscarriages first. Three were on the earlier side, one was second trimester, and the first ones were hard, but that last one was a death in the family. Completely.

Twenty-six weeks old our little girl was. Stillborn, the doctor said. I had to go to the church and get her buried myself since Leya refused. We weren't gonna try anymore after that. It was too hard.

When Felix came, it was natural. It was a surprise, and we didn't take any chances. Leya was thirty-four, on bed rest almost the whole time. I got paranoid.

I'd check her stomach every second I could to make sure there were still kicks in there. I was so scared he wouldn't make it that I don't think I even believed it until he came out crying and looking like he hated everything about air.

Every minute's a blessing with my little boy. I even try to put my words in Felix's dreams. Every night, I try. What I do is, I tell him what I hope for him. I tell him what I want him to be, how he needs to be better than me.

I feel like there's a secret room inside him, a room inside a room even, one that I can fill up with good things and advice, stuff he should know if I talk to him at night like this. The more I do it, the more I can build a voice in the back of his brain that will guide him through everything even when I'm not here.

Tonight, I'm telling him if I ever have to go away and never come back, he'll be okay. I tell him maybe he won't get over it, but he'll overcome it.

I tell him that he'll always know, deep down inside him, that his father loved him more than everything. His father loved him so much he wanted to change and he tried to change.

After, I'm swiping my face with my shirt while the dog looks at me with her head up and eyebrows tweaking like she's worried about me. I pat her head and duck out. I'm not even all the way back down the hall when Rooster's phone rings.

I stop right where I am. Leya's scrambling to switch off the TV and turn around to look at me. This phone just about never finds me at home.

I pick up on ring two. *"Bueno."*

Terco's running his mouth on the other end about how something's wrong since Elvia just called him out of nowhere, asking all sorts of questions she shouldn't have, and then telling him two people are coming to where he is and to open the garage.

He don't hear it, but I swallow hard. I got expletives going in my head then. His house was on the list I gave Collins.

I know it's Ghost now. It has to be.

He got that list somehow. He's going straight down it.

Terco says, "Did you *hear* me? What should I do?"

I got to make a decision now. A call that will blow up everything I been working to build, but I'm in a corner and there's no other decision to make.

"You know what to do," I tell Terco. "Better be quick."

I hang up before he does. I call Collins. He don't pick up. Nobody does, and I don't know what I'm expecting since it's late but I leave a message.

I tell him not to hit the spots I gave him. Whatever he has planned, don't do it. There won't be nothing there to take if he does. I'll explain later.

I call Lonely. He answers on ring one, like always.

"Send your boy to the store by Avalon and you come scoop me up," I tell him, and then hang up.

The store is Terco's place and Avalon isn't the street with the same name. It means Big Danny's gonna pick Rooster up, since he's the king like Arthur.

And Lonely's coming to get me since we live close. I don't need to say right now to him, he knows right now.

Leya's got brave eyes when I turn back around and go back into Felix's room. What I do is, I don't wake him but I kiss his forehead. I smell his hair as deep as I can. I try to get the smell of his little molecules so deep inside my lungs that he'll never leave me, even if I have to breathe shallow the rest of my life.

I rub the dog real good on her ribs where she likes it, and when

I come back out, Leya's standing in the dark of the hallway, lit up like a silhouette with the living room behind her. She signs *I love you* in my direction since she picked it up from me, and it puts half a sob in my lungs I can't get out. It just sits inside me like a bubble that won't pop.

Me and her, we put our fingers on a map of California once and picked a place we'd never been to, talked about, or even heard of before. She knows she'll have to go there without me and wait.

"Empty the safe," I say. "Wake him up and go to Cardiff-by-the-Sea."

Before she can respond or say no, I go right up to her and kiss my wife with all I have, since I know it might be the last time I ever get to.

This is me telling her, you're the mother of my child and I respect you and honor you and put you above even myself.

This is me telling her, if something happens to me tonight, you go, you survive. You have to live past me. You have to, or I can never rest in peace.

And then I have to let go. When I do, she makes a little sound like I'm hurting her by going, and I know I am. I give her a look that says, *I'm sorry and I know, since I'm hurting me too.*

At the open front door, I give her a last look as the headlights of Lonely's car swing past me and push into the living room, lighting my face up before hitting the far wall and disappearing. I send Leya's sign back to her then, *I love you*, and I'm gone.

Ghost

Monday, September 15, 2008
Late Evening

46

On the drive over I'm wondering if I did Elvia harm by bringing Blanco in. How maybe I'm responsible, how whatever happens to her might be on me. My stomach thinks it's all my fault. It's kicking and punching at me from the inside, saying, *Yeah, dummy, it* is.

We get through "L.A. Girl" and almost all of "She." They're Rose's songs. Always will be. But on the drive, I'm thinking about Elvia too, worrying about her getting through all this when we roll up on the Clark Street house.

It's obvious that this is the kind of place where anything could go down. It's right off Atlantic, a big main street, so there's quick ins and outs. The property borders on an alley, which means you can do drop-offs and pickups from multiple angles and not always have it looking the same or suspicious to neighbors.

It's a good spot for doing invisible business. As good as one can be, anyways, because it's not just dark around here. It's the dark putting on sunglasses and a black coat and going to chill in a cave. Like, dark-dark.

Of course that's on purpose.

About twenty feet off the ground, a long streetlamp arm clamped to a power-line pole has its bulb out because somebody put it out.

Apart from that, it's got good vantages. You can see from all directions. Up and down Clark on the front, down an alley on the side all the way to Carlin, really. The driveway's not out front. It's at the back, off the alley. Across that alley, there's an apartment building with a high metal fence. All heavy with bad stucco, that place looks exactly like the kinds of spots I used to get high in not far from here. And just thinking that, I feel those memories in my throat, but I don't say it. Don't need to. They burn enough on their own.

I pull a left into the alley and then drive past the house before throwing it in reverse and backing up into the garage, which is open when we get there. Just for us. I don't pull all the way in, though. I leave the Jeep's nose poking out just in case someone wants to shut the garage and try to lock us in.

"Demolition Girl" is starting on the speakers with a shouted, "One, two, three, four," before guitars and drums come in just as I kill the engine.

The door to the house is partway open and there's a light on inside.

Blanco leads, he's got both guns, and I'm right in behind with my tools.

The kitchen's different here than most drugs houses I've ever seen. It's clean.

And it actually looks like somebody lives here. Car calendar on the wall. This September's a '65 Mustang with a girl on the hood. New microwave. There's an oven with a green towel hanging from its handle. Fridge is old but clean. There's a broom beside it, leaning on some cabinets that don't look banged up. In the middle of it all is one of those tables you go to a warehouse to get and then come home and build it yourself. Sitting at it is Elvia's man.

He's got two hands on the table. A cup of coffee's steaming in front of him. Even when he's sitting down I can tell he's six foot and a solid 180, 185. Tight fade on the hair. T-shirt fitted. Nose crooked like it got broke a few times. If he was a Hollywood actor, people would say his face had character. But where I come from, it just means he didn't have enough money or sense to see a doctor.

From over that nose, he's staring all kinds of evil at Blanco too.

I don't blame him either. I just met Elvia and I understand how somebody could kill for her and not think twice. And I definitely get how she's so valuable that her man would do anything, including going *vendido* on his boss to keep her safe.

Blanco's got one gat in his back waistband and one in his hand. He's not pointing it, just holding it. And he's dipping down, looking like he's taking a knee, or trying to tie his shoe, but all's he's trying to do is see under the table to make sure dude doesn't have a piece hidden there.

I don't look, but he must not, because Blanco's up and planting his gaze back on the dude sitting in the chair.

Blanco nods up at him and says, "What's shaking, Terco?"

It means a lot in three words.

It means *I got you, huh?* With a little gloat on top. It means *Where's everybody else?* It means *They better not be hiding up in here or you're first and Elvia's next.*

Stubborn. That's what *terco* means.

And I'm sure he's that, but he's definitely not stupid either. He gets it.

"I sent them all out," Terco says. He's staring at his coffee cup like he's about to pick it up and break it in his hands. Like, he really wants to and maybe he won't be able to help himself. "I'd say you maybe got ten minutes."

Blanco plops the mag bag on the kitchen table and says, "Phone in the bag."

"I don't got a cell." Terco nods behind him to a landline phone sitting on its cradle on the counter. "Only that one."

I ask him where the safe is right then.

He looks at me, like, *Find it yourself.* Which is fair enough.

So I turn into the living room to get looking.

47

All the walls are drywall and all of them are empty. There's no safe in the main bedroom. There isn't one in the front closet either, just shelfing and household things like Ziplocs and trash bags. It's *organized*. Like, eerie organized.

Nada again in the laundry closet. There's some nice-ass new machines in there though. Stacked one on top of the other. Some sort of steam-cleaning kind. And the more I'm going through here, the more I'm thinking, *This is new*. Making a business house all clean and undercover is like nothing I've ever seen before.

Room to room, it looks like a family house, just a little emptier. Less personal. Not as many pictures up. No dings around its edges and little things piling up like you'd get if people were living here full-time. But, then, it must be so easy to bring stuff in and out when it's like this. Grocery bags full of stuff. Backpacks too, maybe. Nothing strange.

It's genius, in a way. Invisible, almost.

The kind of thing you could run just about anywhere with nobody noticing.

And it's close, but it's not completely safe. I mean, it's obviously not perfect or it'd never be identified on the DEA list and getting warrants put out for it. So what that's saying to me is that somebody's a rat. Somebody snitched on this house because there's just no other way it gets made. It's too good.

I'm standing in the back hallway, with its too-white walls looking like someone actually scrubs them, when a cat walks by me, arches its back, and rubs itself on my shins. Little dude walks a few more steps, does a U-turn, comes back, and rolls up on my shins again. He's got two different-colored eyes, one green, one blue, and a crick in his tail. He's a little bit scruffy for this place, with bits of dirt showing in his orange-and-white fur.

And I'm thinking, *What the hell kind of drugs house bothers keeping a cat?* Cats are too much damn work with their boxes and all that. A dog, I can get with. It can look out for intruders and keep the spot safe. Dogs are no-brainers, but a cat?

No. It's confusing is what it is. I don't see the point. All work, no payoff. That doesn't make sense when you're running this type of game.

Down at my feet, little dude meows at me and flops over on my shoes, showing me his big white belly. Like he wants me to pet it or something. The whole thing reminds me of a guy I used to know. A real stone-cold kind of homeboy, he would have sat right down and been petting this cat for hours. Apache, his name was. He used to love cats way more than people. Would do anything for them. Rest in peace to him.

Right then I'm noticing there's a stack of what look like clean towels sitting on the carpet not far from little dude's fuzzy head, and I know that's strange, so I head straight for that linen closet and open it up.

Inside, at the bottom, falling over onto my foot as soon as I pull the door all the way out, is what looks like half a fake shelf. It was there to sit in front of a safe and disguise it with stacks of towels.

But in this case, there's no towels, and no shelf, and no disguising that I can quickly and easily see the safe on the floor.

It's an electronic keypad Pentagon, and not a bad one either. It's a 2007 consumer-magazine best buy, almost brand-new and definitely badass, sitting there looking shiny in this burnished metal glaze that looks like silver but isn't. I can see somebody's been reading up on the trade magazines because it's the kind of thing that'd take time to punch.

There's a problem with this one, though. I can see it straight off.

The kind of problem that makes me sick to my stomach, the kind that brings my concrete right back up, because, see, it won't take me any time at all to figure out what's in this particular safe.

None.

Because the door's already cocked a bit.

Because it's already *open*.

48

I know there's nothing inside it, but I got to be stupid and pull it anyways. So I do. The moment just as I'm putting a hand on the handle and pulling still has some hope in it, like maybe there's still something in there, but I know that's just my heart being stupid. It *wants* there to be something there, but my brain knows there isn't.

There's no squeak on the hinges when I swing it wide enough to see my brain is right. I knew it was coming, but still it feels like I got punched right out of the atmosphere. Just lifted up and out.

Like I'm the coyote and a roadrunning bird just found a way to hit me with a boxing glove bigger than my body and smack me right off a cliff.

Just, *bam*. And then I'm feeling like I'm falling even though I'm standing still.

I'm floaty from it. Sick and hot and heavy at the same time.

And I got too many thoughts playing bumper cars in my head: the towels, I'm thinking, *They were out, and with everything so damn ordered in this house, that's definitely not right, so that must have been done recently, real recently.* I look back toward the kitchen and I'm still not hearing anything, so I got no idea what's going on there besides Terco and Blanco just staring at each other and playing it tough. *But Terco knows*, I'm thinking. He knows I'm going to find this safe open and empty and he must have some plan for a move when I come back and say so. I just wish I had some damn idea what that move is before I walk back in. I look to little dude. He's now sitting on his furry ass at my feet, using his teeth to work on something he's got stuck between his toes. He's a little chubby, but I'm seeing he's got a tag now, hiding in his neck fur. I'm reaching down nice and easy so I can tilt the little round metal tag up and read it. I got to lean down a little to see.

LIL GARFIELD, it says.

Ha. Of course it does. But what's underneath isn't so funny.

It's an address that isn't this one. Isn't even this fucking *street*.

And that's when that concrete in my stomach tries to break off chunks of itself and cut its way out of me.

Because this's bad.

As bad as it gets.

This ain't their cat.

He's an outdoor cat, a neighborhood cat, just rolling through.

And then I'm wondering how Lil G got in here, how it must've been a window or a door or something, and as I'm looking down the hall to the bathroom at the end of it, a little breeze hits me.

And I get it.

Glasses

When me and Lonely pull up to Terco's spot, we stop two houses down on Clark and I get out quick. Lonely's right behind me with a empty gym bag over his shoulder.

I make a line for Rooster's Chrysler. It's parked sideways in front of the little alley so the Jeep with black plates that's parked halfway in the garage can't get out without ramming it.

As I'm getting closer, I seen how the far side of the alley is blocked off with a truck too. Big Danny gets out of the driver's side of the 300 with his own empty gym bag, closes the door real quiet, and then him and Lonely head to the back to grab what they need to grab.

Some homies are setting up a reflective ROAD CLOSED sign and some cones at the end of Clark so no one can just accidentally roll in off Atlantic. I get in the backseat on the shotgun side. Rooster's already there, looking ready for answers.

"I know I'm not the only one thinking he hit other spots, maybe even your other spots," I say. "We need to shut it down tonight. Everything. Got to be safe."

Rooster nods. He knows I'm right. "If it goes shoot-out in there, we do what we have to." Rooster nods back at Lonely's car for me to go get my *cuete* since he never allows any types of guns in his car. "But I want him alive. I'm serious. I got plans for him."

"All right," I say.

I want to ask what those plans are, but it's one of those things where I'll find out if it ends up being an option. If the main reason he wants this Ghost alive ends up being that Rooster wants to know how the safecracker knows these addresses and somehow that leads back to me, then that's it, and then at least I got my kisses in.

Make the calls, Rooster signs before he gets out and walks towards the front door of the house.

I'm right behind him, walking to Lonely's car and going in the backseat for what I need to grab. I make calls as I go.

First one is to send somebody to look out for Elvia. Next ones are going house by house, telling all of them to shut it down tonight with no questions asked.

If Collins don't get my message and kicks doors at any of those addresses, he'll see there's nothing left. They're all cleaned out. No drugs, no cash, no nothing.

He'll be red and raging and I'll be first on his list of people to seriously mess with, but that's a problem for later. Right now I'm putting a gun in the back of my pants and crossing the front lawn of Terco's house to stand right behind Rooster.

Ghost

Monday, September 15, 2008
Late Evening

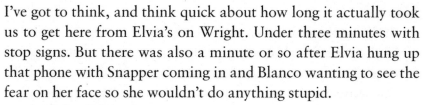

I've got to think, and think quick about how long it actually took us to get here from Elvia's on Wright. Under three minutes with stop signs. But there was also a minute or so after Elvia hung up that phone with Snapper coming in and Blanco wanting to see the fear on her face so she wouldn't do anything stupid.

And she didn't.

But her man sure did.

After he hung up that phone with her, he must've put another call in, because there was enough time for Terco to call the boss—this Rooster dude—get told what to do, and, most likely, get the product out of the house as quick as possible. And after he did that, the motherfucker *still* had time to make coffee. Like, some kind of last little fuck-you to us that's just sitting there, steaming.

I'm already moving down the hall, moving towards the bathroom, and every step towards it, I know, more and more, that that's how everything in the safe got tossed out into the backyard, into the grass or something.

I'm pushing open the bathroom door, not even bothering with

turning on the light. The smell of bleach punches me in the face before I'm even all the way inside, and my first thought is *Were they cleaning in here?* Because if so, that's some thorough shit, but not out of character from what I can see about this whole setup.

I'm pulling the shower curtain back and looking inside. There's a little ledge in there for shampoos and soap, but above that?

A little rectangular window just above where I can see out, and it's all the way open. There's no screen on it either.

Definitely it's big enough for a cat to jump through if he could get up there from the other side.

And I don't even want to hoist myself up on my tiptoes to look out of it, but I know I have to. Just to be sure.

And when I do, my heart forgets to be a heart for a second.

I swear to God it stops inside me.

And I'm trying to breathe but that's not coming either.

It's just me. Frozen.

Watching two guys with little flashlights, projecting them onto the ground so they can comb through the grass and pick up packages.

Ziploc packages.

With little silver things hitting the light and shining.

Fuck.

Those are exactly the same kind of tinfoil wraps that the black tar was in from the last place.

I finally get a breath in as I'm taking a big step back without even looking where I'm going, and I'm putting my foot down, and damn if I don't step on Lil G's tail so hard that he lets out this screaming kind of meow and takes off running back down the hallway, back into the house.

I'm right behind him, grabbing my gear, knocking into walls, going as fast as I can back towards the kitchen with my cases in my hands, and I'm thinking, *Maybe we got just enough time to jump in the Jeep and bust the fuck out, hit Atlantic, and be gone like we were never even here in the first place,* but right as I'm turning the corner, the doorbell rings out of this little plastic speaker box right near my head.

Like, *bing-bong.*

Real crisp. Real clean.

And the sound, I swear, it goes straight through me, breaking every hope I got inside. *This is us caught,* I think. *Done.*

I know right away that if there are guys at the back, there are guys out front, and on the sides, surrounding the whole place.

And whatever's coming now, there's no escaping it.

51

I'm in the living room when I set my gear down where I'm standing. As I'm letting it go and saying goodbye to it, it feels like something's ripping inside me, like I'm cutting ties I shouldn't be cutting. All this gear I inherited. Gear Frank gave me as presents over the years. As hand-me-downs. That's worth more to me than the almost fifty grand inside.

My heart's going nuts inside my chest. Banging on ribs. Acting all trapped and crazy. And maybe that's jacking with my lungs because I'm not really breathing too good either. It's too heavy.

And I've only gone a few steps.

The doorbell goes again.

But all's I'm hearing in the sound is *Ohhh, shit.*

Blanco's out in the living room with me now, looking at me, like, *Explain.*

"Safe was open," I say, trying to get it out quick. In the fewest words. "*Chiva* got tossed. Back window. Guys were out there snagging it."

Blanco's face is different now. He's taking it in. And he's nodding. Like, *Okay.* Like, *That's how it's going down.* Behind him, I see Terco, standing up from the table. Walking forward. Coming into the living room.

Blanco's eyeing him. Hard. "How's it feel killing your girl?"

"This can be easy," Terco says, but the way he's saying it, he's wishing it won't be.

He doesn't have a gun or nothing, not that I can see. It's just he knows we're got, and that it can be crazy or clean. The choice is ours.

I know it. And Blanco knows it.

And more than that, we know there's somebody big behind that front door.

And we know they're not going anywhere till we open it.

Because the doorbell goes again.

Terco tells it like it is. "You fucked up, Blanco. You fucked up bad."

Blanco smirks at that. He gives Terco a complicated look right then, one that's kind of saying how Terco just got his girl popped, and how that's on Terco for doing something stupid and not protecting his own, how all he had to do was be smart and keep his mouth shut, and everything would've been fine, but now Terco's worse than a bitch and Blanco would shoot him right here in the stomach if he wasn't about to work some magic with his mouth and dance right out the door in about five minutes because he was Blanco, and he was protected on high, and to punk motherfuckers like Terco he was completely untouchable, but he'd remember what Terco did. Hell yes, he would. He'd remember everything. And he'd get him back. That was a promise.

All that in a look.

On the receiving end of it, Terco's not having it. He's throwing his own right back, and it just says, *Yeah, we'll see about all that.*

Right now, it's about odds. And we don't even need to see how many they got outside. They've got more bodies and guns than us. Shooting everything up is no kind of option for anyone. If it was, they would've come in when we weren't ready. But putting on a show like this, ringing that doorbell, it's not for me.

It's for Blanco.

It's *respeto.* Even if they don't like giving it, they are.

But it's also a way of saying, don't even think about doing something stupid.

Blanco knows this. He's got the guns out. He's ejecting their chamber rounds, pulling their clips, and putting them in the middle of the living room floor next to the mag bag. It's all a peace offering. A way of saying, you won, and we acknowledge that shit. Now, let's talk. Let's handle it professional.

"No point waiting," Blanco says to me, and it's obvious from how he's talking that he wants me to open the front door, not him.

I look to Terco, but he just stares at me like it's not on him, so I walk over to the front door, taking each step over the carpet like I'm walking on a high wire and it doesn't really matter which side I fall off.

When I get to the door, I unlock it and open it.

Outside is a guy about five inches shorter than me. And I can tell right away I never knew this dude back in the day. It hits me then how almost everybody I knew back then is out or dead. How sixteen years is a lifetime in Lynwood. More than a lifetime. And even I know not to bother dwelling on all that loss. It'll be my time to exit real soon too.

Rooster's eyes do a circuit of the room, looking past me to the guns in the middle of the floor, and then to Lil Garfield sitting on his ass and licking his tail all sad like I broke it, then coming back up to me.

He's Chicano for sure, but maybe a little bit of something else too, around the eyes. Hard to tell because he's got on a Dodgers hat, all black on black with that *L* anchored to the middle line of the *A*, where the logo's just a little bit glossy from the silk thread. He's got a dark beard and mustache, close trimmed.

He smiles at me. And it's not cold or weird or anything. It's just a smile.

And it's polite somehow. Like he's happy I opened the door. Like he's been waiting to talk to me and now he's glad to see my face.

This could only be Rooster.

Because he's looking square at me and saying, "Mind if we come in, Ghost?"

52

Wow, he knows my name. That's as bad as it gets. I don't really give an answer to his question about coming in, so much as step back into the living room and make way, because the *we* is three homies he's got behind him. Two big motherfuckers. Like football linebackers or something. They're the ones that were digging out in the grass, picking up everything that got tossed from the safe. The last one is a funny-looking dude with a messed-up eye and glasses. He's skinny, and I get a vibe just looking at him. I'm sure Glasses is his street name. If it's not that, it's Gafas. Guaranteed. But I'm also getting a feeling like he knows pain backwards and forwards. It clicks for me right then. The big two are just for show. It's these other two that are no joke.

Rooster comes through the door first. He takes his hat off when he steps into the house. His hair's tight to the scalp but not clean shaved. Dark, maybe black, with a little gray at the temples. He's around forty, wearing a black T-shirt, no logo. Black jeans at the waist. Not baggy. Relaxed. Not Cons or Nikes. Some simple black leather tennis shoes, the kind I can't tell the brand on just by looking at them.

The only thing real remarkable about this guy is his tattooed sleeves.

It's expensive shit too. The best ink around. Chicano-style. Black and gray. Art from Pint, a crazy-eyed skull. Big Sleeps with some insane letters I can't read from here. But I can see Chuey Quintanar did some work on there with a portrait of a Bernini sculpture on the forearm, just the face of the girl as she's turning into a tree, and it's so clean that it looks like it was cut out of marble yesterday. Probably this guy has all kinds of terrible old-school tattoos on him, or maybe he lasered them or had them covered with better stuff when he really came up, but either way, right now, his arms are sending the whole room messages.

And they're saying that he's sure-as-shit real.

They're saying he's a grown-up gangster. With taste. Class. Like he knows all about expensive tequilas but prefers *mezcales*, even knows about the different agave types and has a favorite region. Guerrero, probably. He still pounds a King Cobra every now and again, though. Like, it don't matter, whatever.

They're saying he embraces pain so long as it's in service to goals, and when he starts in on something, he fucking finishes it.

So, that's when I know.

In this moment.

This is it for me. The end. Let there be no doubt.

But I also know he won't be the dude that kills me. Just the one ordering it done.

"Rooster," Blanco says.

"Heard you were in the neighborhood, Blanco." Rooster nods at the guns on the floor and his linebacker homies pick them up with the clips while Rooster moves to the couch to sit down. All casual. Like he's an invited guest and we're just hanging out. Like this isn't a big deal at all.

The TV's off and black, but I see a reflection of Rooster in its screen, and he's looking dead at Blanco. He hasn't stopped looking at him. And Blanco hasn't stopped looking right back at Rooster.

We go a rough moment like that.

A moment for everybody else in the room to soak in that whatever's about to go down in here is going to be worked out between these two, and the rest of us will have to just deal with the consequences.

It's Rooster that fires the first shot with his mouth, though.

"Bring me my phone," he says to the dude in glasses. "Get them to text me that one thing."

Glasses pulls a phone out of his pocket, and all's I can think right then is *Wow, man, this Rooster is something else.* I mean, if a dude doesn't even use his own phone, if he pays someone else to take all the risks using it, it's not going to go well for you. And it's about to get a lot worse.

Instead of the little ding that signals a text coming in, Vin Scully's voice pops out of Rooster's phone saying, "Home run!"

And then Glasses is clicking on whatever needs to be clicked, and he's holding the phone up to me and Blanco, so we can see the screen, and as soon as I see it, I wished I hadn't, because I'm looking at *evidence.*

I barely met the dude, but even I recognize the picture of Snapper on the carpet of Elvia's place with some thick-looking blood all over his face. I don't know what it is, a brutally busted nose or a gunshot or what. He's too messed up to tell. But I don't need to be able to tell either. It's bad. And it's safe to say he won't be snapping on anybody anymore.

"Delete that," Rooster says.

Glasses presses the screen once, twice.

And like that, Snapper is gone.

53

That was Rooster just setting the tone. Like, showing us how high the stakes were and how rigged the game was. He's the house. He'll take our bets, but he's always going to win. Terco can't keep himself from smiling at that too. He's overdoing it a little, even if he is just grinning at carpet. Blanco's not showing anything.

To him, Rooster says, "So what's going on with you, big man?"

Rooster's tone adds all kinds of questions for Blanco. Like, *What the fuck were you thinking? Were you feeling bored, or what? Why even do this?*

But Blanco only answers the actual question: "This and that."

He doesn't say anything more, just stands there, head held high. Eyes still glued on Rooster. He's not justifying shit, never going to give anybody easy whys about his life. Never will. And I find it hard not to admire that.

"You can play it however you want to play it," Blanco says. "But I brought him here. So you can give me his price, I walk, and we can be done with it."

Figures there's a price on me dying. Figures Blanco would

know that and not tell me, just keep it in his back pocket till he needed it.

I don't find any of it that surprising. It confirms everything I was thinking about the drugs house in Rancho San Pedro when I was down there taking all its money, that the people in that neighborhood definitely saw my Jeep, definitely noticed how I was walking out with a bag, definitely saw my face. Word must've gotten spread.

Figures even more that Blanco wouldn't say anything about it till he needed to. It's part of his Get Out of Jail Free card.

"If you want the price," Rooster says it nice and slow like it's the most logical thing in the world, "you have to do what the price asks."

They're talking about killing me.

Casually.

Using euphemisms.

It's how I've always known when I'm in a room with some for real bad people. They say more with what they don't say than what they do. And most of the time, they make decisions without saying anything at all.

Blanco looks to me.

He's weighing up putting a bullet in me against whatever the number is for doing it. I'm looking right back at him, sending the mental message to do whatever it is he has to do, since I know he's going to do it anyways. It feels like we're looking at each other a long time.

"I'm good," he says, and sniffs, putting his eyes back on Rooster. "But I'm gonna need to tax you on all the *chiva* you threw out that back window. I'll take my third and be on my way."

Rooster's impressed by the bravado of this, if nothing else. "So what is it that you'll be taking a third for?"

"For hitting you before *la DEA* hits you. For making sure none of your people go to jail. For making sure there's no case on you. This address's on the list. There's more of yours on it too."

Rooster blinks. He takes the information in and thinks on it before saying, "I'm happy to know how you know that."

And then he spreads his hands. Like, *Impress me.*

Blanco points a hitchhiker's thumb at me and says, "This motherfucker's an officer of the court. His connects told him four warrants came today. He got all the addresses."

"This one?" Now Rooster's pointing at me too. "Almost nine hundred is what he took from some South Bay homies. Could've disappeared after and maybe been good, but this is him, Greedy Gus, back for more."

Blanco's trying to help when he says, "Maybe look at that money like it bought you something smart. No arrests. No court cases. No DEA. No lawyer bills. That's a lot of fucking nothing."

Rooster sniffs and nods. Like, *Fuck you, Blanco, you talk too much.* And he turns his face to me even though he's still talking to Blanco when he says, "Or I could look at it like he's a thief and that never gets forgiven."

"Yeah," Terco says, like it's even his turn to speak. "Cuz this is Lynwood, motherfucker."

Blanco doesn't bother replying to that. He knows it's decided, that there's no helping me now.

And Rooster just nails it all in. "You're going to walk out of here without him, Blanquito. He's mine now."

Rooster using the *little* suffix doesn't escape notice in this room. It's a slap. It's Rooster putting himself on a higher rung than Blanco. Being magnanimous and disrespectful at the same time, and it's pretty good, but it's an act. Nothing more.

Rooster's just playing like he's in charge of Blanco walking out of here unharmed, but they both know he's not. Not even close. It's a show for Rooster's little ones. To save face. To keep looking tough. Strong.

See, with Rooster and Blanco, it's feeling like they're both on the same level. They're both big. Above this neighborhood bullshit, really. Nothing's happening to either one of them here. Their fates are for bigger homies to decide. A case will be made at a sit-down that they probably won't even be invited to, and it just might go Rooster's way, and I can see Rooster feels confident in that, and I get why. Blanco overstepped. He came in and took what he shouldn't have. He disrespected. But the thing with big homies is they own the big picture. People like me don't even get a picture.

People like Terco and Glasses have a tiny scrap of it. People like Rooster and Blanco have chunks of it. Like, little kingdoms. Big homies see the whole landscape, all the Southland, and beyond too. It's what they do. And if Blanco's going to stay valuable because of that Armenian and Russian business, then it doesn't matter what he did tonight. If the business he's bringing is bigger than this fuckup, he'll do something to atone and he'll keep breathing. Simple. He'll keep making bigger people money, and that'll be that. Rooster will live with it because he'll have to. And nobody else will even get to have an opinion. Not Terco. Not Elvia. Not the little homies probably still leaning on that couch in zip cuffs waiting for somebody to save them. Not *anybody*. That's how this whole game works. The big people make the rules. The rest of us just deal with it.

Rooster nods to Terco, and Terco's got explosions blowing up behind his eyes when he has to dig out a third of the *chiva* that went out the window and hand it to Blanco. Blanco takes it without so much as a thank-you.

To Rooster he says, "You tell Big Fate I said what's up."

Rooster doesn't react. Won't give Blanco the satisfaction.

But I feel a little pain go pop in my chest. It's been so long since I heard that name. Too long.

"*Fuck* dying," Blanco says as he nods to me then. "Give a big hello from me to your girl when you see her."

He means Rose because he knows Rooster's going to send me to her soon. And this's him saying he's sorry but also how he knows it'll be a relief for me. All these years without Rose. Too many.

"Fuck dying," I say back to him. Like now it's our thing somehow. And in this moment, I guess it is. And I'm okay with it. And I think Rose would be too.

With that, Blanco just turns and goes.

The door closes behind him. Gets locked.

And Rooster leans forward on the couch and says to me, "Now let's discuss how you're about to pay me back for every penny."

Glasses

Monday, September 15, 2008
Late Evening

54

The room's getting warm with so many people in it. And it's interesting words Rooster uses when he says he wants Ghost to pay him back too. I don't let my surprise for that show. I'm still tripping on the showdown with Blanco.

On my life, the last person I thought I'd see when that door opened was him, and that forced me to have to reconsider Ghost, like what else don't I know about him if he has a guy like Blanco to reach out to?

I don't take my eyes off Ghost through the whole thing. I know it's him the second I see him. He's five-eight and brown, like the description said. Wood brown and weathered, the way fences get from lots of sun.

He's skinny but muscled. *A fighter*, I'm thinking. With his puffy boxer's eyebrows from old scar tissue and his sharp eyes underneath, the type where you know he's thinking all the time. Weighing odds. Trying to shift things and maybe make it so you don't know it's him doing the shifting.

What's off about him is the dark circles under both eyes. Big ones, almost like black eyes from getting punched. They make him look all worn-out, like the world is heavy, but also like killing him is the only thing that will ever make him stop fighting.

He's no joke. I watch his eyes all throughout the negotiation and exchange between Rooster and Blanco. Agitation, I seen. Nervousness too. What I didn't see much of was fear.

It was mostly acceptance. I mean, he didn't even look upset when Blanco gave him up. He knows how this is about to end. He's known for a while. I can tell just by looking in his eyes. They look tired but ready, like whatever it is we're about to do to him will finally be an opportunity to rest.

That messes with me too, since I know how exhausting it is to put plans together, to put things in place to be able to roll out at a moment's notice, to have to keep heavy secrets from crashing down.

Just looking at him, I see how he knows all that the same way I do. What I'm guessing the only difference is, is that I have people close to me, sharing my everyday, and he don't. He's got books and records in boxes. He's pure solo when Blanco sells him out.

Blanco saying what he said about warrants tells me Collins put my addresses in, and by the time they came back out the other side, Ghost knew every one.

I been trying to think of who might be able to pass that information on, but it's just a waste of time. It don't matter. That's a done deal. What matters now is what happens next, and what Rooster means when he says he needs Ghost to pay him back.

I'm fidgeting where I'm standing, feeling the barrel of the gun getting warm against my tailbone, just waiting for his response.

We all are. It feels like the whole room's waiting on a cliff-hanger.

So I guess it's funny how the next thing to come out of Ghost isn't actually words. It's blood. His nose just starts bleeding all down his front.

Terco looks like he can't even believe it. He's about to blow up and lose it, but that don't change that it's happening, that Ghost's just sitting there, about to drip all over the living room carpet.

Ghost

Monday, September 15, 2008

Late Evening

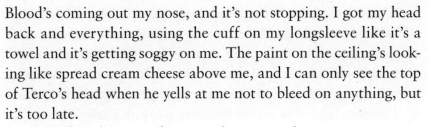

Blood's coming out my nose, and it's not stopping. I got my head back and everything, using the cuff on my longsleeve like it's a towel and it's getting soggy on me. The paint on the ceiling's looking like spread cream cheese above me, and I can only see the top of Terco's head when he yells at me not to bleed on anything, but it's too late.

Dabs drip down my face, my chin. Onto the carpet.

Terco says, "Fuck!"

And right then I know which one is the clean freak around here. Maybe it's not by design. Maybe it's just the dude Terco is.

"Get him a towel," Rooster says.

The top of Terco's head goes away and I hear him stomp off down the hall to the linen closet with the empty-ass safe in it. Soon after, I've got a big brown fluffy thing stuffed in my face too hard.

I almost laugh that it's brown, because of course he picked that color so I don't stain it.

I decide to sit.

Why this is going down right now, I don't know. I mean, I've definitely been up for hours and hours. I've not been drinking much water. Could be that the Santa Anas' dryness is hanging around in the air. Could be the tumor giving up and popping or something. But if that happened, my whole brain would go with it. And I can see. I can hear. I'm not fuzzy or nothing. I'm just bleeding, all down the front of myself.

Rooster's standing above me now, not smirking exactly, but almost. Close enough to reach down and choke me, stab me, whatever. My throat's exposed too. *Oh, well*, I'm thinking. *At least it'll be quick if he does something.*

He says, "How'd you manage not to blow your ass up in Rancho?"

Rancho San Pedro Projects, he means. The safe with the $887,000 and the dynamite dust in it. And I don't know why Rooster's playing it like this. Maybe he's trying to throw me off or something, because this is all preamble. That's a Frank word. To him, it means a bunch of dummies saying dumb stuff before they finally talk around to the important shit. And me and Rooster both know we're about to play Let's Make a Crazy-Ass Deal where I basically give him everything in exchange for going out easy.

"Oh," I say it muffled, because I'm saying it around the towel. "Was that for me? I'm flattered as hell, man. Thank you."

I don't tell him I actually missed the explosives in the safe door the first time, or that Collins had to point it out to me later. Hell no. Besides, there's no way those Dracula-teeth explosives in that safe were for me. For DEA maybe. For another crew trying to steal, maybe. But no point in coming at me. They know this. Because if it's not me, it's Frank or it's Glenn fucking Rios driving his ass into town from San Bernardino. DEA will always get somebody. They never stop coming.

But Rooster keeps going. "How'd you do it, though?"

I get it. He's the type that likes to know things, likes scaring people enough to tell him. But fuck him. I pull the towel off my face and more blood just comes out, goes down over my mouth before jumping off my chin. I smirk through it. Not like it's the first time. Any boxer that ever boxed enough knows what his own tastes like.

"I'm a professional," I say, and then, under my breath loud enough so everybody hears it, "dumb motherfucker."

I don't see the punch coming. I see a flash of black on my right, duck a little but not enough, and my whole world explodes.

I'm flat on my back in an instant. Ears ringing and all.

There's a banging in my blood as my cheekbone's screaming red alerts at my brain. I feel the pain bounce around me on my pulse, each and every heartbeat, going as far back as the base of my neck. It's a fiery thing inside me as I'm rolling over onto my side and pushing myself back up to sitting. I shake my head to get the cobwebs off me, but that just puts more of my blood everywhere, which doesn't make the pain any better, just makes Terco curse again.

In my peripherals, one of the linebackers is shaking his hand out because it must have hurt punching my hard head, while Terco's staring death stares at my bloodstains on the carpet. He's more mad at them than me. Good. Fuck him too.

"No call for that." Rooster's sitting back on the couch now.

I say, "You got the blood of an officer of the court all over a known drugs house. There's no explaining that to them. And why'd anyone even bother with that shit in Rancho? If it explodes, nobody's business goes good after that. DEA kicks doors for a year on nothing but some bullshit. Smart guy like you, you'd never do that."

Rooster says to me, "You got a mouth sewn onto you."

But we both know I'm not wrong.

I shrug. I test my nose. I'm not bleeding as much from there so I bring the towel down and tilt my head back to normal.

"I kill it at parties," I say.

I'm getting looks now. Like, *How can you be so chill?* Terco's wondering. I can see it. Glasses too. The linebackers only wonder if Rooster tells them to wonder.

The answer is, I don't fucking care anymore.

I'm scared, sure. Scared like I'm wired up and steady electricity's going through me, but most of what I've been scared about my whole life is the unknown. Now I got a bunch of knowns standing in front of me, and I don't care what they do to me. My body, they can kill. They only have power over my mind and my spirit if

I let them. They can never have those. Not even shreds. They can't take what's invisible unless I straight up give it to them. And that's not me being brave. That's just a truth of human existence. The kind of thing they've been saying at group since forever.

Because, see, I already *been* dying before. Been on operating tables. Been shot. Been chemo-ed. Overdosed three damn times. *So, fuck it,* I'm thinking, *what's one more?* They're getting me this time, and when they do, it'll just be doing me and the world a big-ass favor.

Glasses leans over Rooster by the couch. They're taking a time-out for a conversation. Some, I'm catching. Most I'm not. They're talking about how I'm not the type that gets beat and tells anything about anybody and something-something, I don't catch the word. And they're back to talking about how if I was that type to talk, they both figure, Blanco would've made me and then he'd have the Rancho money right now to himself. Rooster's looking at his hat in his hands, and then he's looking at me. His eyes are saying my life isn't worth what I owe.

A few whispers go back and forth that I don't catch after that, and then Glasses steps back and Rooster says, "I need the list."

I could try to negotiate on this, drag it out. But there's no point. They'd just shut all their shit down anyways. They're probably even doing it right now. So I give him the list. One address I struggle remembering. I try to find it in my head, but it's not there. So to cover up on that, I start spelling street names of the ones I know and get told to shut the fuck up. Glasses writes it all down.

I only gave them three. They don't ask for more.

After, I say, "I see how you run things here. It's a good spot. Clean as hell. And I've been in a lot of these over the years. Would be a shame not to keep franchising it."

They're all waiting for me to get to the point, so I do. "You got a *ratón* creeping around, telling tales."

Rooster's interested. Every boss's interested in hearing about that, but he's eyeing me like an actor, all like he doesn't believe me for the benefit of the rat if he's in this room right now.

"That's a problem I can't help you with," I say. "I don't know who it is. But I know this house never gets made without someone telling on it."

Rooster's not going to say anything to that.

He's been thinking it already. I can tell.

"Get him to his car," Rooster says as he's turning for the door. "Make him drive."

56

This is a problem. I had a whole speech planned in my head. About how I was going to convince them to let me drive myself to San Pedro. Because if you kill an officer of the court, I'm on record, and how the authorities don't forgive that, and how there's nothing but nonstop running afterward for whoever did it. Because they'll come for you. And I was going to talk about the ways to avoid that, the ways to give me some freedom, but then Rooster wants me out in my Jeep, and driving for some reason, and to where? And then I have to play it like a rag doll and just go limp on the carpet I already speckled with blood.

Because fuck dignity. *¡Sin vergüenza!*

They want to kill me somewhere else, they'll have to carry me out of here. They might even have to knock my ass out first. It's not like they can't do it, though. Not like the linebackers don't have it in them. But that doesn't mean I have to make it easy. And for what it's worth, Lil Garfield's still in the house, and he comes out of nowhere, because he must be thinking I'm playing or something, so he walks right over to me and stands on my chest. So I pet his bumpy skull. Because fuck it, why not? When am I ever going to get to pet a cat again?

Never, that's when.

And he's warm and furry and soft, and I'm memorizing how that feels on my fingers, and watching him closing his eyes like he trusts me, just wanting to chill in this moment and lock it up inside me.

Rooster walks back over from the door, his face going red above me when he leans down and says, "You're a thinker. You like being one, and you think you're smarter than anybody. So, I got to ask, you spent any of your thought time wondering why I'm still here?"

He opens his eyes wide at me to emphasize how I've been an idiot.

And I'm thinking, *Shit*. I'm thinking, *No*. I haven't thought about that.

But I should have.

He keeps going. "Blanco's gone. Shouldn't I be? Because what's left for you is just a cleanup job, no? And you *know* I'm not about to be near that."

He's not wrong.

Things are clicking in my head but not connecting, not falling into place, and all's I'm coming up with is he's got something he needs from me. And I *know* that's true. The thought falls out of my brain and catches in my throat quick. It goes cold and hard inside my neck, this feeling. Like I swallowed an ice cube and it got stuck.

I still have one hand on Lil Garfield. And he's purring now. I feel the vibrations of it inside my lungs. I wish I could sink into it and disappear. But a new thought won't let me go. A heavy one.

"You need me for a job," I say to Rooster. With my free hand, I'm rubbing the cheek that one of the linebackers mashed. I don't think it's broken, just about to be bruised purple and swollen two sizes too big. "But I'm not about to be killing anybody. You can just shoot me now if that's what you want."

Last, do no harm. I can't go out any other way.

When I go out, I go out clean.

All five of them laugh right then.

And that's when the stuff that's been clicking around in my head actually snaps together into something: Nobody here is stupid enough to kill an officer of the court in a drugs house that's on the record. That's never going to happen.

"No." Rooster's looking at me like he pities me. "Something else."

What that something else is, Rooster's not going to say, and neither is anybody else. It's one of those things I'll have to see when I get there.

"Something about to get me out of debt, huh? That's cool," I say.

I'm playing, but I'm not. There's just a little bit of hope in what I'm saying, because I'm thinking that whatever this is must be a big deal, big enough for Rooster to need it, and if he needs it, maybe I got more room to negotiate and somehow twist this back my way.

But all five of them laugh again. Like, *No*. Like, *Forget it. This's not about to get you out of that debt. Not even close. But you're doing it even if we have to drag you.*

And you know I'm not moving from where I'm sprawled out, so they do.

The two linebackers come over to me, they both take hold, pulling my hands off Lil G and my cheek, and right before I'm lifted into the air, a shocked Lil G opens wide eyes—one green, one blue— digs his claws into me, and jumps off, scratching me good.

I don't even mean to, but I say, "Damn!"

Because I think he drew blood under my shirt. But that doesn't matter now.

I'm up and floating and I'm helpless, getting carried through the living room air by both linebackers. This's what drugs used to do to me, but worse. They'd puppet my ass all over the place. *This isn't the worst it's ever been for me*, I'm thinking.

But it's really fucking close.

The linebackers have got an arm and a leg each and I got my head all the way back, watching the house upside down through the front door as Terco stays. He's already got gloves on. And a yellowy sponge. And a white bottle. Bleach.

And he's kneeling by my blood, about to make it all go away.

57

Outside by the garage, I'm light enough that one of the linebackers drops my right foot, keeps holding the top half of me up with one arm, and opens the driver's door of my Jeep. Both of them kind of hoist me up and shove me in the front seat after that, but when they do, I just keep doing what I've been doing, acting like I never had any bones in my whole life, and I just slide down into the place where your feet are supposed to go.

The back door opens and Glasses gets in behind me. He wants to get this show on the road. Needs to. Because Rooster said so.

You can tell because Glasses hisses right near my ears when he says, "I need you to sit up and be a man."

I laugh.

He doesn't like that very much.

See, Glasses must be used to these kinds of things working on people that want to keep living. And I just need to keep making it clear to him that I didn't care in the first place, and I sure as hell don't care now, and what's even funnier is that he thinks I'm just playing tough. I mean, he must be thinking that because that's when the cold mouth of a pistol that I never even seen him with cuddles up to the side of my head.

It's a wide O of a mouth. High caliber.

He pushes it into me, right on my temple, hard. Like he's trying to bruise me with it. Teach me a lesson. I can't see his face, but I know he's frustrated and mad.

So of course I laugh again, because that's me getting to him, and I say, "This's not about to make me sit up, Gafas. C'mon, man. Act like you done this before. Rooster's waiting."

And Glasses has *got* to know that I'm not about to drive us somewhere quiet so I can get shot through the head and be dead on my steering wheel, honking a horn for people to wake up to. No thanks.

Both linebackers are just staring at me like they don't know how to fix me and make me obey. I like that. This shit is almost comical.

We pass a few seconds like this, obviously with Glasses thinking about what to do, how to make sure I get where I'm supposed to be, and he must make up his mind about how that's happening, because the gun goes away.

"Backseat," Glasses says to the linebackers as he gets out.

He's switching to the front, about to be the one driving instead of me. I don't have much time to celebrate that little victory because I'm getting yanked out and thrown in the back, smashing my leg on the doorframe in the process. It hurts like a little explosion in my kneecap but I don't say anything. Don't give Glasses the satisfaction. I just slide right back down again, holding my cheek where I caught that punch.

"Make him sit straight," Glasses says to the bigger guy.

The door across from me opens and the dude gets in. The only way he can think to sit me up is to grab me around my shoulders like he's half hugging me. I slump against him. I can tell he hates it but he does it. He snags my keys from my pocket too, hands them between the seats, and Glasses starts her up.

The beginning of "Demolition Girl" jumps on the speakers. The Saints.

It's the beginning bit right after the *one, two, three, four* all good punk songs need to have.

Lyrics come in, all about how I'll be so sad I was Rose's. How she'll make me cry. How she'll make me wish I could die.

All of it was true.

All of it except the line about how she wouldn't let go till she was through. That never happened. When she was through, Rose never let go of me. She stayed with me. On magnetic tape. And inside me. All this time.

"Hey," Glasses says from the driver's seat, "I bet you wanna listen to this, huh?"

My heart spikes up quick inside me, thinking how if I show him it means anything to me, he'll destroy it, throw it out the window or something just to get at me, so I don't move.

I just meet his eyes in the rearview, right where he's staring at me, trying to see if he can find another way to fuck with me, to hurt me.

And I don't say shit.

I just smile. A real one. One, like, *You can't hurt me*. Like, *You can't touch me. I'm here and I'm not here*, my eyes are saying. And I'm just trying to stare into whatever soul he has till Glasses blinks at me and looks away, uncomfortable.

"Whatever," he says.

The tape goes off, the radio comes on, and we drive.

Glasses

Monday, September 15, 2008
Late Evening

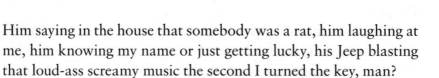

Him saying in the house that somebody was a rat, him laughing at me, him knowing my name or just getting lucky, his Jeep blasting that loud-ass screamy music the second I turned the key, man?

I swear, in my whole life, I never wanted to blast somebody so much as this motherfucker right here in his own backseat. Having the gun on his head like that, it felt good to me. If felt like it'd only be a little thing to pull the trigger.

Hey, if anybody deserved to take him out, it should be me, that's what I was thinking. I wanted to make him true to his name so bad, and I would have too. The only thing stopping me was Rooster, how he'd feel about that if I did it, how he said he needed him alive, and how he'd know for sure I was the traitor for doing it.

I bet I could just say Frank's name and Ghost would straighten right the fuck up, but I can't do it. And that's messing with me. I know keeping that information in my back pocket is smart, but I'm also caught up in something that's feeling like respect, seeing as I'm still tripping on how Blanco sold him out, how Ghost looked like he *expected* it and still made it out of there alive. That shit was a miracle.

I'm hearing Leya in my head now. How I need to quit with the cursing. How I need to slow down. How I need to watch and think.

There's a tap at the driver's-side window so I roll it down. It's Big Danny.

He says, "You good?"

When I nod, he gives me a address and tells me to follow the 300.

Lonely says if I lose them, he can navigate me. He knows the spot. He's been there before. I haven't, which makes me wonder what it is exactly and why Lonely's been there but I haven't.

I say, "What type of spot is it?"

"Storage."

This could mean anything, prolly even that Lonely's hauled stuff there before, but rather than ask for more, I let it drop. I'm too busy adjusting my glasses on my head and pulling out on Clark.

The ROAD CLOSED sign and cones have been taken away and the brake lights of the 300 look super shiny in the night. Already I feel a headache coming on, so I close my right eye. It's not good for depth but it's good for me actually being able to get us somewhere.

To Lonely, I say, "How far is it?"

"Not far, like ten minutes."

I'm not happy having to drive at night like this but I'm not about to be holding Ghost up instead. What I'm feeling right now is, I'm dreading how this's gonna turn out. This Ghost is the first person I've feared in a long time.

Normally, I know what's happening or how things will break down. With him, I feel out of control, like I might do or say something I wouldn't usually. He's throwing me off.

I'm rolling windows down as I take us the back way to the 710 on Clark, right on Millrace, left on Carlin, right on Olanda, left on Gibson, left on Rosecrans. I'm getting dizzy a little, sweating even. Ghost's got his eyes on me the whole way too, studying me.

I'm figuring by now that Collins got my message and DEA aren't coming, but right now I'm second-guessing my call, thinking I should've told them to come and arrest everybody and me too.

Ghost dropping the bomb about somebody being a rat in the room? Man, it was just over at that point.

Terco's gonna clean and go. They all are. The houses won't just close temporarily now. It'll be permanent.

Business will shift, and what's burning in me is how I set Terco up so nice for a fall and now everything is falling but him. Everything I've been building for months is gone. This whole parachute I'm putting together for myself? It burned up around me tonight.

The dog will have no busts, no dope on the table, no money, and he will be hungrier than he's ever been after so many meals set up right in front of him got taken away. He'll eat somebody after that and it's gonna be me if Leya don't grab those call logs out of the safe.

The worry of her forgetting hits me hard. *If Felix was crying or fussy with getting taken to the car,* I'm thinking, *it would've been easy not to check twice that she had everything.* The thought of it just balls my stomach up.

I've got to call her somehow, to check and make sure she has them, but it's not possible right now, not with Lonely in the backseat holding Ghost up. I reach for my pocket but my antacids aren't there.

I left them at home in my jacket, except I have to remind myself now how that house isn't my home anymore and that's all on some safecracker sitting in the backseat right now, looking smug as shit.

Ghost

Tuesday, September 16, 2008
Early Morning

59

We're in Carson, I think. At one of them office parks with nothing but one-level buildings filled with orange-doored storage units as big as car garages, and we're pulling through the guarded front gate after Rooster's car, and Glasses is nodding at the dude and the guy just straight shuts it down. Puts the little gate down behind us, turns the lights out in his booth, and walks away from it. Nobody else getting in now.

But we're way outside of business hours anyways. This place closed at 1800, and it's going on 0138 in the morning now. My dash clock says so. It's bouncing as we're going over speed bumps to the back of the lot, into this alley of units that only faces a concrete wall about a hundred feet long and twelve feet high.

Besides the one carrying Rooster, two other cars are here, some old Chevy and one of those ageless Toyota trucks that never stops running no matter how much you beat on them and make them carry shit. Frank calls them modern-day mules. Anyways, the lights of both of those are pointed at a garage unit that the other linebacker is opening right as we pull up, and as the door

slides up, disappearing into the building and I can see what's inside, I finally get it.

Well, what I get first is chills going up and down my back and
neck, all over my head too, and right after, I know they're not
about to kill me.

They *need* me.

And I'm sitting up now because I know I'm not about to end
up dead in a Lynwood alley after all.

At least, not yet. Not here.

See, inside this storage garage is more safes than I ever seen in
one tiny place before. Not even a showroom. It's safes on top of
safes. Stacked up three high, and I'm looking at them like they're
the Egyptian pyramids and I'm thinking, *How the fuck did they
even* do *that?*

It's sinking in why Rooster was asking me all those questions
about safes before. He wants me to *open* these for him. And maybe
some that might be booby-trapped. And it's making even more
sense why the linebackers are with us, not just to deal with my dumb
ass, but mainly to lift some heavy shit.

I'm getting out of the car, on my own steam. Frank's phrase.

Rooster's walking up, his hat down real low over his eyes,
saying, "Make sure homeboy has a socket for his drills."

And then, looking over to me and up a little, with the same
first smile I ever saw him with, he says, "Time to do what you do."

We're talking twenty safes, maybe thirty.

Hours of work. The ultimate marathon.

Now that he's showing me what he wants to show me, Rooster's
got a different tune to him. He's lighter, more relaxed.

He says, "You need some water or anything? You hungry?"

"Sure," I say, still feeling fuzzy looking at all these safes in
front of me—a bunch of Sentries, some American Securities—but
smart enough to know this might be my last meal, though where
the hell is open this time of night around here, I don't even know.
Norms maybe.

I say, "Where'd you even get all these?"

Rooster nods at one of the linebackers to go take orders and
grab food, then turns to look at the safe stacks with me, the two

of us putting long shadows over the open cave of the garage while an extension cord gets plugged in and spooled out all the way to my feet and dropped with a little clack.

"Here and there," he says.

So I come back with "I'm going to need fifty percent of any cash and gold I pull out of these."

Rooster laughs.

"So," I say, "forty then. Look, I got no use for the other metals, no gems, no guns, no dope. Straight cash and gold, that's it. If there isn't any, I don't get any."

Rooster looks to Glasses and says, "This one, owes large and still thinks he can be the one negotiating."

They stare at me. Together.

But I know something they don't know I know. See, a lot of safes went missing in the '92 riots. And I know me and Frank flat out refused to open stuff when it didn't have papers or the people coming in asking seemed shady as hell. I'd always heard there were some janitors out there during the riots who just didn't give a fuck. They were more than happy to tell crews where safes were, even unlock gates and doors, let people in, and point them out. And that information got acted on. I'm standing here staring at the living proof. Every last one of these is stolen. Guaranteed. There was only one problem with that, though. Once you got them out, you had to get them *open*.

Obviously, they didn't figure out that part. Shit. It's obvious they've been trying, for *years*, to get these popped, and nobody could ever do that for them till tonight.

And now that they got me, they're going to need to pay for my services.

"For me it's simple," I say. "How many years have these been sitting? More than a decade, at least. So, how long was it really before you gave up on a more private office space with a bigger door and more storage and just dumped them here in an eight-by-twenty garage? I bet you couldn't believe your luck when you heard about me getting wild tonight. You saw the angle *quick*."

Rooster's not saying anything, but his eyes are. They're angry at me for seeing him, for seeing *through* him.

"Forty percent," I say, "or you can just kill me right here and these motherfuckers stay closed forever."

The game just got real.

Everybody knows it.

The eyes of this crew are on me hard now, and on Rooster too. They're going back and forth like ping-pong. I got sweat creeping up on my lower back. I got both linebackers and Glasses and the silhouettes from the other cars all looking at me and itching to do whatever Rooster says.

And when he sniffs, they shift.

Like it was almost a command. Almost.

Rooster looks at his fingernails. "You really don't want to live, do you?"

I decide to be honest. A hundred percent.

"I'm not living anyways, so whether I do this or not doesn't matter to me." Then I lower my voice and keep it lowered, just for us. "I got cancer. Brain tumors, back for more. Couldn't get enough of me when I was younger, I guess."

Rooster's looking at me like he already knows this. "Okay, so what's the money for? Where's it all going?"

That's Rooster. The dude needs his whys.

"Families," I say. "It's paying off houses."

He shoots me a look then. Like, *You* cannot *be serious!*

But I am. And he sees that and shakes his head.

So that's when I say, "I need something else too."

"You're just full of those tonight," he says, and he's not exactly gritting his teeth, but he's close. The important thing is, though, he's lowering his voice too.

So it's just us now.

"I do this for you," I say, "and you let me drive myself down south."

He's not even looking at me now. "Where you looking to drive, thief?"

"San Pedro." For Rose. But I don't say that. "Everybody knows the cancer's back. My boss. DEA. FBI. Everybody. They've all seen how I've been acting weird lately. Uncharacteristic, they'd say."

Rooster's not saying stop, so I keep going.

"You let me drive my own way down to Pedro, and I'll kill my own damn self. You can send people with me to make sure I do it. After, there's no questions. No investigation. Cops think I got depressed and killed myself over the disease. It's the perfect crime. Nobody in your crew catches a charge. Business keeps going. You got my obituary to hold up to anybody that knows I took what I took in Rancho."

He cuts in with "That doesn't pay back the money, though, does it?"

"That's sunk cost at this point. Perils of doing business. Besides, you must not've loved that money too much if you had it stuffed in there with the explosives. You were already ready to lose it, I think."

And I don't say why because I don't know why. I don't speculate on how either. I just finish with "And I know you'll just have to pay it back in installments if I can't cover it on your cut of what I bust out of these."

I wave a halfhearted hand at the safe stacks. Like, *Only if I feel like opening these.* And I keep going, voice low, "But if you at least let me do it my way, you'll have something way more useful: the story of it."

He screws his face up then, like, *Fuck you.* Like, *Stories are worthless.*

But I'm on it, still keeping it down so nobody else hears, "Dude like you already knows how that's the best thing out of all this. I mean, nobody needs to know I'm dying. Just think of the story your people will be spreading after this. How you talked an officer of the fucking court into killing himself after giving up those raid addresses because that's how damn cunning you are. How psychological. You got a guy to do himself so nobody in your crew would go to jail for it. That's criminal-mastermind shit right there. That's untouchable crime. Crime done with the mind. You'll be a legend."

I know this appeals to someone that doesn't even carry his own cell phone for safety's sake, but this is me just priming him for the knockout, aiming straight for his ego.

"And I bet that story unlocks a lot of doors for you. I mean, people wouldn't be talking about Blanco beating some kids with a baseball bat twenty years later then, would they? They'd be talking"—I pause here, building up just the right amount of anticipation before saying—"about *you*."

I swear, I don't even have to watch that fly through the air between us and land on him. I *know* it sinks in. Heavy. Deep. He's looking down. Furrowing his brow, I'm sure. And in a hot second, he's sniffing and smirking, and right then I can already see it. How the story has him. How it's grabbing him and lifting him up inside.

I don't go on about how they can make you. Rooster knows this one can turn him into a king. All he has to do is give me that dignity to do what I need to do myself. Just me going out, not hurting anybody but me. How clean that'd be. How good.

"Twenty percent," Rooster finally says to me, and puts his hand out before whispering, "and just so we're clear, I'm also going to let you keep what you took off my other house tonight too."

"Forty," I say, and shake his hand, "or you can kill me and not get shit. You've never had anybody this good come near these safes, and you never will again either."

His eyebrows go up and I let go. I give him a look that says, *Tell me I'm fucking wrong.* Rooster sniffs and nods at me. He doesn't say anything, but it's forty.

When he does that, and I see my toolboxes get set down in front of me, relief runs up and down my spine like cold spiders with extra legs. Rooster's giving me a look then too, like, *If this were different, I might actually* like *you.*

Glasses

Tuesday, September 16, 2008
Early Morning

60

Lonely's driving to go get everybody food. Normally, I'm not getting sent on runs like these since I'm above that, but I volunteered since he hadn't left by the time Ghost and Rooster had finished negotiating.

I said I was hungry but didn't know what I wanted. Being on the road now gives me some time to think about how Ghost said he wanted to save homes for people, and when I heard it, I didn't believe it, but the more I think about it, there's no other explanation, and I'm not sure how I feel about that, him pulling a ghetto Robin Hood.

What I wonder after that is, how true he is to his word. Ghost killing himself will solve a lot of problems for me, but that's only if he actually pulls a trigger. It'll mean I can go back to Collins and blame it all on Ghost having access, snagging all those addresses, and hitting Rooster before DEA could come.

I can turn it on Collins how there's leaks in his house, and that made everything unsecure, including and especially me. It's not my fault if they can't keep my information safe. That's on them.

On Rooster's end, it looks obvious that it's all Ghost's fault, that those addresses couldn't possibly have come from me. And I'm liking that, since it's no longer about me being suspect. It's about Ghost being wild. It's about how he screwed everything up.

If he does what he said he'd do on top of that, he's giving me my life back. He gets all the blame and I can keep going as I've been going, getting new addresses and feeding them to Collins on *my* schedule. I can even make Terco look like the rat while I'm at it. Then I don't have to be out to Cardiff for real until there's a SWAT team knocking down Rooster's door.

Hey, it could work. But it's all depending on Ghost doing what he said. If he does, it fixes everything. I can drive right to Cardiff and bring Leya back. That'd be good too, seeing as how us disappearing right now is the only thing that would 100 percent convince Rooster I'm the rat.

But if Ghost don't kill himself, I'll have to. Rooster will make sure of it and that's a whole different scenario to deal with, since Collins would never help me if it ever looked like I had anything to do with a body.

All I need to do is talk to Collins. I need to hear a good explanation from him on how he could've gotten the addresses without me, and I'm thinking hard on that until Lonely breaks my quiet.

"I got this alert on my phone."

I ask him what he means by *alert* exactly. Rooster's strict about certain homies never having phones on them, and since Lonely does so much, he's one of them.

"News alerts, that kind of thing."

"You're not even supposed to be carrying your own phone when we do what we do. You know this. It's a smartphone, man! It has trackable GPS!"

"You're right. I shouldn't've brought it. It's just that things happened so fast tonight. I get that call from you while I was in the bathroom, and then I had to dress, and then I'm in the car in a minute, already driving. It's only halfway to your place that I even realize it's in my pocket, and it was too late to turn back then."

His last few words hit me. We go a couple blocks in silence.

"Can't change it now," I say to him.

Lonely pulls up to a red light and hangs his head a little. There's no cars coming the other direction. I'm about to tell him not to tell Rooster about having a phone, that he can maybe just run the battery down and leave it in the trunk of the car, but a cop car pulls up beside us on the driver side.

We're in the middle lane, going straight. They're in the left, going straight. I can see the logo just fine where I'm sitting and it makes me go cold inside.

It's Sheriffs. On my right, I never would've been able to see it, but on my left, I seen it too good. It makes my mouth dry.

I'm looking at the one riding shotgun looking at Lonely, taking in his polo and his shaved head looking straight forward before moving his look to me. It takes a lot to do it, but I nod down at him and do a half smile. He turns away.

And I think we're good since my glasses can be helpful that way sometimes. Nobody up to no good would wear them, I guess. But right then, the sheriff in the shotgun seat says something to the driver, and then the cruiser's roof lights pop on. My heart jumps inside me.

I'm thinking about how I've still got a gun on me. Unregistered. But my heartbeat gets back to normal again when I see they're just running the red and turning the flashers off when they get to the other side of the intersection and speed off.

Me and Lonely look at each other. It wasn't an escape exactly, but we know we're lucky. And Lonely nods at that before frowning.

"This news alert," he says, "it's saying how something happened in Morelia."

The tone he's got makes me worry. He has family from Michoacán too.

I say, "What type of something?"

"A grenade attack."

I still got a aunt there in the capital, my uncle that got deported, my cousins, my grandparents. My mind goes to them, to their faces, to the time I got to visit and eat roast-pork tacos in a dusty backyard before I got my record and couldn't travel. I got a pain in my chest now too. A bad one.

"Seven people dead. They don't know how many hurt, maybe a hundred."

"But it's Independence Day," I say.

"Yeah. Whoever threw those grenades waited until a crowd was in la Plaza de Armas for the *grito* too."

I feel sick at that, a hot type of sick. My voice's high and angry, coming out of me so fast I can't stop it. "So somebody planned throwing grenades at innocent fucking people?"

"Yeah."

I don't have words for a second. I'm just staring at the street ahead of us, the red lights stacking up.

I'm biting my lip so hard I'm drawing blood, but I'm liking the pain, since it's something for how I'm feeling inside. I got Felix in my head now, how his hair smells like peanut butter sometimes, and I put the back of my hand up to my face like the way he does when he sleeps.

"Kids," I say from behind my hand. "Did it kill any little kids?"

"Too early to tell."

"Who did it?" I want to know. I *need* to know.

"Looks like one of the cartels. Nobody's sure which yet."

"Well, if there's maybe a who, then there's prolly a why, right?"

"Calderón's from Morelia," Lonely says. "There's a theory on how attacking there might force him to rethink how he's doing his drug war."

Felipe Calderón, *pinche* president of *pinche* Mexico, is who Lonely means, a target sitting however many miles away in DF when it happened. This type of thing, it wasn't aimed at his body. It was pointed at his heart, his soul, not just his, but at all of ours, and it still hit.

I say, "This was some terrorist shit."

We stop at another red.

"Yeah," Lonely says after a while.

Hey, this right here, it's a line that just got crossed. I feel it. Innocent people? In public? *On purpose?* That's straight out of bounds. It's the type of thing I prayed would never happen, but now we're here. It happened. The world's different now.

You put people in barrels long enough and get away with it,

eventually you must get to thinking that you can do whatever, whenever, wherever, to whoever, and that won't matter to anybody. Fuck.

The whole world just stepped over a line it never should've crossed, and I feel it moving me over one too, just the opposite way. I got Lonely's words from earlier bouncing around nonstop in my brain. *It was too late to turn back then.*

I'm feeling that, since I can't turn back now either. I can't go back to being a double agent or whatever it is when both sides think you are one. I can't set this all back up again.

Can't wait for new houses to come back up and be moving product again. Can't keep doing it like I've been doing. I need out.

I need the money unfrozen right now and making that happen means making Collins happy. I need to give him all I can give him and be done. There's no other way to be out. But I already know something else needs to happen first.

I need to make sure Ghost does what he says he'll do, for my sake, and then I'm gone for good. I have to be.

Ghost

Tuesday, September 16, 2008
Early Morning

61

Food from Norms comes without anybody asking me what I wanted. There's all sorts of stuff. Burgers, mostly. The turkey. The Cowboy BBQ. Those go quick. There's quesadillas, even a couple green chile and chickens, but all those go too before I can pick one. I'm last, which makes sense. I get stuck with the ultimate meat loaf and I don't even like the mushrooms it's topped with, so I scrape them off, but fuck it, what am I going to do? Complain? At least it's still halfway hot.

Glasses is the one who brings it over to me as I'm scoping out the safes, and he's got this look on his face like if it were up to him, I'd starve, but Rooster comes with him, so he keeps his mouth shut. It's just the three of us. Away from the others eating off hoods of cars and trucks.

Rooster didn't grab a container. *A guy like that, he doesn't eat Norms*, I'm thinking. He's above it. When he eats a steak, it's Dal Rae or something. It's Pacific Dining Car. Maybe even San Franciscan if he's into prime rib. A guy like that travels all over town. You can tell. To wherever the good shit is. It's not like how it used to be, growing up in the same eighteen blocks and never going anywhere. Now the city's wider, and if you got the money, it'll give you whatever you want.

"I know I don't got a right to ask anything else of you," I say to Rooster, "but this bad-loans shit that's coming down, it's going to wipe a lot of people out. A lot of families. It's a tidal wave coming."

Keep talking, Rooster's look says, but I might be misreading it.

I go on anyways, with Glasses staring at me, not blinking.

"Pay off some houses for folks." When I say *folks*, I'm hearing in my head how it's a Frank word too. "It might only be a few thousand here or there. I'm hearing a lot of shit will go into foreclosures and you can scoop it up cheap. But, just, if you could, help the people that need helping. That deserve it. The others? Just be watching because a lot of people are about to drown."

Glasses is staring at the ground now like it's about to jump up and run away. Rooster shifts his weight from one foot to the other. I overstepped. I feel it.

I mean, Rooster's face is stone and it's making that real clear. It's telling me I had a right to negotiate when it was about me, and he let me, but this, talking to him about his business, suggesting he do something like charity without getting something in return, is just plain stupid.

"I'm not saying it's for free, just—"

Rooster looks to Glasses and they both make the same frowning face before Rooster turns and waves his hand at a figure standing over by the truck lights where everybody's eating.

"All right," I say to the back of his head, as a way of saying, *This is me shutting up now*, because I get it. I tried to give him a heads-up, and he's not taking it, and that's okay. That's up to him.

The silhouette becomes a person when it gets closer. And it starts looking familiar too. It's a guy. And when he's about fifteen feet away from us, I can tell it's the little homie from the first house me and Blanco hit earlier tonight. The one getting down with the girl. When he's a few feet away, I can still see zip cuff marks on the kid's wrists.

He sees me seeing them and nods at me, like, *Yup*. Like, *That's where we know each other from.*

Rooster knows this. This is him giving the kid an opportunity to redeem himself.

And this close, with the two of them standing side by side, I can see the resemblances. They're obviously related, probably cousins, not brothers, and the kid is about twenty years younger than Rooster. A younger, handsomer version with sharper cheekbones and some greenish eyes.

"We need a little one of you running around, safecracker," Rooster says to me. "This is Lil Tricky. Teach him up."

My first thought is *Hell no.* Mainly because it's impossible to learn to do what I do in a day. I mean, even if I knew how to explain it, I couldn't teach it. My second thought is *I'm not going to, because that's not the deal I shook on.*

Rooster doesn't care about any of that, though. Because he's already walking away with Glasses, the two talking for a few seconds before Rooster gets in a car. It pulls out right afterwards. He's getting the hell away from here, which is smart.

And I'll never see him again. I know this.

But his word is his word.

And I'm going to have to trust on it to somehow get whatever I pull out of these to Mira at our drop-off.

62

When everybody's done eating, the linebackers take turns going Q*bert and climbing up onto the pyramid, putting their whole weights behind safes and pushing them off the top row, smashing them straight onto the ground. Three-hundred-plus pounds coming down with sharp edges from four or five feet high. Yeah. That'll bust your concrete up pretty good. Each one landing is loud too. Car-crash loud.

But then again, it's not my floor. And whatever fall guy they got listed on this paperwork is about to get sued for this, but Rooster'd never care. This kind of shit doesn't touch him. The rental agreement is definitely in someone else's name. A guy like Rooster is too careful for that. He doesn't even carry his own phone.

When a safe is down, the linebackers both fight it out of the divot it just made, place the door facing up to the sky, and go get another one to line up next to it.

This is how it goes.

When it comes time to get to work, it's like my brain is thanking me, because I don't have to think. I can just let my hands go. Get relaxed. Get into a rhythm. Not worry about what comes after. Just do the work.

Thirty-one safes are in two side-by-side storage spots.

I can't believe it myself.

Twelve of them got fucked up so bad by terrible crack jobs that they're completely inoperable. Frank word. Work done not just by amateurs, but by idiots. Making it obvious Rooster had somebody try to crack them. Nobody any good, though.

But I guess it makes sense. There wasn't even an Internet giving advice on shit like this to anybody that could read in '92. Still, there are haphazard holes all up and down the sides, trying to drill hinges, and that's just on the old ones—before safe designers got smart and put them all on the inside. The worst ones, though, are the ones that got blowtorched. Got one safe looking like a dalmatian dog it's got so many damn spots on it, but the worst is from when they took the torch to some mechanisms and basically got the tumblers so hot they all melted together. Oops. Maybe you can get in by blowing them, but I'm not about to be that guy, especially with Collins finding explosives in a safe door not all that long ago. So like I said, inoperable. Forever. Dumbasses.

Nineteen left to see what I can salvage.

Ten of these are drop safes. That means they have little drawers or slots at the top so you can deposit money into them. You close the drawer or the door and the money *drops*, down a hole into the locked safe. It's possible these came out of restaurants, but are more than likely from bars. Two are old as hell, good old U.S.A. steel from the 1950s or '60s.

I do these first. Not showing this little Tricky kid shit. I pop six of them when I'm asking him to get a random tool for me before he figures out I'm actually waiting till his back's turned to do it. I just mix it up afterwards. He's hyped about it. Going back and forth. Always asking to use my scope to see in, but even when I let him, I don't tell him what he's looking at. It's what Frank used to do to me. To test me. To see how much I could actually pick up on my own. I had three years of that.

Glasses does inventories and runs math. He types it all up in his phone.

From the first six we get more jewelry than I expected. Weird for drop safes. Lots of stone necklaces and rings. All of it looking old. None of it looking like anything I can shift to Mira. One is nothing but cash and gold coins, though. And that alone makes this worth it. I make the coins easy for Glasses. Out of every five, I get two. The take on that is four hundred gold coins in their little plastic containers. I don't know enough about pressings and what-not to fight for certain years, so the ones Glasses parcels out just go in my Jeep. The cash take on all six of these safes is damn good at $632,000, nearly half of it in little paper-banded $1,000 bundles. It was a little more but I just told him to round up to the nearest whole. Of that, I get $252,800, which is more houses.

And even better, that's me nearly paid off to Rooster.

The next two are gun safes. Stand-ups. Six feet. They aren't easy, which is good. Because I make a show of it. I blow through six drill bits on those, and the punches never take because I'm too busy making sure they don't take. Last, do no harm. I'm not about to hand these fuckers a bunch of untraceable guns, so I spout about the kinds of locks they are and get real technical. I also get frustrated and loud. I make it clear how I hate wasting time when I could be popping the littler ones. Eventually, even Glasses agrees that I should just open the others.

When that's decided, I rest.

Six down. Two gun safes I messed up on purpose so no one else can ever open them. Eight done total.

Everybody else breaks then too. The safes are all lined up. Breakfast food is coming by, but I don't need any.

What time it is, I got no idea. Past four in the morning, probably, because I'm sitting on the hood of my Jeep and lying back flat and watching the sky going that kind of color where black is letting go of the night and what you're left with is just this dark gray hugging onto purple. And I'm so tired I'm a little sick to my stomach, and my eyelids are heavy, man.

I could sleep. Right here. Right now.

But something inside me is saying, *Nope.* Saying, *Don't you dare. You got to be down by that ocean*, it's saying.

And I'm up again, and I'm taking the coffee Lil Tricky brings over with too much cream in it, and I start hitting a flow then.

I mean, I'm just *on.*

Like, I walk up on one and just Jedi the shit out of it. I must punch it in under two minutes all by myself. Everybody's staring at me from the cars, faces full of food, or mouths hanging open, but they don't know I've popped a Sentry just like it probably a hundred times, and I know the guts of it by feel. I can picture how it's built exactly inside my head, and I know where the little moats around the mechanism are, and I just go right into it and make my space and then, *bam*, I'm making miracles happen.

Glasses puts his English-muffin sandwich down, comes over, and does numbers on the phone.

The rest are the rest. When they go, it feels like they're falling like dominoes, one going down just gives me momentum into the next one, and the next, and the next.

And my arms and legs are so tired from putting all my weight on my drill that I don't even know how I can stand up anymore, but I'm in this zone, and magic just keeps happening. And the office safes are done, and the drop safes are done, and the gun safes are staying fucked, and there's nothing left except for a bunch of openmouthed safes lined up in a row like dead whales on a beach.

Out of one comes papers, old letters. Years and years of tax forms. Basically, a whole lot of nothing.

Out of another comes something that looks like maybe it's cash at first, but it's really old-looking stock certificates and U.S. Treasury bonds. I try to fight Glasses on these, but he sees me coming and lets me know. No. Only cash and gold. And he's right. That wasn't the deal, and it burns, but that's how it is.

Out of another the linebackers grab out a mess of seashells. Obviously sentimental. But there's cash in it too.

And the final tally's coming in. Glasses is double-checking it. Carrying 1s and tapping at the phone's calculator as purple is coming through in the sky, poking big holes in the gray, taking it over.

And every time I see green paper coming out of metal mouth after metal mouth, I'm thinking, *More.*

Every time I see that *verde*, I'm thinking, *¡Más, chingón!*

For the people about to be homeless by Christmas, the ones that don't deserve it.

For them.

For their houses.

Their families.

And for the home I never even really had growing up.

For the city housing I got booted out of.

For the foster home I got booted into and never stopped running away from.

For everything I ever been through.

For all the bad shit I did.

For Harlem Harold.

And all the people I hurt.

Especially the ones I can never say sorry to now.

More.

Glasses

Tuesday, September 16, 2008
Early Morning

63

The drill goes and goes. Ghost moves between looking down this thin little microscope and punching holes into the doors. It has a rhythm to it, so I stick close since I'm on notes duty, checking everything in the safes, tapping it all in.

This's supposed to go to Rooster, but I'm not exactly sure if we'll be seeing each other again, so I take notes on whatever comes out of all these metal things with their doors open in case it's gonna be useful to Collins or me down the road.

It's a weird sight. All these secrets and hidden things coming out in one big swoop. I know I'll never see anything like it again, and I wish I had a picture of it, but that's never happening.

As I go from safe to safe, I can't shake the feeling that it's a mess of time capsules, that with each one we're bringing something back to life that maybe should stay buried. I even smelled the air in one right after it got opened to see what it smelled like twenty years ago. What it smelled like was paper and stale cigarette smoke.

Ghost just pops, looks in, and then he's on to the next. But I log everything. The numbers are looking crazy too. I focus on those instead of how bad I want to call Leya and make sure she's okay and that my little peanut-butter boy is okay too.

I know I prolly could do it now with Rooster gone, but I hold off since it's not 100 percent good to talk here. I don't want to take any chances of any homies hearing me, so what I do is, I log. I check and double-check numbers.

In one real old-looking safe with a twist handle, we find a fake drawer with a sliding bottom to it that has some weird family secrets inside, like photos of two different families with the same dad looking the same age in both sets of photos.

Lil Tricky was yapping around like a puppy when I pulled them out, and he said how they might be identical twins, but then we took them over to look at each one under the light and we couldn't see any differences in the faces, not even little details, so we think it's one guy being shady. I wonder where those families are now.

I catch Lonely's eye sometimes as I'm going through and he's helping move things. We read a mess of news in Spanish while we were waiting for the food, and we ran the battery all the way down on his phone. When it was dead, I made him put it in the trunk with the gun I was carrying so it was two less things to worry about.

We didn't find out more about the grenades in the square or if any little kids got hurt. After, we didn't talk about it.

Ghost's slick. I mean that. I don't want to compliment him, but credit where it's due. He's real. I get how Rooster wanted Lil Tricky to learn something, but being able to stand here and watch Ghost do what he does, you can tell it's the type of thing that takes years and years of experience.

It takes feel. He makes it look easy too. I never seen anything like it. I can tell he's messing with Tricky. He'll send him off for a wrench or something, something dumb, and he'll pop when the kid's back is turned. It's like he's always keeping some trade secrets that way.

The more I think about it, I have seen something like how Ghost pops safes. The face he makes even looks like Kobe's, like when the black mamba is mad and taking you one-on-one and there's nothing you can do to stop him.

242

He's going right through you, like it or not. *They're the same that way*, I think. Both top of their game, unstoppable on their days, almost unstoppable anyway.

I'm not buying what he's saying about the gun safes at all. I look at how he does everything else and I know he's doing it on purpose. He don't want Rooster to have more guns, simple as that, and I get it.

Since I don't exactly want Rooster to have more guns either, I don't bother calling Ghost out. Besides, what would he do if I did? Go limp on the asphalt and quit? No thanks. I just let it slide, so everyone else lets it slide too.

By the time Rooster finds out and thinks to ask me why I let Ghost get away with some weak-ass excuses for not doing it, I won't even be here to answer. I'll be in Cardiff, packing us up into a rental car or a used car I just bought, getting ready to drive us somewhere else as fast as I can, somewhere safer.

Ghost

Tuesday, September 16, 2008
Early Morning

64

When the tally comes down, I'm tuning out a little. Feeling jittery and light in my boots. Also, I don't even want to know how much drugs there were. They can just skip all that. I already feel bad enough about giving those poisons a way back into hurting people's lives. Not just addicts, but their families. Their friends. Shit, even random-ass people unlucky enough to get caught up in drama. I know all that too good, and it burns in me. Up and down my arms. Because it's been feeling like I opened a bunch of Pandora's boxes, and some evil that was shut up and not hurting anybody can go right back into the world again and it's all my fault.

C'mon, Glasses, I'm thinking. *Get to the fucking money.*

Let there be some good to come from it.

I keep telling myself, *Bad money can do good things.*

Glasses does jewelry next. I'm not listening. I'm watching the linebackers and the guys that came with the truck loading everything of Rooster's into the bed. It's got a hard-shell cover over it, but it's open and propped up and taking it all in.

Gold's next. My cut's the four hundred coins and sixty-four

little one-ounce bullion bars. I don't know what that's worth, maybe $750 an ounce, but the coins are heavy going down into my lockbox. Maybe it's $300,000. Give or take.

Last comes cash. I do my own math real quick first.

$897,000 from the Rancho San Pedro Projects, already to Mira.

$48,000 from the first house tonight. Still in my tool cases.

And Glasses does one last recount before setting out my 40 percent on everything that came out of storage.

$1,133,284 it rounds up to. All that goes in a giant hockey bag that one of the linebackers carries to my Jeep like it's not even heavy.

But I'm thinking, *In California, in L.A., that's not enough. It's not enough houses.*

Still, it totals out to—hang on. I'm not thinking so good.

I grab a pen out of the Jeep. I work sums out on my palm, fuck up, and start over. What I end up with when I'm finally done is: $2,078,284 in total.

$2,078,284 point 00, plus whatever the gold's worth.

I can't shake the feeling that it's not enough, though. Even if Mira's paying off scraps of what's left on mortgages in parts of town most people wouldn't dare to live, it doesn't feel like enough. Especially with the money out to Frank. Especially with the trust money. *Especially* when 60 percent of this night's work right here went to Rooster for almost $1.7 million.

I got to take a breath on that. A forced one. And I'm hearing Mira in my head asking me if I know what the word *enough* even means. It burns a little because the answer's no. My whole life it was always a finish line that kept moving once I got something else. But it has to stop somewhere. Has to stop here. And I have to be good with it. Somehow.

So I think about people I'll never meet getting to keep their houses. Ten, or maybe twenty, and not just them, but also their families. Kids. Uncles. Grandparents. I think about Frank not having to dodge calls from the bank anymore. I think about him living without that weight and how I lifted it off him. I think about Laura going to college, being whatever she wants. I think about young women, survivors, getting to go to college because of the trust. To help them start again. To *live* again.

When I push that breath back out, I'm feeling empty without it, but good empty. Like, I did everything I could. Like I couldn't ever have done more if I had a whole lifetime. And maybe it's not enough, because I don't know if there's any such thing, but it's close. It's something.

"*Fuck,*" Lil Tricky says, looking over Glasses's shoulder.

Glasses shrugs him off and looks at me and nods like, *Damn.* Like, *Did tonight even really happen?*

I'm too tired to even nod him back.

$2,078,284. All that is what Rooster paid. Everything I took out of Pedro, everything I took out of the first Lynwood house, and then some. And that's good, because it knocks something off my list that I've been stressing about but too scared to even entertain the thought of. That if I didn't cover tonight, Rooster might go after Frank and Laura thinking they had the money.

But now, that's off the table. Rooster got a good deal on me, and he's going to see it that way. And that's that. Now I just got to hold up the rest of mine.

The truck's done getting loaded, and my Jeep's buttoned up too.

As I'm trying to think on how best to coordinate meeting Mira at the drop-off spot, another car arrives. The driver splits off into the one that's been here. It's not explained to me what it is, so I wait. It's not too long before Lil Tricky comes up to Glasses and me with a request. He wants to see me blow my brains out, he says. Glasses tells him maybe, he'll think about it, till then though, drive the follow car. And that explains the extra car.

I go to the driver's-side door of my Jeep. Glasses comes with me, moving to the other side and opening it up to get in.

"Oh," Glasses says, "now you're about to drive?"

I let that one sail right past me, don't even react.

I get us out from under the gate one of the linebackers gets lifted, and onto the street. Glasses tells me to go the speed limit. To stop at all yellows. Under no circumstances am I to try something stupid to attract attention or get the cops to follow. I say that's not a problem. I don't say, *Why would I?* Because I don't feel like I even have to.

What I do, though, is put Rose's tape back in and finish out

"Demolition Girl" before counting the five seconds with Rose, and then Bad Religion comes in with "Quality or Quantity" and how that's some kind of choice I have to make, and I feel like today of all days, I actually did. I traded whatever time I got left for quality.

It's a fast combo of a song. Over before it's almost even begun, and I guess Glasses is being respectful because he waits till it's over and quiet and I'm counting with Rose when he says, "You shouldn't have said that about there being a rat."

I push stop on the tape. I've got a headache coming in that's going to be off the Richter scale. It's been coming. All the ones that start where my neck connects to my skull do that. The last thing I need is to have any kind of conversation with Glasses about this shit.

And I'm not defending myself or anything, but I say, "Wasn't telling him anything he didn't already know."

But I'm also wondering why Glasses is bringing this up right now.

"Yeah, but you should know not to. Seeing as how it could endanger an officer already in the field."

That's when it clicks. I might be slow right now but I get it. I'm nodding. Glasses doesn't need to say it's him. Not flat out. He's the rat. Undercover or informing. He's the reason the DEA knows about those houses. No other explanation.

I get how he's not been found out, though. I mean, he fooled me. He comes across scary real good.

"You're right," I say. "You got me on that."

And we drive a bit after that, saying nothing. I'm starting to feel my heartbeat at the top of my neck, hitting me with little slaps of pain.

We're driving over the 110 on the 405 North, into Torrance, towards the drop spot Mira and I said a few weeks ago we'd use only in case of emergency, when I say, "You think Rooster's word is good?"

"It is if yours is."

"I need to hand all this off." I look at Lil Tricky following us in an anonymous little Nissan. "Can't have Rooster going after the person I'm giving it to, though. Not ever. And I can't have any-body else knowing who's got it either."

What I'm saying but not saying is, I can't have you knowing the person this goes to. Because I put everything on the line for this and I can't have you fucking it up for whatever rat reasons you may have.

He comes back with "It's got nothing to do with me."

And he could be lying to me, though.

It's possible.

And there's this little look in his eye. Like, maybe it's regret that he told me too soon about the dude he was. But it's good for me to have. Because we got something on each other now, and besides, it's not like I've got a choice.

I decide to risk it, to call Mira.

My prepaid's in my hand and I'm dialing.

We're turning onto Grant from Kingsdale, pulling up near the giant box of a concrete parking structure of the South Bay Galleria mall, when I go one more left and stop the car by the front entrance to it. Parking's free here. Not like other parts in L.A. And there's no little guard station, just a ramp that goes up. The morning's turning orange around us. There're no other cars. Nobody's at work yet.

"You need to get out," I say to Glasses. "There's only one way in and one way out. I'm not going anywhere. I'll be right back here to pick you up when I'm done."

Because I can't have him seeing Mira, or her car, or anything about anything.

He gets it.

He must not get it too well though because there's a second exit that she'll be taking, the one for East Artesia to go straight onto the 405, and he must not know I'm lying about there only being one.

Glasses looks at me like he doesn't think I get to decide where he goes before getting out, and I roll the window down and tell him I'll be standing up there with my back to a wall so I can be watching stairwells and looking down at him from above too.

For the last thing, I say, "Give me that phone you've got on you."

He gives me a look like, *Really?*

My look tells his look, *Yes, really.*

He hands it over.

When Lil Tricky pulls in behind me, I get out and I go and take his phone. I also take his keys. I tell him the same things I told Glasses. Stay here. Don't move. He doesn't look to me, though. He looks to Glasses, and Glasses nods like, *It's cool*, and goes to take something out of his pocket but his hand comes out empty and he frowns at it.

Then I go up. I watch both of them in my rearview and then floor it to the top, screeching the whole way.

On the top level, I see her, arms crossed hard beneath her breasts, looking like she's trying tears on before wearing them for real.

And I'm completely exhausted and thinking, *Not hurting people is impossible.* You can't go through life with that as a priority. I mean, you can try. I tried. But it's happening anyways. Pain happens. Despite best intentions. That shit's inevitable.

I pull past Mira and park out in the open-air part so I can get out and look over the edge of the little wall to the garage entrance where Glasses and Lil Tricky are at. They're cool down there. Glasses, smoking, then looking up at me, waving. Lil Tricky, in his own world, reenacting some story for Glasses, and he's doing some shitty kung fu kicks and laughing.

Mira's behind me, walking towards the Jeep. I'm doing the breathing exercises they taught me to push my headache back down and get me ready to see her face-to-face. I don't think they're working for either one.

I knew she'd get here before me. She lives closer. She'd put a sweatshirt and jeans on. She'd come. As fast as she could. I didn't tell her to put the magnetic covers on her plates that I got her, but it's good to see she did it. When she leaves here, she knows to sell her car and get a decent used one. Something reliable and cheap.

When I take her keys from her and pop her trunk, she says, "What'd you do?"

She's saying it over and over, staring at how fucked-up my cheek looks. At the blood on my shirt.

No use telling her what I did. Or that I did it because I had to. And it's good she's at least not asking about the cancer, and just to make sure she won't, I give her everything. One point one million dollars and change isn't as heavy as you think it is. Feels like twenty-five pounds, maybe.

When Mira puts her face in the hockey bag and starts going through it, her "What'd you do?" turns into "What the fuck?"

And she's thanking me as I dump the gold and the toolboxes in her car. I tell her to take the cash out of them before giving my tools back to Frank.

I give her the address of the shop. Tell her when to go by and do it.

After that, I don't give her words. I can't. My headache's starting to take me over.

So I just kiss her like, *Please.*

I kiss her like, *Be better without me.*

And when I break it off and turn to get back in my Jeep, I don't look at her. And when I drive out, I keep myself from looking in the rearview because I can't be looking back. Not now.

Because this's me. A ghost. Floating in and floating out.

Glasses

Tuesday, September 16, 2008
Morning

66

Ghost's even smarter than I give him credit for, taking my phone like that and taking the keys? He's on it.

I was thinking I'd have the opportunity to call Leya and I was getting excited for it, just to hear her voice and hear if she had the call logs so I could stop worrying about it so much, but then Ghost's taking it and speeding off into some parking garage.

He has to know that I know there's another exit. I'm not exactly sure why he thinks he's fooling me. When we were coming in, I actually was looking at the parking structure next to the mall and thinking to myself how if I had to plan a drop, then that was where I'd do it since there was a clear exit onto Artesia, and that means a clear exit to the freeway too.

I'm sure there's entrance and exit security footage on this garage. Most all malls have them these days. When I get my phone back, I could make a call and we could put a push on somebody for security footage of the parking lot for about the last hour.

I bet there's no other cars, so it'd be simple to find a license plate number and go meet this partner of his if we wanted to.

I shake my head at that. It's not even worth doing that when I'm trying to get out, and I'm thinking how lucky Ghost's connect is and doesn't even know it.

Lil Tricky asks me what I'm thinking about, since he's sixteen and stupid, the type to ask dumb questions when he has no business doing it, and like most little guys, he's only asking so he can get to talking about himself.

I don't bother telling him anything. I figure if I just stay quiet long enough, he'll jump into saying whatever he wants to say anyway, and I'm right.

"Oh, man, Glasses, you don't even understand what this night was like for me. So, I was getting with this girl, and I'm thinking it's all good, right? My boys are next door, and things are going hot, cuz you know she's down for whatever, but then like I hear this whistle, and I look up and see some guns with dudes behind them, and I'm like 'Oh, shit!' and I'm trying to get up off her and she's screaming . . ."

He goes on, but I tune him out. After he's done telling me how, if things had gone just a little bit different, if he'd looked up sooner, he would've jumped up and kicked the big guy in the dick, and then he does some kicks in the air right in front of himself to show me, like it would've been easy.

I smile at that since he's being funny but he don't know how he's being funny. If Lil Tricky tried that on with Blanco, he would've had a hole in his head before he finished swinging his leg back.

Lil Tricky tells me he stayed there with his hands tied for a long time, maybe an hour. He's not sure. The other guys tried to get up, but they weren't getting far, not until the door opened and somebody they'd never seen before rolled in and cut them loose.

He was there to clear the house and empty the safe, this guy, but there wasn't anything worth taking in it, so he put his hand up in the top of the closet and took the three pistols from in there instead. He made sure they were safetied if they had safeties and put them all in a bag.

After, he went to the garage and got a ladder. He took all the cameras down and put them in the sewage services van he was driving before telling Lil Tricky a car was waiting at the curb.

It was from his uncle since he was needed somewhere and that somewhere ended up being the storage spot in Carson.

I'm nodding, but not at what he's saying. I'm nodding since I'm looking at the follow car and I'm remembering how me and Lonely took it out last week on some errands, and I'm smiling now since I know there must still be a gun in it. Under the driver seat. That's lucky.

Lil Tricky notices me smiling and says, "You smile a lot, you know that? You might need to fix that. It's not making you look so tough."

"Sure," I say, like what this kid thinks about me or anybody else ever meant anything, "I'll see what I can do about that."

It's not much but that gun is my new peace of mind just in case Ghost don't do what he said he'd do, or even if he does and I need to take care of Lil Tricky to get away. I'd rather not, since he's Rooster's little nephew and all, but if I have to, I have to.

Besides, it's not like Rooster won't already be looking for me. He'll just have one more reason on top of all the others.

Ghost

Tuesday, September 16, 2008
Morning

67

At the bottom, I give them their phones back and I'm about to give the follow-car keys back to Lil Tricky, but Glasses swipes them and tells Lil Tricky to switch it up with him. Next thing I know, the kid is making himself all comfy in my shotgun seat and I got to tell him to buckle his ass up right as Glasses's getting in the follow car. At first I'm thinking it's because he wants to try to follow Mira, but he doesn't. When I pull out towards Hawthorne Boulevard, he's right there behind me. Good.

As I'm speeding up, Lil Tricky's rubbing his hands and saying, "Okay, break it down for me, like, what else do I need to know to kill safes like that?"

I don't feel like answering, so I don't. I'm mainly just squinting at the road and pushing one of my thumb knuckles into my forehead to offset the pressure.

The respect in this kid's tone is good, but I'm thinking, *What else? You never learned anything to begin with.* I don't say that, though. Instead I'm looking at this little dude for the first time. I mean, *really* looking at him. Mustache playing on his lip. Eyes all lit up because he's still buzzing about all those locks getting done. And right then, I'm thinking about how this little dude probably isn't even eighteen yet, and how he grew up where I grew up, and so I'm looking for some sameness in him.

Because in Lynwood, growing up in them eighties and nineties, safety was for other people. For white people not named Blanco. For people with money. For people living in Bel Air with the Fresh Prince or some shit. Safety was for people on TV. Not us. Never us. All we got handed was risk and running.

And so, not growing up with anything like safety, I'd get all confused when I found it in unexpected places. In a hospital bed with some nurse looking down on me, telling me they just took some kind of tumor out of my head. Or with Rose, at the beach in Pedro where I'm aiming us now, in the aquarium down there with her touching sea hares in the touch tank, and up by the Bell.

That was the kind of safe I didn't know I'd had till it wasn't there anymore. Of being with someone that you care about. Knowing you're a team. There's promises in that. How you'll look after each other. Do *anything* to protect each other.

And when that happens, there's this funny thing about it, it doesn't feel right. It feels like maybe it's fake and not worth it. The first few times, feeling anything like safety made me anxious. Nervous. Sweaty. Because I thought it was me slipping. I thought I wasn't allowed to feel it at all.

The lights are going our way as my head's thumping me like the road thumps the tires. We're flowing down to PCH as I'm wondering if Lil Tricky's the same somehow. If he's a little me. And I'm wondering how to angle him, maybe, so he can't go my route, and while I'm thinking about that, all's I say to him is "I'm going to need you not to talk."

I don't know how he feels the weight of it, selfish as he is, but he does.

And while I'm pulling up to a stoplight that goes green for us, I put Rose's tape back on, rewind to the end of "Quality or Quantity," then count the five seconds with her again, but right this time.

While it's quiet.

68

We're not even to Crenshaw when "Please Don't Be Gentle with Me" by the Minutemen starts, and that's a tough one, because I remember how Rose said something almost exactly like that when we went out. It was a kind of thing where I didn't know if it was a date and she didn't either, but we went to Santa Monica Pier and tried to cut fishing lines and we laughed about how I was seeing more white people than I'd ever seen in my life before, and at the end of it all, I went to hug her and it was awkward and I was thinking how I'd hurt her if I hugged her for real, and that's when she said she was human, not glass. I couldn't break her, she said. But it looked like it, I swear. Eighty-eight pounds she was. Right near the end. Not even ninety.

The song ends and me and her count the space between together before "I Love Playin' with Fire" by the Runaways comes on, riding on guitars, and then Joan Jett's growling and I remember how Rose would smile with half her mouth whenever she heard this and kind of swing her head side to side. This song was always Rose's way of saying to me that she wasn't scared of me, or scared of the things I'd done. But I knew it was because she didn't know them all.

Lil Tricky's looking at me now, bringing me out of it. He's watching me listen. Watching my face.

"Don't be getting crazy on me," he says. "Don't be, like, driving us into a concrete divider or something."

And cool and calm despite blinking through pain, I say back, "I'm past crazy. Now I just want to end where I need to end."

He's still looking at me.

I don't take my eyes off the road, but I say, "You still want to see me blow my brains out?"

"Hell yeah," he says, with the kind of toughness that isn't toughness at all.

"Why?"

And he doesn't have an answer to that. He tries, but gives up pretty quick and just watches Lomita businesses scrolling by outside his window because looking at the Thai-massage and food places, a donut spot with Cajun food, a pet shop that only sells reptiles, is easier than giving me a real answer.

I did up a will last month. Lawyers charge way too much for that shit. Mira's guy, Willis-Jackson, doesn't give discounts.

I would be giving the Jeep to Mira, but when I'm done with it, she won't want it. So it'll go into a lot somewhere and then maybe get auctioned off.

All the rest goes to Frank and Laura. Everything I ever got.

I've been saving a long time.

One of the virtues of living in the past, I guess. Once I had the Jeep, I was good.

Never bought a house or a condo. Just rented an apartment off Frank for less than he ever should've been charging me. He bought my building for rental income back when everything went down in the eighties. Savings and loan or whatever. Smartest financial thing he ever did, he said.

I've never had hobbies or collected anything. Some vinyl, maybe. A record player to play them on. It had two tape decks in it. I tried to make some tapes for Rose on it, but it never felt right, so I stopped. Instead, I just listened out for stuff I figured she would've liked. Always tried to listen with her ears to new stuff. Propagandhi, maybe. Less Than Jake, also a solid maybe. Anti-Flag, definitely.

Saving half my salary every year for the last, what? Thirteen years.

No. Fourteen.

Frank's going to be surprised when so much of what he paid me comes back, and my stipulations are for it to help pay for Laura's college. Wherever she wants to go. There was never enough to buy a building, but it's enough to help with Stanford.

I'm going sixty-five on the 110 South, watching Glasses in my rearview, following tight.

That's when the Buzzcocks come on, and I've been waiting for them, dreading them, because this's one of the songs where it's

Rose's true sadness. Her frustration. And it always hits me hard, like the years in between didn't dull her pain one bit.

Because what did she get? She wanted a lover just like in the song. Didn't really get one, not how she might've liked and needed. Putting this song on the mix was her way of saying, *I'm a teenage girl and my life's supposed to be in front of me, but "What Do I Get?"* Cancer, that's what she got. Chemo. Insomnia. An erratic stomach. A hood boy, too late. An early fucking death.

By the time the song's over, we're driving past refineries you can smell, and Lil Tricky's screwing his face up and covering his nose while Rose's trying to rescue the mix with the Clash, her trying to tell me "I'm Not Down," but I never believed that, and I don't think she ever thought I would.

In San Pedro, the 110 Freeway dead-ends at a stoplight and I turn left onto Gaffey. It's hilly down here. We go up, down, up, and then before going too much up again, I turn on Twenty-Second and go down to Pacific, where I turn right.

When the song's over, I'm counting five with Rose again and stopping the tape because I can't handle the Raincoats right now. They're last.

Down by Cabrillo Beach it's so early that I can't park in the lot because there's no one there to open the guard gate, so I have to park us on the hill on White Drive.

"I got to see something," I say to Lil Tricky. And I leave him in the car.

Glasses, already parked behind us, has the phone in his hand, probably calling someone to tell Rooster where we're at.

When I get to where the sand is, I take my boots and socks off. I get it between my toes.

It's the best I can do, because I can't smell the salt of it. I've got some kind of flowers in my nose now. Lavender, maybe. The scent of something long gone.

The first time I was here, I was seventeen, and it was because I couldn't say no to Rose's face. I got in her Jeep, with the seat leather hot like a grill, and her fingers on my neck making me jump, I was that nervous.

But then she took me to the sea. This part of it. This exact part.

And she gave me new eyes to see it by talking about how the light hits the water. The way the ocean arches its back and throws sun everywhere, the way it tumbles and spits, the way it hits the beach and rolls back into itself.

I'm looking out at Terminal Island, thinking how it's my turn now, and I got to close my eyes and stop feeling all sorry for myself.

Because all's I'm thinking about right now is how my heart has been broken a really long time, since before I was even an adult, and how I'd never thought that before.

Only now. Only here.

Glasses

Tuesday, September 16, 2008
Morning

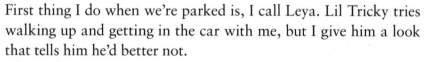

First thing I do when we're parked is, I call Leya. Lil Tricky tries walking up and getting in the car with me, but I give him a look that tells him he'd better not.

He don't look happy about it, but he don't push it. He stands out in front of the bumper with his back to me, looking at the sea.

When Leya picks up, I can't ask about the log first. I got to build to it. We jump through the right hoops. Is she there okay? Yes.

Is the little man okay? Yes, he's sleeping.

How's the puppy? She's not a puppy anymore, but I'll always call her that. She's good. After all that is when I can ask about the log and not hurt feelings.

"Of course I have it. It's the first thing I grabbed, the most important thing." I hear her unzip something and push some things around in a bag before she says, "I'm looking at it right now."

"Prove it."

Pages flip and she starts reading a date, a phone number, where I was when I took it and who it was from. She skips the part about what it was about, which is cool, since I'm already good.

I don't need to hear any more. Relief comes at me and jumps on me like my dog when she's happy to see me.

"You're real good to me," I say to Leya, "too good."

She argues that, since she's kind, but she shouldn't. I know I don't deserve how she takes care of me and how she sticks with me through whatever. She could've had a normal life if she wanted, a husband that didn't have a messed-up eye and a messed-up face and worked at the DMV or something, you know? Somebody safe.

But Leya always says that life's not about deserving. It's about making choices and dealing with what comes, especially things you can't control.

I say to her, "Did you hear about that thing that happened in Morelia?"

"No, what happened?"

She's got a tone like she's distracted and tired. I get that. My stomach has been decent for a couple hours but I'm starting to get real dry eyes. That happens when I stay up too late. I also got some nausea creeping on me when I say, "Three grenades got thrown in a whole crowd of people there just celebrating Mexican Independence Day."

She's not distracted now. She sort of yelps before hushing herself since Felix is nearby. "That's terrible, Rudy! Do you know about your family? Are they okay?"

"I don't know."

"Does anybody know why it happened? Was it crazies?"

"It was some organized crazies."

My wife, she's quick. She knows what I'm saying when I say that. "Did that make up your mind about anything?"

"Maybe it was a shove, another one, but my mind is already my mind."

"I get that. Come home, *amor*. Come be with your family."

I'm about to say something about how there's no home to have anymore, but it's like she's reading my mind when she says, "Home is where we're together." She knows that hits me, so she locks it in by saying, "We only look forward. We don't look back."

When you're younger, when you're stupid, you can't appreciate a wife. When you're old enough to know enough, you get how you need one to be better, to even make it through. I wouldn't be here right now without her. That's just a fact. I feel like only when I had something I couldn't stand to lose did I see clearly where I was and what I was doing. And when I saw that, I had to change.

"With my one eye," I say, since it's a thing of ours that started when I was trying to cheer her up after the miscarriage, "I'm looking forward to seeing you soon."

"How soon?"

"Soon as I can. You know how I feel about you."

"I do," she says, and then, "Say bye to Felix."

The phone rustles and stops, so I tell him to be good to his mother, that I'll be there soon, and when I am, it's about figuring out a new life. I stop after that since I don't know what that looks like yet and it feels weird having said it.

When Leya comes back on the line, she says, "Bye. Drive safe. We're right here waiting for you, at home."

I tell her bye too. I hang up with my heart heavy in me. I know she's putting on a brave face, being a little too nice, camouflaging how she feels, how scared she is we're doing this.

I check the premarket price on BBY. As soon as Ghost does what he's supposed to, I'll make a call, promise Collins the logs, but make it a condition that the stocks get thawed out. As soon as it's unfrozen, I need to place a call to sell all of it at the opening.

If I can get a buy for it at $42.40, then it's worth $655,000 today, give or take. Even with capital gains, that's a whole new life. A whole new world.

Lil Tricky sees me fussing around with the phone and walks up to the car again, but I wave him away for a second time. He looks like he's not sure what to do with that, so he just stands there on the hill, staring down onto the beach where Ghost is walking back towards us like he's trying to memorize all that sand with the bottoms of his feet.

Ghost

Tuesday, September 16, 2008
Morning

70

Oranges. That's what I'm smelling when I leave my boots at the beach, get back in the car, and drive us up toward Korean Bell Park with sand grinding between my toes. I go up one last big hill on Gaffey and pull us into the parking lot across from the basketball court in the last space on the middle so no one can block my view of it. Or the cliffs and the sea behind it. Glasses rolls in two down from me on the same side with nothing parked between us.

That court is where Rose used to steal people's basketballs and toss them to me to boot over the fence, down onto the cliff below. I only ever got one gone, but when I did, Rose pulled a damn brand-new basketball out of the Jeep and handed it to this high school kid, like no problem. You should've seen the look on his face. Like, he'd thought he lost everything and then it all came back and better this time.

The first time I tried to kill myself, not really on purpose, but if it happened, it would've been okay with me, I did a bunch of downers and got in a bath at a motel room that wasn't even mine.

263

That was a week after I'd seen Rose Grace Stenberg's obituary in the *Times*, and I figured I'd just fall asleep and drown. Obviously I didn't. There was something loose about the old rubber stopper, and maybe I kicked it when I sunk down, but I woke up later in an empty tub. Cold and puckered up like a raisin.

Rose and I never ate oranges together or anything, but I feel like she's here with me now, in the car, trying to hold me. It's a heavy-blanket kind of feeling.

Lil Tricky's looking at me again, but now he's nervous.

"Rose wanted to die looking at this sea, wanted her soul to just drift out to it," I tell him. "I don't think she ever did."

He doesn't ask about Rose or who she was, so I don't drag it out. I'm looking down at the steering wheel when I say to Lil Tricky, "I need you to give me the gun Rooster had somebody give you, and then I need you to get out."

I know he has it. I saw one of the linebackers give it to him to give to me.

I look up and he's freezing on me. Worried the whole deal will change, but not sure how it would.

I say, "Slide the gun down into that little holder on the door by your foot, and then get out that door, shut it, and get in the other car."

I see it parked a few spaces down from me. Glasses's wearing sunglasses now, looking out at the orange morning over the sea, arm out the window.

Lil Tricky does what I ask. When I see the gun come out, I'm relieved it's got a silencer on it. There was a time when all I ever wanted was to go out with a bang, but now I just want to slide out without anybody noticing.

Before he goes, he says, "What you did tonight? *Damn.*"

It's one word, that last one, but it's respect. Lil Tricky's eyes are all big and he's smiling. He doesn't mean getting interrupted and tied up and robbed. He means me busting all those safes, and I'm actually glad that's what's sticking with him instead.

With that, the door closes and he's gone. I watch him get in the other car.

I don't take the gun from where it is. I get out my prepaid because there's something I need to do.

I close my eyes. I take a fast, big inhale and get oranges on top of oranges. Up my nose. Down into my lungs. And then I call Stenberg Locksmithing because I know it's not open yet.

There's no possible way Laura will pick up, which is for the best.

It rings through to the old tape machine because Frank never wanted to switch to voice mail. He just loved tapes. Like daughter, like father, I guess.

And hearing his voice, low and slow, explaining to me where Stenberg Locksmithing is, I don't expect it to make me feel all overwhelmed, but it does, even when it's going on about operating hours that I already know by heart, and if I have a message to leave it after the beep, and I never planned on leaving one, but then I am.

"Frank, uh, it's Ricky. I just wanted to say that—"

There's a click and a scramble and that rough voice, Frank's voice, saying, "Ricky?"

"Uh," is all I can say because the words I had are gone now.

And so I just say, "Yeah." Like an idiot.

And he's saying, "You just say whatever it is you need to."

And I didn't expect this. Didn't want to do it this way, but here I am trapped in it, so I struggle out with "You were like a dad to me."

And it sounds so stupid in my ears. Like, it doesn't come close to how I feel. But I know he's hearing in my voice how this's the last conversation we're going to have.

"I know," he says, and in the weight of those two words I'm hearing how he took being there for me pretty serious. "It's my turn to say something back, so you listen."

He pauses there, like he's getting his gumption up, because that's just how he'd say it if he was on the outside of this.

"I know about you and Rose," he says.

I make a noise into the phone like I just got hit. Words never felt so much like a gut punch.

But he's still going. "She told us, Rose did. Not a name or anything, but that there was a boy. Well, she told her mother, but I've read her diary a fair few times, and there was the Jeep too, that same model she drove."

He takes his mouth away from the receiver and coughs off to the side. "The day I saw you in Hawthorne, I thought it had to be you. But I *knew* it was you at Marcy's funeral.

"Just so you know, I'm glad she had you before the end, and I'm glad I got you afterwards. That's all I really have to say, Son. That's it. And just, thank you. For everything."

He's never called me son before. Never called anybody that.

Not even Glenn fucking Rios before he got that middle name for betraying.

Then Frank's voice gives like it never has before in all the time I've known him. He says, "I'm going to hang up now, but it's not goodbye. I'll still be with you, and you'll still be with me because that's just how it works."

And hearing that breaks something in me. I feel splinters when I breathe frozen oranges. All up and down my rib cage. In my throat. I'm thinking how those words were spoken by a man that had to endure more than anybody should ever have to.

"Thank you too, Frank," I say, before the line goes out with a click.

Those words aren't enough, but they're the best I could do.

I have to just sit after that. I have to look out at the sea.

And I'm stuck on something, how Rose had a diary, and how much I want to see what she wrote, maybe what she even wrote about me, but it's too late. I'll never see it. And that feels like I got an anchor on me. Dragging me down.

That makes me put my key back in the ignition and turn on the tape deck and push *Fuck Dying* in one last time. I rewind to the end of "I'm Not Down" and let it play out, and then we count together. Me, here and now. And Rose, back then.

One. Two. Three. Four. Five.

And the Raincoats come on, with their offbeat rhythm and seesawing guitars and singing like sobbing.

"In Love," the song is called.

It's what Frank's daughter most wanted to leave me with.

It's what I've carried in me all this time.

And that's enough.

71

When the song's over, and since I still got my phone in my hand, I dial 911. The line clicks in and the woman on the other end asks me what my emergency is. I tell her I'm about to shoot myself in the parking lot of the Korean Bell Park. I tell her I'm in a white Jeep Wrangler right next to the basketball court. I tell her they need to send somebody so a family doesn't find my body and mess their kids' heads up for life. I tell her I have to go now. This isn't a prank call, and I toss the phone to the floor with a thump. I hear her faraway voice asking questions, but I don't hear words.

I take one hand and squeeze the back of my neck hard against the ache there before leaning over to get the gun. I check the clip and chamber. The thing is full even though I only need one.

I'm tugging the collar of my shirt away from me so I can look down on the rose I got over my heart when a van with kids in it pulls into one of the spaces across from me, and I'm thinking, *Don't they have school or something?*

But they must not, because they get out, and as three kids make a dash for the grass, the mom minding them nods at me. And I smile back. Grateful they didn't pull in a minute later. Or two.

I make a check there's nobody else around and I slide over to the shotgun seat so that when I do it and I lose control of myself, I don't fall forward and hit that horn so people come running. I can't have people seeing this.

Except for Glasses and Lil Tricky. They're still watching.

But they can't see how I got the gun over my heart now.

How the cold metal of its end is sliding down my shirt, over a rib, and into the divot beneath it. It doesn't fit right in there, between two ribs. The silencer end is too wide, too big. The space between my ribs, too small. And the problem with having my shirt on is I can't see where the rose is on me.

From the sandy mat by the pedals, babble's still coming through the phone, but the operator knows I'm gone so it's more spaced out, maybe talking to an ambulance driver. I take my shirt off. I try again.

The gun's colder this time when I find my spot below Rose's rose, and I angle it down a little so I know the bullet'll go straight through me and down. Into the seat behind me, down into the floor after that, into the Jeep's undercarriage if it has to, but not into some little kid walking by.

Never that.

My palm's sweating, and the crisscrossing grip of the gun is digging in, but all's I can think about right now is how all people got holes in them. Holes nobody can see. Not even doctors. Holes that need filling.

We're born with those. Everybody is. My problem for the longest time was not knowing this about myself. Maybe I got more holes than most people from how I was raised. Or not raised. Maybe having parents stick around fills you up somehow, puts love and kindness into you and builds you up inside.

And maybe if you get cracks in that foundation later it's up to you to patch it up. But if you never had that foundation, maybe you're just a facade. You walk around and people *think* you're whole because they see you upright, walking and talking. But they can't see down inside you. They can never know what moves you or makes you do what you do.

My holes are bigger than most people's. They're bottomless. They can't be filled. I've learned this about me. I'm not blaming anybody, just saying it's true. I still did what I did to Harlem Harold. I take accountability. But I lived almost my whole life hungry, always looking for any kind of fill-up, not knowing that whatever I put in just flowed right out.

In meetings, I've always had to get up in front of my peers and my people and say my name and that I'm an addict. Being sober sixteen years doesn't change that fact. I'll always be one and I'll always have holes in me too.

They'll never be full.

So, I guess what I'm trying to say is, what's one more?

Glasses

Tuesday, September 16, 2008
Morning

72

Even right up to the end, I didn't think he'd do it. I thought he'd find some way to get slick and wiggle out of it. But then he pulled that trigger. I heard it.

There was a little bumping sound when he shot, like a rock hitting metal inside that Jeep, but you wouldn't know what it was unless you knew it was coming or you were looking straight at it.

I wasn't looking since that just seemed like private business to me, especially after all he'd been through to get to this spot, all he'd done. I made Lil Tricky go see it. To be sure. I made him walk over and look in.

Next to me now, Lil Tricky's holding his stomach. He's not gonna puke, but when you see someone give it up for real, or you see a dead body, you feel it in the absolute middle of you, like your body takes a picture using a piece of you as the paper. Your soul, prolly.

That's why it sticks with you. It's inside you forever after that. It walks around your dreams, looking just as clear as the day you saw it.

I say, "You expect something else?"

"No," he says, but the way he says it, he didn't know what to expect.

"Is that what you wanted to see? Why you wanted to come down here? He hurt you so you thought it'd feel good to see him go out like that?"

Lil Tricky's shutting down now. He's staring at his shoes, leaning forward, almost holding himself up by his stomach.

"Yeah," he finally says, sounding like the little kid he is.

"But you feel terrible now?" I look in my side mirror and angle it way out to see this lady and her kids playing on the grass by the basketball courts.

"Maybe."

"That means you still have some human in you. I think you should walk home. Nail that in some."

"What?"

The lady and her kids have got some type of balloon ball and they're hitting it back and forth to each other. It floats in the air, gets hit by weird gusts, and they adjust to it. The object of the whole thing is just to make sure it don't touch the ground. That's what it looks like anyway.

They're going pretty good at it too. Seeing that, it makes me think of how I been trying to keep everything in the air myself, all the winds I've been dealing with. Not so far away, coming towards us maybe, I hear a siren.

"Now you seen a man die," I say to Lil Tricky, "I need you to get out of the car, walk home, and think about it."

He's wide-eyed, looking at me like Felix's green frog hat before he opens his mouth. "I don't even know how to get home!"

"Hey, you'll figure it out. Men figure things out."

He's gonna say something else, but he stops himself and I'm glad. He can't see it, but I got the pistol in my left hand, hidden down by my leg. I'm gripping it harder as he's sitting there trying to make up his mind, and I'm almost about to bring it up when he moves his hand to the handle and opens his door.

The little ceiling light pops on above us. I see how white his face is looking then, as he's getting out, and I nod at him to get his attention as the siren's getting closer.

"Think about whether or not you need to be doing what you're doing," I say.

He just stares back at me, blank, checked out.

"You're not made for this. Now I need you to close that door."

He does it. He puts his head down and starts walking back to the road.

He'll never know it, but I'm real grateful to the kid for not making me do something I didn't want to. I put the gun back under the seat and I'm about to start up the car and pull out when a ambulance comes rushing into the parking lot with its red lights spinning and that siren going. It could only be Ghost that called it. That must've been the second phone call he made. What I'm thinking about that is *He didn't want the kids playing with the balloon ball to walk up on it by accident and see his body like that.* All I can think of then is how honorable that is.

From where I'm sitting, I look back to my left to see the lady grab her kids and all three of them stare into the parking lot. The balloon ball they were playing with has nobody to catch it then and it drifts, pushed by a little wind, and hits the ground, but it don't stop. It goes on a little ways from there, skidding over some grass before stopping against the pole holding up the basketball hoop, but not for long. With a little more wind it's going again, rolling over the basketball court as the paramedics jump out, try the door handle, and then break the driver window of the Jeep to unlock the doors.

Glass smashes out onto the parking lot. I watch Lil Tricky watching from near a fence at the other end of the lot. His face balls up as a blond paramedic rips open the shotgun door and blood drips down from the baseboards as he puts gloved fingers on Ghost's neck, looking for a pulse, but the guy's staring at the chest wound while he's doing it and knowing it's done. I see the body clearly for just a second, a rose tattoo on an unmoving chest in black ink, and the blood beneath it almost looking like it's coming out of it, but then it's gone. The paramedic steps back between us and puts Ghost's right arm up onto his lap before closing the door.

I been around a lot of crazy stuff. *A lot.* But Ghost doing all he did is the craziest thing I ever seen. Anybody else would've ended up done in a few hours, but not him. I'm shaking a little replaying it in my head. And what's going on right now is, my hands don't want to stay still where they are. I'm just watching them on my lap. Twitching. I can't remember the last time that happened to me. I thought this life couldn't touch me like that no more, not with me seeing so much. I guess I just figured I was all dead inside from everything, but here I am, finding out I'm not.

I'm still tripping on how Ghost was stealing that whole time for other people, some he didn't even know. That's just crazy. I didn't know him that much, but already I can say he earned what he took better than anybody ever could have in the circumstances. He put something into the world that's gonna stay here even after he's gone. And it's hitting me how I might want that same thing. To leave behind something better when I'm gone too. Not for no strangers. For my family.

My hands aren't stopping, so I grab the wheel and squeeze it until my pulse's jumping up and down in my fingers. What I can't get out of my head is how he saved me when he pulled that trigger. When he saved me from having to do it, he saved my whole family too, and he'll never know it. I start up the car and put it in reverse while I'm thinking on it. I back right up. Maybe too fast. But I know I could be in his shoes pretty soon like that, so I'm braking, slapping the shift down into drive, and going out the way I came. I'm nodding my head the whole way, like I'm bobbing it to a beat only I can hear, as I'm leaving the parking lot, hanging on to the wheel, aiming myself towards Leya, towards Felix, towards the place that isn't home yet but is about to be.

Author's Note

I found *Dreamland: The True Tale of America's Opiate Epidemic*, by Sam Quinones, invaluable to my writing of this work. Without Quinones's insight on the prescription pain-pill epidemic, and the heroin cells that capitalized on it, I'd know significantly less about the ranchos of Nayarit, the Xalisco Boys, and Operation Tar Pit.

Acknowledgments

Álvaro
Marisa Roemer
LAFD Battalion Chief (Ret.) Ron Roemer
Brandon and Karishma Gattis
Evan Skrederstu, Chris Brand, Steve Martinez, and Espi
Gustavo Arellano
Charles Farrell
Carlo Rotella
Luis J. Rodriguez
Jenn Eneriz
Ryan Hammill
Patrick Hoffman
Sara Nović
Paula Hawkins
Chaz Bojorquez
Chuey Quintanar
Sam Tenney
Sam Quinones
Bill Esparza
Nick Cimmento
Daphne Durham
Paul Baggaley
Lizzy Kremer
Simon Lipskar
Harriet Moore
Steve Younger
and
The Men Who Drive Trucks with Black Plates